THE EARL'S IRON WARRANT

The Dukes' Pact Series
Book Six

By Kate Archer

ARE YOU SIGNED UP FOR DRAGONBLADE'S BLOG?

You'll get the latest news and information on exclusive giveaways, exclusive excerpts, coming releases, sales, free books, cover reveals and more.

Check out our complete list of authors, too!

No spam, no junk. That's a promise!

Sign Up Here

www.dragonbladepublishing.com

Dearest Reader;

Thank you for your support of a small press. At Dragonblade Publishing, we strive to bring you the highest quality Historical Romance from some of the best authors in the business. Without your support, there is no 'us', so we sincerely hope you adore these stories and find some new favorite authors along the way.

Happy Reading!

CEO, Dragonblade Publishing

PROLOGUE

White's, London 1818

T HE SIX OLD dukes had settled themselves round a roaring fire in their favored room of the club, each man aiming his feet toward the flames. The rain had come down in buckets since dawn, the morning no brighter than twilight. To a man, they were uncomfortably damp, despite expensive greatcoats and finely-made umbrellas. At their time of life, the wet was a cold serpent twisting round their arms and legs and slithering through their bones.

Still, they had all roused themselves and ventured out into the wretched weather to meet with one another. These gatherings had become usual to discuss the pact between them meant to spur their sons on to marriage and heirs. So long a time had they met in this manner that the Duke of Carlisle already had a grandson, by way of his daughter-in-law, Lady Hampton.

The pact between the dukes, conceived and launched in desperation, had cut funds and made things very uncomfortable for these errant sons. The strategy had seen success after success. To be sure, there had been bumpy roads and twisting byways to that success, but most of them had now had the pleasure to sit at a wedding breakfast.

Yet, at this moment, the men were strangely silent. As footmen silently swirled round them, handing out cups of warmed wine and setting up trays of meats, cheeses, and hot rolls, the gentlemen looked everywhere but in the direction of the Duke of Bainbridge. This should have been that gentleman's moment for congratulations. But was it? They'd all read of the upcoming nuptials between Lord Grayson and Miss Dell in the newspapers. But had it really come off?

The Duke of Bainbridge suddenly laughed. "Gentlemen," he said, "you look as though you attend a funeral. Yes, I know the cause of it— recent events seem most improbable. You may ease your minds, my friends. My son is married, I watched the ceremony with my own eyes."

The dukes breathed a collective sigh of relief. The Duke of Wentworth, who now found himself the unfortunate owner of *two* gouty feet as opposed to one, stared at those swollen appendages that just now rested together on a stool.

"Penderton's daughter, though," he said with a note of incredulity. "I only say…that is, I had heard, I think it was hinted at, that she is rather, how shall I say…bookish."

"Yes," the Duke of Gravesley said, "I heard so, too. A veritable scholar just like her father. And of course, your boy is…well, how would one describe it? I suppose one might say, that is, he is generally understood to have…an aversion to books."

"I do not claim to comprehend it," the Duke of Bainbridge said, "but they appear delighted with one another. I expect they share eccentricity as a common trait, as they have gone off to Sweden of all places for their wedding trip."

"We congratulate you, Bainbridge," the Duke of Carlisle said. "Perhaps there is a lesson in this. We must understand that there are any number of ways a couple may find they prefer one another. At least, we must hope so, as we approach the end of the road regarding this pact between us."

"A most difficult end," Gravesley said.

The gentlemen round the fire all nodded, as if they had been dreading this day for some time.

"Well all right," the Duke of Glastonburg said. "He's the last hold-out. How do we get that devil's spawn of mine married?"

"Dalton? God knows," the Duke of Carlisle said. "I fear it will take extraordinary measures."

"Then extraordinary measures it shall be," Glastonburg said. "I will not be left behind on this matter. I will not sit idly by while the rest of you bounce grandsons on your knees. By God, that rogue will come to heel!"

"Hear, hear," the gentlemen murmured, though it was not particularly rousing or imbued with the confidence one might have wished for.

CHAPTER ONE

M ISS DAISY DANWORTH clutched Mrs. Jellops' hand. They stood in Daisy's bedchamber in the house on Grosvenor Square, a rather sad affair of dull furnishings, worn carpets, and old curtains. Her father, Viscount Childress, never cared to spend money on anything a visitor would not see and so, above stairs, they lived in whatever the owner of the house had left for their use. Daisy might be dressed in all manner of silk and fine lace, but behind closed doors was decidedly shabby. It was also decidedly uncomfortable—the fires might roar in the drawing room and dining room, but they only sputtered in her own.

Though she and Mrs. Jellops had often bemoaned the discomfort of the sparse and cold chamber, the two ladies had not a care about the state of the room at that moment. They were at the window, watching for signs of anyone arriving to the house. The news had been coming in fits and starts all morning and they had been on tenterhooks to discover what was to be the end of it.

A cart pulled up to the front gate, driven by a gruff old farmer from the countryside. Surrounding the cart on horseback were her father's particular cronies, none of which Daisy would allow into the house had it been her right to bar them from it. They were the worst sort of men—heartless and careless, crude and loud, and usually drunk.

As Mr. Gringer dismounted, Daisy glimpsed into the cart. Her father laid there, just as she expected. What she had not known was in what condition he would arrive.

"A sheet covers his face," Daisy said quietly. "He is dead. My father is finally dead."

Mrs. Jellops peered down and whispered, "I can hardly believe it. Can he really be dead? I half expect him to suddenly sit up and punish us for being at the window."

Both ladies shivered at the thought and Daisy was shaken from her confidence. Mrs. Jellops was right, nothing was yet proved. It seemed impossible that anything could kill such a man. How could a horse and a fence kill the beast that had been the bane of her existence?

Perhaps he only pretended as some cruel joke? Or worse, perhaps he pretended so he might glean what her feelings would be on hearing of his demise? She had been careful, always, to hide her enmity. But might it not have been unmasked somehow and now he sought proof of it?

He had always been vengeful and spiteful, finding slights in everything and punishing those perceived slights from whatever direction they came. He'd been in more than a few duels and men stayed well clear of him when he was in a temper, lest they be forced to meet him at dawn over some ridiculous matter. He was unhappy with the world and went through it with his sword raised.

Lord Childress had been convinced, long ago, that Penny's mother, Lady Childress, had been unfaithful. He had tormented the woman into a sickbed, and then harangued her into a grave. It had taken years to do it, but Lord Childress was nothing if not determined.

As a girl, Daisy had listened to it all from around doorways, through open windows, and sometimes in the very room she cowered in. She'd heard the insults and threats, and she'd seen the bruises her mother tried so hard to hide.

She'd dreamed up so many plans to rescue her mother from the beast. One fond imagining was that she would save her pin money, hire a carriage, and take them both far north. They might live in a forest with kind faeries and if her father ever came for them, the faeries would beat him about the head and drive him out. They would live in peace and her dear delicate mother would rest and recover under the cool shade of greenery.

Her mother was dead before Daisy could enact any kind of escape. She was ten, and told it at breakfast by a governess, as if she were being told the weather. Weeks later, that same governess left abruptly. Daisy always suspected her father had meddled with the woman. Mrs. Jellops arrived in her place and it was Daisy's understanding that she'd been sent by a concerned cousin, Lord Mayton. She was certainly not a lady her father would have hired, but she was installed all the same.

In those days, Daisy had clung to Mrs. Jellops like she was a lone buoy in the midst of an Atlantic storm. When she was too old for the schoolroom, the lady had become her companion. Mrs. Jellops might have been driven out like all the rest, but she was a distant poor relation and even for Lord Childress, that might have been a step too far. He would not have cared for Daisy's opinion on the matter, but he would not have liked to be whispered about in his wider family, or worse, in wider society. He held a great regard for titles and one's place in the world and that regard was the only thing that kept him in check. In any case, Mrs. Jellops, though seeming a comfortable and round sort of person, had a determination to stay by Daisy and would not have been driven out anyway.

As for his daughter, Daisy was nothing more than a commodity on the market. She had been told, in no uncertain terms, that she'd better marry well, as her only use to him was for the connections she might bring. She was never left to forget how unfortunate it was that she'd been born a girl, and how her mother had failed in producing a son and heir.

It was also supposed Daisy's fault that her grandmother, Lady Alicia Polworth, had settled a great deal of money on her, cleverly locked up and overseen by trustees. It was a source of near constant aggravation that he could not get his hands on it and he was determined to at least find a way to claw back her dowry in some distant future.

She and Mrs. Jellops had gone on in such a house, always careful not to aggravate and to stay out of the way as much as possible. The house was like a tomb and had never seen laughter. The only servants who ever stayed more than a month were those who did not mind being constantly berated. She had sometimes dared to tell people that her at-home day was on Wednesdays. There were some, from time to time, who even ventured to come. They were those who did not know and had not heard of the awful Lord Childress. Always, Daisy listened for footsteps, fearing her father would arrive and say something scathing to a person he did not feel was suitably elevated.

Just now, though, Daisy began to hope her father had been silenced forever. Mr. Gringer had looked up to their window and shaken his head sadly.

The other men began to haul Lord Childress from the cart to carry him inside. Daisy could see now that the sheet that covered his face was tied securely around the neck. The men did not have a care for how the head lolled to one side as they dragged it off the wagon. A person alive would never be carried in such a manner. Not even as a ruse would they dare it.

"He is truly dead!" Daisy whispered. "My mother rejoices in heaven, while *he* travels in the opposite direction to pay in eternity for his crimes against her."

"And against you, my dear," Mrs. Jellops said.

"Yes, and you too," Daisy said. "But *we* have outlived him. In a year, I will be twenty-one and have access to my grandmother's money. I will have three thousand per annum and you and I can go and live somewhere in peace."

"By the seaside," Mrs. Jellops said, "as you have always spoken of."

"Yes, though not Ramsgate. Not anywhere near that house, or any other that my father ever called home."

"Agreed," Mrs. Jellops said. "We will go somewhere that does not contain the taint of him. Brighton, perhaps?"

"Yes, it must be Brighton, I think. We shall swim every fine day and be as free as dolphins," Daisy said, the relief of shaking off her father's yoke coming upon her in waves, just like the sea she yearned for.

Mrs. Jellops staggered back over the suggestion that she would one day find herself bobbing in the sea. She was a very circular person, her waist belying her fondness of cakes, but though there was little doubt she would float sufficiently, she did not seek out exercise of any sort.

"Never mind it, then," Daisy said, laughing. "*I* will swim and you will wave to me from the shore."

"As has ever been my habit."

"And I shall give you your own money," Daisy said. "I am certain my father has been stingy with you. You will have no household expenses and I will settle on you three hundred pounds a year to spend of fripperies. I know how fond you are of pretty things—you can fill our house with them."

The lady gently sighed, no doubt thinking of all the pretty little trinkets and gewgaws she'd seen in this or that shop that she'd not had the means to pay for. She smoothed her skirt, as if to dismiss that pleasant reverie. "Until then, though," Mrs. Jellops said, "I wonder what will happen to us?"

Daisy could not care less. Whatever it was, it would only be a twelvemonth.

"You don't suppose," Mrs. Jellops said, peering down to the street, "that he'd name a guardian from *that* group of scoundrels?"

"Oh no, I do not think so," Daisy said. "You know how he was always such a stickler for titles. It's bound to be some cousin or other with as lofty a title as he could wrangle. I am certain he approached the Duke of Glastonburg, he is the entailed heir. But he would not have found success there, for the duke never liked him. I think it must be Lord Mayton, he is a cousin *and* an earl."

"Ah yes, Lord Mayton, he sent me here to begin, very pleasant fellow. I suppose we will do very well under his roof. Though, it is just like your father that he would not have ever informed you of the circumstances," Mrs. Jellops said.

"Oh, but why would he? What man like my father would believe he would ever die or care what happened to me if he did?"

Mrs. Jellops breathed a sigh. "And yet, he has died, and thank goodness for it. Now, I think we'd better go downstairs and see what must be done."

Daisy turned and grasped Mrs. Jellops' hands. "We must appear suitably devastated, though. I am not certain either of us is that talented of an actress, but we must try. It would be unseemly to appear relieved."

Mrs. Jellops nodded and attempted an expression that might indicate her sorrow upon discovering Lord Childress had perished. It was wholly unsuccessful and only ended up appearing absurd and sending Daisy into fits of giggles.

It was near a half hour before they could compose themselves, go down, and claim that they had been crying too heartily to attend the men below.

CHARLES BATTERSEA, EARL of Dalton and heir to the Duke of Glastonburg, had been stewing for weeks. He'd not much choice, as far as he could see. All of his friends but for Burke had been reckless in the extreme and now found themselves in the marital yoke. His funds had been cut off, his creditors were no longer as awed as they once had been and came knocking whenever it suited them, he was reduced to attending tedious dinners just to *get* a good dinner, and the season was coming to a close. Even Marty Destin from his club was beginning to inquire when he might get paid. He could not afford to open his house in Brighton and would not dignify his ridiculous married friends with his presence at their country houses.

He might go to Burke, of course. But then, he could not spend the whole summer there without looking like a charity case. And what was he to do with his staff? He supposed he'd leave them here, and they might scrounge whatever they could for food. Bellamy could go further afield to find a butcher who would extend credit or he could sell off some silver for ready money. He would not feel sorry for them, as he knew full well that Bellamy would help himself to the wine cellar, as he always did. As for his stable, what little money he had left was put aside to pay for it. People might starve, himself included, but as long as he breathed, his horseflesh would never have a hint of anything gone wrong.

That old scoundrel of a butler opened the door softly and said, "Lord Burke to see you, my lord."

Charles waved his acquiescence. He did not particularly want to see anybody, but if he were going to decamp to Burke's house, he'd better not bar the door to him now.

Lord Burke walked in and Charles noted him surveying the chaos of his library. Opened books and strewn papers littered every surface.

"I fail to see why you employ servants," Burke said. "I have yet to enter this room and find it at all in order."

"As that is in no way a surprise, why do you bother to mention it?" Dalton said.

"Very well," Burke said, "I will say why I have come. I wondered how you got on now that Grayson has married Miss Dell. I know you quite counted on him to remain a bachelor holdout with you."

"Grayson," Charles said bitterly. "Do you know where he's gone with the little minx? Sweden. A wedding trip to Sweden. Who ever heard of anything so ridiculous?"

"Lady Grayson is not a minx and I do not think it is Sweden that has put you out of sorts."

Charles shrugged. Burke had known the lady a very long time and was unlikely to be swayed by all he could say against Miss Dell. Or, *Lady Grayson*, as she had somehow made herself.

Still, she was a minx. She must be. How else had the lady librarian seduced Grayson? Giles Grayson, who never opened a book? It was unaccountable, and therefore, her fault.

"Really, Dalton," Burke said, "if you intend on living in poverty rather than marry, that is certainly your purview. I simply do not understand why you are so irate over your friends' marriages."

"Oh, I see," Charles said. "You are to be next. Who is the lady?"

"There is nobody," Burke said hurriedly.

Charles looked at his friend critically. There was something odd in his tone. "I am glad to hear it," he said.

"I am not certain *I* am," Burke said mysteriously.

Charles decided not to pursue the matter. No doubt Burke had been disappointed in love. He only wished his other friends had found such luck. Unfortunately, those other fools had met with endless successes—one after the other had willingly trotted into the parson's noose.

"In any case," Charles said, "I will need to force myself upon your hospitality this summer, as I do not have the funds to open my house in Brighton."

Burke looked up in surprise. "Oh no, my good fellow, I won't open the house in Somerset until the shooting. I have been invited to stay at Ramsgate with the Minkertons."

"Ramsgate? Who stays at Ramsgate?"

"A large amount of people do, including the Minkertons. They have a large and rambling cottage by the sea, it is very charming. Lord Bartholomew is a baron whose land borders my own. They are longstanding friends."

"I've never heard of them."

"I do not doubt it. Belle Minkerton will only be out this coming season and Lord and Lady Bartholomew do not like town. Further, as they do not love the habits of the regent, they would hardly place themselves in Brighton."

"Friends or not, I do not see why you should spend months with them."

"*You* were just proposing to spend months with *me*," Burke said.

"Deuced inconvenient, is all I say," Charles said.

"Yes, it is, for you," Burke said drily. "Why not go to Cabot and have a look at his horseflesh? He and Lady Cabot have expanded the stables to a remarkable degree."

Charles folded his arms. "I will not visit any of my friends who have fallen to the Dukes' Pact. I have vowed it."

"Vowed it to who?" Lord Burke said, looking amused.

"To myself!" Charles said. "They are weak."

"They are happy, and you are ridiculous."

"I should throw you out, now that I know I cannot stay at your house."

Before Lord Burke could throw *himself* out to be done with the conversation, Bellamy hurried in with a letter on a silver tray.

Charles looked at him in some annoyance. Bellamy said, "Sorry to disturb, but it is from the duke."

As a usual matter, a letter from his father did not bring good news. Most of the old man's letters were long and heated diatribes over how much Charles spent on a horse or a gambling debt or, his father feared, an actress.

That could not be the case this time, though. Charles had been cut off for some months and so there was nothing the old fellow could complain about.

"Ah," Charles said, "I will wager he writes to call off this pact business. He sees he cannot win and he does not like to imagine his son begging dinners or setting himself up in other people's houses. It becomes embarrassing and he wants no more part of it. I knew the old boy would come round eventually."

"Perhaps you ought to read his letter before you relay its contents," Burke said, settling himself into a chair.

Charles took the letter. "He is my father, I know how he thinks. He is too proud for this shameful nonsense to go on indefinitely."

He tore the letter open and read through it. Charles could feel his temper rise with every word. "That motherless son of a—"

"Stop this instant," Burke said, holding his hand up. "I do not know what your father has written, but there is no cause to throw *those* sorts of insults around."

"Oh yes there is," Charles said, handing the letter over to Burke. "Read it for yourself."

Lord Burke took the letter and perused it. As Lord Dalton's fury had increased word by word, Burke's surprise kept apace.

Dalton,

As you may have heard, or will soon, Lord Childress has gone to meet his maker. (I cannot imagine God actually made him, so I assume he goes to the devil in the fastest conveyance possible.) He misjudged a fence and his hard head hit an even harder rock when he was thrown.

As you are aware, I am the estate's entailed heir. What you most definitely do not know, as I cannot ever remember agreeing to this but there are papers that claim I did, I am now guardian to Miss Daisy Danworth, Lord Childress' only child. It is all most irregular, as it ought not be the heir that is named guardian, but I have consulted with Spinks and he says we'd best just get on with it. He says the Chancery is so slow that the girl will be of age and married before a case is even heard.

Finding myself in such circumstances, I am determined to do right by the lady. However, I am much engaged with the estate at this present moment as we are set on doing long over-due renovations. The duchess and I will be moving into the dower house with your grand-mother until the work is completed. Obviously, there will be no room for another person in that house, never mind the lady's companion and her maid. As it is, we will find each other underfoot at every turn and I pray the duchess and the dowager do not strangle one another. (Yes, they get on perfectly well at a distance, but trap them in close quarters for too long a time and it will be like a couple of leopards tied in the same sack).

Therefore, I will require you to conduct this business on my be-half. Childress' house in town was rented and the landlord wants them out. The estate in Shropshire is said to be in disarray and needs attention. I have been informed that the butler and housekeeper, who served both the estate and the London house, have run off together, and the cook has taken other employment. I presume there is still a footman or two lurking about. There is also a house in Ramsgate which is said to be in rather better shape.

You will escort Miss Danworth and her companion, Mrs. Jellops, to either of those two places, I care not. If you go to the estate, rectify its deficiencies. If you go to the house in Ramsgate, send me news of its real circumstances as I think the agent sounds over-enthusiastic. I have been informed there is a hunting lodge on the estate and a small cottage on the grounds at Ramsgate—those will be your choice of abode while the lady stays in the main house. You will bring your own staff for Miss Danworth's use until suitable replacements can be found. Write weekly to tell me how you get on.

You will do as I ask, or I will see that every piece of unentailed property I own goes to your cousin Herbert. Consider this not a friendly request, but an iron warrant.

I will presume, though you are pressed into service, this is a wel-come development. You cannot possibly afford to open the Brighton house, town shall be empty and dinners dried up, and I hear there are creditors banging on your door day and night.

As a last note, I am not so foolish as to give you funds directly to provide for the care of Miss Danworth. I will put the household kitty in the hands of her companion, Mrs. Jellops. Good luck prying gambling money from her sensible middle-aged fists.

Glastonburg

Lord Burke roared with laughter and set the letter down. "Good God, he is positively Machiavellian!"

Charles drummed his fingers on the desk. "He claims the dowager and my mother will be at odds in close quarters. A bit of nonsense. That makes me believe it is the two of *them* got together to launch this scheme. Yes, it smacks of them. My father is no more Machiavellian than a turnip. But those two? Machiavelli, himself, would be fuddled to find himself in the middle of one of their plots."

"Who is this Herbert who is to inherit your land?" Lord Burke said, hardly containing his laughter.

"A lump of a fellow who could no more manage an estate than fly to the moon. Nobody knows what's to be done with him."

Lord Burke composed himself and said, "However this plan came into being probably matters little. The question is, what will you do? Your father has issued what he terms an iron warrant—will you give up so much to Herbert? All the while starving in your house in town?"

"I know what they think," Charles said, ignoring Burke's questions. "They think, put me in close quarters with Miss Danworth and surely I will drop at her feet and beg her to marry me. Ha! Of course that's what they think."

Burke shrugged. "You do seem well-suited," he said. "She is as…cool…as you are. And you cannot claim she is not a beauty."

"I do not deny it," Charles said. "Though I will point out there are beauties everywhere to behold and most of them causing far less trouble than a lady of the *ton*."

"Do they cause less trouble though?" Burke asked. "Marberry told me your last light o' love threw you out when the money dried up."

Charles did not answer. It was true that the actress he had spent a few pleasant months with had not been over-sympathetic in discovering that jewelry and rent were no longer to be forthcoming. She'd moved on to a more fertile field and he'd not been particularly broken up about it.

In any case, he had a far bigger problem on his hands. How to circumvent his father's orders without losing a large chunk of his inheritance to mealy-mouthed Herbert Conway?

He could not say he was opposed to Miss Danworth's company. She was one of the more interesting and intelligent ladies of his acquaintance. She did not fan herself or pretend at delicacy or engineer false laughter. She was not always working hard to be gay, as if all the world was a marvelous place. She was also *exceedingly* pleasant to look at.

He also could not claim that finding a comfortable place to reside for a few months, until he could make the rounds of shooting parties, would be so very terrible. What he was to do with the lady when the shooting started, he knew not, though he supposed he could drag her along from place to place. None of it was insurmountable.

However, what he *was* opposed to was this flagrant attempt to push him into a marriage by hook or by crook.

How little his own parents understood him! He would never marry. He would never bring life into the world. Not when he'd seen what men at war could do.

As it often did when he thought about the war, the scar that ran down his cheek began to burn. He could smell the smoke and the metallic stench of blood running into the ground. And then, as always, his memories led him back to Quatre Bras—that place that would never leave him in peace.

The battle had ended and the night had been cold. He'd lain in his tent, but despite the weariness of his limbs he could not sleep. The sounds of drunken men celebrating king-sanctioned murder while corpses lay rotting just a mile off had never disturbed before. After a battle, he'd been in the habit of forgetting, or reminding himself that it was war, or that it was a matter of survival—it was either the enemy or himself. That night, the whoops and howls, roars and curses, laughter and back-slapping seemed to surround his tent as if the gates of hell had opened. Closing his eyes did not erase what he had seen or what he had done. As if the tableau was still before him, two eyes filled with abject terror stared unblinking and final, terrible words were whispered. He'd watched it in his mind's eye like a play, over and over again as the night wore on.

Sometime near dawn, the awful truth of humanity had stolen over him. They were all animals. They might drape themselves in fine fabrics and hold sway over the kingdom of beasts, but they were little better than well-dressed wolves. They were bloodthirsty predators—the war had simply allowed them to shrug off the sheen of civility they'd pretended at.

He had vowed that night that he would never indulge himself to bring in what he'd had a hand in taking out—a life. If one wished to be better than a beast, a price must be paid. He was determined to pay it. He would not create more men who would be sent to war and be turned into raging beasts.

"Now you have drifted far away," Burke said, pulling Charles back to his library and the present day.

"I was just thinking," Charles said.

Burke rose and said, "I will leave you, so you may think in peace. I am sure this will be a difficult matter to mull over."

"There is nothing to mull, I have decided," Charles said. "I will not allow one sovereign that is rightfully mine to go to Herbert Conway."

Lord Burke smiled. "Your father will be delighted, and poor Herbert devastated."

"I think I will go to Ramsgate, since you will also be there. If I am to be saddled with Miss Danworth, I might as well become acquainted with your precious Minkertons and you will be on hand to entertain me when I become too dull. In any case, it sounds a deal better than a run-down estate in Shropshire—Bellamy would be useless in a house that needed any real work done to it."

"And so Bellamy comes to Ramsgate," Lord Burke said softly. "I hope Childress has left an extensive wine cellar."

CHAPTER TWO

THE HOUSE IN Grosvenor Square was as it had never been before. The heaviness was gone, and Daisy felt as if she could finally breathe. One would have thought, seeing the black curtains in every front window, that the interior would be gloomy. The windows facing the back garden, however, had all been thrown open to let in sun and air. Daisy and Mrs. Jellops had taken to using a sitting room facing that garden to have their tea.

The days following her father's demise had been chaotic. A hatchment was attached above the front doors, a minister secured and mourners hired, Daisy and Mrs. Jellops were fitted for dour mourning clothes, announcements were made in the newspapers, and personal notices were written. Though, as Daisy applied the dark wax to each black-bordered missive, she wondered who among the receivers of the news would weep.

There were a hundred other details to attend to and her father's librarian, Mr. Crackwilder, was instrumental in seeing that all got done properly. Though he was soon to be Lady Grayson's librarian, his last act for her was to ensure that the valuable Palaskar collection of books was safely moved to the Shropshire estate.

A funeral service, which she blessedly did not have to attend, was given. The minister had explained that though ladies did not usually attend the service, there was nothing in the church teachings that forbid it. He'd wondered if she had strong feelings about saying a last farewell to her father. Of course, her feelings *were* rather strong, though she did not dare reveal their joyfulness. Rather, she'd said she did not trust herself to stay upright during such a proceeding. The minister had nodded knowingly and appeared relieved. He could not possibly have been more relieved than she was.

The funeral was about as well attended as she would have expected. Lord Childress' few close cronies made an appearance and arrived drunk, according to one of the church wardens. However, those who had nodded to the lord on the street or gambled with him at his club, or invited him to large affairs, stayed away. They may have wished to keep the peace with the bad-tempered gentleman while he lived but felt no compunction to honor him now that he was dead.

The committal was to take place in their own churchyard in Shropshire. Daisy was vastly relieved to see the body finally leave the house covered in heaps of flowers to overwhelm the smell of decay. It had lain in the drawing room for some days like a constant threat. She and Mrs. Jellops had slept in the same bed every night he remained downstairs, in case his ghost struggled out of his body and came to terrorize them.

Her father's solicitor enlightened them as to Lord Childress' will, and of course it was as meanspirited as the man himself. He left Daisy nothing from his unentailed property, not even her mother's jewelry, though he left all sorts of insults to be paid out. Lord Grey was to get one shilling as a testament to his miserly habits at the club, and a feather duster was to be purchased and handed to Mr. Johnson in recognition of his weak and ineffectual nature. Daisy had not been disappointed in any of it as she had not expected any other result. She *was* surprised that the Duke of Glastonburg had consented to be her guardian, but she supposed she would not mind spending her mourning period on his estate.

As to the items in the house that were now rightfully owned by the duke, quite a few of them had fled in the pockets of the butler and housekeeper, who had run off together. Though it meant the loss of a good amount of silver, Daisy was not sorry to see them go. They were miserable creatures, both of them, and deserved one another.

Of course, it was rather difficult to go on without those two senior servants. Daisy had not the first idea what was to be done about dinners or what the maids ought to be doing all day. Considering the recent quality of the dinners, she knew well enough they took advantage of her ignorance. Mrs. Jellops did what she could with them, but they were all soon to be out of employment and so they were not particularly awed by the lady's directives. They might have revolted entirely if Daisy had not held back their letters of recommendation until they began answering advertisements.

None of it could make her unhappy, though. The beast, the murderer of her mother, was dead. *She* was alive and twelve months away from total, absolute, and permanent freedom.

The only thing they waited for now was a summons from the duke. He would let Daisy and Mrs. Jellops know when they were to be packed and travel to his estate in Somerset. Her only qualm, when she'd first heard that the duke was to oversee her affairs, was that his son, Lord Dalton, might be in residence. She'd dismissed the idea, though. It was unlikely the lord would be hanging round his father's house when he might be in his own, which she understood to be in Brighton. She was both relieved and vaguely unhappy by the realization, though she assured herself it was only the expected dearth of company her own age that depressed her spirits.

A footman had finally delivered the waited for communication to her hands.

Daisy tore open the sheet and read its close scrawled message.

My Dear Miss Danworth,

My most fervent condolences on the recent passing of Lord Childress.

As you know, I am the entailed heir of that gentleman's estate,

and have also been named your guardian in his will. It is not altogether usual, and my solicitor tells me that you may challenge it in
Chancery Court if you so wish and I would not stand in your way.
However, he also advises that particular court moves like boots
through molasses. As you only have a twelvemonth until your majority, I suggest we simply proceed.

As it is not altogether seemly to have the entailed heir act as
guardian, I have named my son as my agent. He will escort you to
Ramsgate for the summer months and attend you there, staying in the
cottage I have been told is located on the grounds.

The solicitor has informed me that your father's butler and
housekeeper have decamped. Lord Dalton's butler, Mr. Bellamy, will
take over the butler's duties. You may hire any housekeeper you like,
or my son will do the duty if you prefer. I assume you have a lady's
maid you will bring with you. The rest can be hired locally.

Mrs. Jellops will go on as your companion and I will place the
household budget, which will be two hundred pounds per month, in
that lady's hands. I understand the lady to be one of commonsense
and that will take the burden off your shoulders. Should you require
more, I am happy to provide. My intention is that you want for nothing and are provided every comfort.

I have arranged for a modiste named Mrs. Belle to come and take
your measurements for suitable mourning seaside attire, as I have
been informed by my duchess that she is the only lady who will do.
Mrs. Belle will send the clothes on to you at Ramsgate once they are
readied.

Lord Dalton should already be making his way to that town. I
will send you there with an escort of four carriages, four armed
coachmen, and eight stalwart grooms.

I pray these plans meet with your approval. My carriages will arrive at dawn on Tuesday.

Glastonburg

Daisy dropped the letter and it fluttered to the carpet.

"Good Lord," Mrs. Jellops said, looking alarmed. "What does he say?"

"His letter is both generous and terrible," Daisy said. "He puts two hundred pounds a month in your hands."

"Two hundred pounds for what?" Mrs. Jellops said.

"Our household. He sends us to Ramsgate."

"Ramsgate! Whatever for? Why do we not go to Somerset?"

"Lord Dalton is to accompany us," Daisy said. "I believe this has something to do with the Dukes' Pact."

Mrs. Jellops was quiet for a moment. She, like most people, was not as quick-witted as her charge. Finally, understanding overspread her features. "You cannot think it is a scheme to marry you off to Lord Dalton?"

"I can, and I do," Daisy said. "What a ridiculous notion! It is skating near scandalous to have him living in the garden, for one. For another, if the duke had bothered to become at all acquainted with me, he would know that I intend never to marry. I have no need to, and I will never put myself at the mercy of a man. It was my mother's mistake, but it will not be mine."

"Lord Dalton also says he will never marry," Mrs. Jellops said. "Goodness, if your suspicions are true, the duke is a misguided creature. He ought to be throwing his son in front of ladies who desperately *want* to marry."

"I suppose the duke thinks himself very clever," Daisy said. "I suppose he does not mind if his scheme results in any talk."

"Perhaps, though," Mrs. Jellops said, "it is for another reason. Perhaps Lord Dalton himself has suggested it. He is virtually penniless after all. Perhaps he needs a place to put his feet up and eat good dinners. He is a gloomy sort, but for all that he does seem to enjoy your company. Or enjoy it as much as Lord Dalton enjoys anything."

Daisy laughed at the notion. "If that is the case, Lord Dalton will rue the day he went to Ramsgate. He is to stay in the old cottage on the back lawn—do you not remember it?"

Mrs. Jellops smiled. "Oh dear, yes. He shall not be very comfortable."

"As for dinners, he may shift for himself," Daisy said. "I see no reason why I must provide them."

Mrs. Jellops tapped her forefinger against her chin. "Except it is now the duke's funds that will pay for everything."

Daisy had not considered that. Still, she did not see why she should be forced to dine with Lord Dalton every evening. *Especially* not Dalton.

She had perhaps allowed herself to enjoy their verbal sparrings more than she ought. She had perhaps failed to understand why people thought his scar marred his looks when it only made him look…more *him*. She had perhaps thought him superior to the posing dandies of the season.

That was precisely why he should not make it a habit to dine in the house. She had allowed herself to find him interesting because he was never any threat to her. Dalton was a man whose real temperament could not be known. It was too hidden; he revealed nothing.

Daisy was certain that was precisely how her mother had made the mistake with her father. The dear lady could not make him out, and so invented a temperament for him that had never been and only later found she was mistaken.

It suited Daisy, just now, to claim she would never marry. She would stay with that attitude for some time or forever, she knew not. She was not unaware of the problems of spinsterhood—particularly the lack of children she very much wished for and the greatly reduced social circle. If she did ever conclude that she might marry, it would only be to a gentleman who was thoroughly known and proved not a man like her father.

She thought she could devise ways to know, because she knew all the little things about her father. How did a gentleman treat animals and children and those who were weak? How did he interact with servants? How did he seem when a delay was caused, or a wine glass spilled over, or an errant ember burned a hole in the carpet? Was he generous or mean? What were his gambling habits? How did he take his losses? Were there any rumors of him having participated in a duel? Did he spur his horse more than he ought?

When it came to her father, she knew the answer to all those questions. And as for his horse, Daisy was certain he had spurred the beast one too many times, and the horse had finally got its revenge by throwing his master over a fence.

The weaker often did get their revenge somehow. The horse would throw, the cook would overbake, the maid would build a damp fire, and the daughter...well, the daughter would simply outlive. Her mother had not had the chance, and Daisy would not waste her own opportunity.

CHARLES HAD ARRIVED to Ramsgate late the evening prior. Now, in the cold light of morning, he stared at the drawing room of the ramshackle structure he was meant to occupy. No, he could not even call it a drawing room, as that would imply there were other rooms of differing uses. There was no library, no sitting room, no dining room, not even a water closet—only a privy some yards behind this hovel. There were not servants' quarters! There was only this room, a lone bedchamber, and a rudimentary kitchen with no cook in it. The roof over his head was laid bare, with no proper ceiling put in—he could see darts of sunlight coming through gaps in the old shingles.

He'd met the agent to open the main house and had, at first, thought it might be pleasant. The house itself was located on the west cliff. It was commodious, of sturdy gray stone, and had a charming view of the sea. The furnishings were not elaborate, but then a seaside house did not need expensive curtains that would only grow moldy from the salty ocean mist or deep carpets that would only trap sand. Its worst fault was that it needed to be cleaned up, it looked as if the occupants had suddenly left without the slightest preparation. For all that, he thought it would do very well, indeed.

He should have realized why the agent paled when he asked to see the cottage and informed the man that he would stay in it. Amongst the fellow's mumblings about its modest circumstances, he'd followed him through the back garden to one of the smallest houses he'd ever seen. It seemed hardly worth the effort of building!

"This is unacceptable," Charles said to the agent standing by the door.

The agent, glancing around the sparse room, did not see reason to argue with the assessment. "Perhaps, my lord," he said hopefully, "you might consider a hotel? Or there are any number of bachelor apartments to be had. You might even rent your own house."

Charles thought he might consider any or all of those things, had he any money to pay for them. The particulars of the Dukes' Pact were so well known by this time that he could not think he would be extended credit by a landlord. Any proprietor worth his salt stayed well apprised of who was in town and what they had at their disposal. They had no choice, else there would be an endless parade of young men who had suffered heavy gambling losses enjoying their rooms for free.

The agent reddened and Charles took that as rather a confirmation that his predicament was well understood.

"This will have to do, for now," he said. "Perhaps there are ways to bring this place up to snuff."

The agent nodded eagerly, as if relieved to hear the lord duping himself in such a manner. Charles well knew he *was* fooling himself. There was not enough money in the world to make something of this place.

It was an ungodly situation. Bellamy, his own butler, would stay in the main house. So would his valet, as there was nowhere to put him in here. His servants would live in better conditions than their master!

His father was a cruel fellow. Or his mother, or his grandmother. Or all of them, whoever had cooked this scheme up.

Well, they might plot and plan all they liked. Living in rough conditions would not be enough to defeat him. He would liken it to his old tent in the war or the camping he had done as a youth. It certainly would not be any more comfortable.

HARRY DALE, VISCOUNT Burke and heir to the Duke of Somerston, knew full well that he should not have accepted the Minkertons' offer to stay at Ramsgate. All in the neighborhood thought him as an older brother to Belle Minkerton. Belle Minkerton, herself, looked up to him as a brother. After all, he was four years her senior and she was not even to be out until the coming season. His parents and hers had a longstanding friendship born of close proximity and similar tastes. It would not have occurred to any of them that there was anything romantic in the air. And of course, there was not, it was only in his own head. Everyone, his parents and the Minkertons themselves, looked forward to whatever assistance he would lend at her launch. What eligible fellows would he steer in her direction?

He would rather not steer anybody toward her. He had been in love with Belle since the moment he'd first set eyes on her all those years ago. Her father, a baron who'd been sent to Antigua by his father to make a family fortune, had found he could not abide the slave trade. Much to his father's surprise, he'd returned not with a fortune but with an Antiguan lady he'd made his wife, after spending some years as an attaché to an admiral. He had brought his bride to England when Belle was just thirteen and settled on the neighboring estate. Her hair was ebony that shined in tight ringlets in the sun, her skin a rich deep brown, her dark eyes perennially amused, her lips always dancing on the edge of a smile. He had stuttered at their first meeting, and she *had* smiled kindly then, as if encouraging him not to make such a cake of himself. He had been certain his face had gone a deep red, though of course later, alone, he assured himself that he would only have appeared sunburnt.

At first, he'd been just seventeen and it was no more than a boyish crush—a deep secret he kept from his friends lest they tease him mercilessly. Over time though, he had grown into man and she into woman and the crush had not left him. It had transformed itself to a more mature love and he did not know what he was to do about it.

Though really, there was nothing to be done about it. It was not their age that separated them, but their relationship to one another. Belle would never regard him as anything but a brother and so as a brother he must act. He wished for her happiness above anything, though it inevitably led to his own never-ending unhappiness. He would assist her during her season, though he'd really rather not.

His resolve was firm on the idea. He knew that he should have stayed well clear of her over the summer. Yet, here he was, in her very house. He cursed himself for his weakness.

It would have been well if he could have been more like Dalton. That gentleman might be trapped in the company of Miss Danworth and yet he would never fall for her charms. Dalton was impenetrable. He was not.

He would call on Dalton as soon as he might. Perhaps spending more time with the hardened gentleman would rub off on him. He would introduce Dalton and Miss Danworth to the Minkertons and thereby keep Dalton's good example of disinterest squarely in front of him.

Burke sighed. If he were to be honest with himself, he did not mind bringing Dalton into Belle Minkerton's sphere because he knew full well she would not like him. She would size him up and find him self-indulgent for his scowling, as she would not know that of all gentlemen, Dalton had been most changed by war. At school, he'd been the one always joking. The transformation was an understood thing among his friends, though nobody thought it right to comment upon. They'd all just become incredibly lenient with him, even forgiving him for endless interference with their future wives. Burke supposed it must be a testament to their friendship that they'd not all broken with him. Not even Lockwood, who he'd imprisoned to keep him away from his lady.

He'd thought Dalton would slowly come out of whatever morass he'd landed in, but the change seemed rather permanent at this point. He should be deeply ashamed that he was happy Belle would not like him. He should be even more ashamed that he would probably fail to mention the cause of his friend's unhappy outlook.

He must get better at wrangling his feelings!

THE LEAD COACHMAN the duke had sent for Daisy and Mrs. Jellops had been convinced that they departed early enough to make the trip in one day, assuming they did not require too many stops. Daisy was not so anxious to arrive to Ramsgate and insisted it be done over two days with a stop overnight at an inn. If she had her way entirely, she might have stretched it to three days, but that would have pushed the already-irritated coachman a step too far. While most travelers would prefer to arrive to their destination as quickly as possible, Daisy would rather be jostled in a carriage day after day forever than reach the house at Ramsgate.

She gripped Mrs. Jellops' hand as they neared the outskirts of the town.

Mrs. Jellops squeezed back and said, "But my dear, it will not be as it was. You are the mistress of the house now and nobody shall come through the doors unless you admit them."

Daisy nodded, knowing in her logical mind that was true. Still, she could not erase the memories of what those past summers had been. Her father was always attracted to low company and the house seemed forever filled with soldiers of some sort. As they caroused downstairs, Daisy and Mrs. Jellops would bar her door with furniture pushed up against it before they dared sleep. Even as a young girl, she'd sensed the danger without needing Mrs. Jellops to tell her.

Her father, thinking as highly of himself as he did, would never imagine that one of those soldiers invited in and served his best brandy would dare meddle with his daughter. But men dared all sorts of things late at night and full of liquor. Sometimes, it might even be in the daylight, as Daisy had found cause to run out of the garden one afternoon after being forcefully kissed by one of those men.

Daisy felt her heart pounding as memories flooded back. "You do not think," she said, "that some of them, those who made their home in the town, might see the house has been opened and come knocking?"

Daisy had no need to identify who *them* were, Mrs. Jellops knew well enough.

"If they have the nerve to do it," Mrs. Jellops said, "Lord Dalton will put them to rights. I suspect they would leave with a bleeding lip or a blackened eye."

Daisy's heart slowed its pounding. Mrs. Jellops was right, whatever Lord Dalton was, he was a refined gentleman and would not countenance her father's rough associates.

"Lord Dalton may not be the most cheerful fellow," Mrs. Jellops went on, "but I think he can be relied upon." The lady hesitated a moment, as if a new idea was presenting itself to her.

"What is it?" Daisy asked. "I can see that something worries you."

"Ah, I suppose it is nothing. I only fear that Lord Dalton may not be in the best of spirits having gained an understanding of his accommodations."

Daisy bit her lip. "That is true, I suppose. But then, would it really be possible to further darken the lord's mood? Black cannot become blacker, after all."

Both ladies did their best to suppress their laughter, silently looking out their respective windows and only the shake of their shoulders giving them away. It was forever a habit between them, born of dark days, to laugh when contemplation grew too uncomfortable.

CHARLES HAD DONE his best to ready the house, and ready the hovel that was to be his own home for the duration. He'd hired a service to straighten both places, wash linens, gather the dust up, and air things out. He'd already spent one dashed uncomfortable night in the cottage, harangued by crickets and beetles and God knew what else crawling around. It had rained in the early morning and he was helpfully informed of that fact by the gentle pounding of drops on his forehead. He'd arisen damp and irritable. The next night, he'd spent in the house in peace, but now that Miss Danworth was set to arrive, he'd be back to his untenable lodgings.

He had not been able to avoid noticing the maids' pursed lips at the endless amount of empty wine and brandy bottles that littered the main house. They were under tables and rolled into corners, standing on bookshelves, and hiding behind curtains. There were cabinets full of them and a bin in the kitchen overflowed. Even for himself and his not particularly fastidious household, this seemed beyond the pale. He shuddered to think what had gone on in the house when Lord Childress was its master, or what Miss Danworth may have witnessed.

Bellamy and Charles' valet, Tate, had arrived several hours ahead of Miss Danworth and Mrs. Jellops. Their reactions came as no surprise to Charles.

Bellamy worked to keep the mirth from his face, especially after he'd got a look at the well-stocked wine cellar. His mirth faded mightily when he was informed that procedures in this particular house would not mirror their own in town. His butler was not to touch a bottle in the cellar without the express permission of Miss Danworth. While it had never bothered *him* that his servants were drunk below stairs, it would not suit a lady.

Tate, a retired Navy seaman, had looked round the ramshackle cottage to see where and how he would do his work. The curses that flew from him would have made any sailor blush. He had marched back to the house to devise a system of attending his lord across a garden each day without even the most rudimentary set-up to aid him. Though he deemed it impossible, Charles was certain he'd come up with some plan or other.

Finally, the ladies' carriages made their way up the drive and stopped at the front doors. Two of the grooms leapt down and assisted Miss Danworth to the gravel.

While many a lady had been made drab in mourning, her black silk dress seemed to suit Miss Danworth. Her person was all blond curls and pale cheeks and seemed even more so in their current dark frame. Her blue eyes shone bright on the cheerless background.

"Lord Dalton," she said, waiting for Mrs. Jellops to descend behind her.

Though she was assisted by grooms on either side, that lady struggled down the steps and landed with a thud. "My lord," she said.

"Miss Danworth, Mrs. Jellops," Charles said, bowing. "I condole on the loss of Lord Childress."

"Then you will be in small company," Miss Danworth said. "And do not count me among the few who will miss him."

Charles had not expected such an answer. Whatever Lord Childress had been, he had supposed his daughter would appear suitably stricken.

"I see you are shocked at Daisy's forthrightness," Mrs. Jellops said. "We have our reasons."

Charles nodded and thought he better not pursue that particular line of inquiry. "I realize the current situation is not usual," he said, "but I hope I have made sufficient arrangements for your comfort."

Miss Danworth swept past him toward the open front doors and said, "Look to your own comfort, my lord. I imagine the cottage will require your full attention in that regard. We shall send over your dinners."

As Charles watched the ladies enter the house quite without him, he felt a veritable steam coming from his ears. She would *send over* his dinners? He was not even to dine in the house? It was outrageous!

He paused. Miss Danworth might think she was to sashay in and send his dinners over, but there was not even a cook hired yet. He'd better tell her, and then she would descend her mighty throne and realize she required his help. Arrangements must be made with some tavern or other and he would see to it. He straightened his cuffs and marched in after her.

CHAPTER THREE

D AISY HAD BEEN both pleased and repelled to see Lord Dalton again. She had always allowed herself to like him a bit too much, but now that he was going to live in close quarters, she felt the need to push him off. She had intended to descend the carriage regally and portray an utter calmness of spirit, and hoped she had at least come close to it.

She'd since been introduced to Bellamy, who was Lord Dalton's butler and was to act as her own for the summer. As well, there was the lord's valet and three footmen of dubious looks. Where were the other servants? She had only brought her lady's maid, Betsy.

"Pardon me, Mr. Bellamy," she said, "I understand there may not be a housekeeper hired yet, but where are the housemaids? The cook? The kitchen maids?"

Bellamy seemed relieved that his master was just now approaching and could answer these uncomfortable questions.

"I have contacted an agency," Lord Dalton said. "They are to send over some promising candidates on the morrow. You may interview them, or I can do it if you prefer."

"Of course, I will do it," Daisy said. "I wish to have a hand in choosing the people surrounding me. Well, I suppose we must just shift as well as we might until then. I presume, my lord, you can arrange something in the kitchen. Eggs, perhaps?"

Daisy did not fail to note the look of outrage on the lord's face. She did not really think he could cook eggs or anything else, but it amused her to pretend that she did think it and that he would act as cook.

"I wouldn't know how to light the stove," he said between gritted teeth. "I'll arrange for something to be sent in."

Daisy nodded as if it were of no import to *her* how a dinner arrived. "As you wish. I suppose, under these unusual circumstances, you ought to dine here this night as an exception. It will only vex a proprietor if we arrange different orders to go to various locations."

"How kind," Dalton said.

Daisy nodded graciously. "Now, as I am to borrow your butler for the summer, I would have an interview. Mrs. Jellops, might you oversee Betsy? The footmen can carry up the luggage and she can begin to unpack. We will stay in our usual rooms, Lord Childress' room may be closed and locked. Lord Dalton? I presume you have other matters to attend to?"

Daisy watched with satisfaction as her directions were carried out, though Lord Dalton looked rather surly over being dismissed and Bellamy looked rather alarmed at being told to stay.

She had resolved to gain a firm hand over the staff. Daisy had always been rather run over by her father's servants, aside from her lady's maid. Darling Betsy had ever been her champion below stairs, while Mrs. Jellops acted the same above stairs. She would hire a housekeeper she felt Betsy could get on with and as for Bellamy…well, it was imperative that he learn to take orders from Daisy and not Lord Dalton.

"You may shut the door," she said to the butler. She seated herself and took her time arranging her skirts, then said, "It is a rather odd situation, to have another's butler act as one's own, but here we are. I presume you know your duties well enough but there are a few particulars I wish to convey."

Bellamy nodded and appeared in deep thought over what particulars might be shortly coming his way.

"My father has had occasion to consort with some rather low individuals over past summers. If any of those people arrive to the house, they are to be turned away instantly and told they need not ever return to it. You will know you encounter one of these rogues by their dress, their manner, and their lack of a decently composed card to send in. Anybody hinting that they are or have been a soldier must be kept out. Anybody claiming to be an old friend of Lord Childress must be kept out. Bring your footmen together to bar the door if necessary, but do not allow any of them to cross the threshold."

"Are there so many of them, Miss Danworth?" Bellamy asked, appearing agitated by the idea that they were soon to be under siege, and he was to be the battle commander manning the front line.

"Quite a few," Daisy said, "though how many will dare to gain entrance now that my father has departed the world, I know not. However, excessive drink, bold ideas, and the lure of a dowry may prompt a few."

Bellamy wiped his forehead with a handkerchief and Daisy thought he looked rather pale.

"Further," she said, "you are to carry out my orders as I direct them, with no consultation with Lord Dalton. He was your master and will be again, but he is not at this moment. That is all for now."

Bellamy nodded, then shuffled his feet and cleared his throat.

"Is there something you wished to add?" Daisy said, certain that there was. She hoped he was not on the verge of attempting to cow her or otherwise override her authority.

"It is only, that is…" Bellamy began, "it is quite right that you are the mistress. There is no confusion as to *that*. Only, I shouldn't like my boys to go all topsy-turvy on me. These footmen have been with me a long time and we have a certain way of going on."

Daisy could see that something was about to be proposed that she was not likely to favor. Nobody hemmed and hawed as this fellow was now doing when they wished to communicate something agreeable.

"Perhaps you might be more specific by what you mean," Daisy said. "What is this *certain way of going on*?"

"Well, me and the boys have the comfortable habit of having a bit of wine after our duties are done for the day. It gives the fellows something to look forward to, you see."

"I am not sure I do see," Daisy said. "What, in your mind, is a *bit* of wine?"

Bellamy stared over her head and out the window. "Oh, a bottle or two a man would do it."

Daisy was nearly dumbfounded. A bottle or two each? Was he mad? They must all be drunk as soldiers every night. Or, they *had* been. They would not do so under her own roof. It might be technically the duke's roof now, but while she lived in it, she would set the tone. She'd just arranged to keep any drunken visitors out of the house, she would not very well condone allowing drunken servants to terrorize her or Mrs. Jellops, or especially poor, dear Betsy.

"I am amazed you would propose such a thing," she said sternly. "I will excuse it as a mistake one might make when one has served a bachelor for too long. I certainly will not tolerate such habits, nor would I subject my female servants who must frequent the downstairs to the inevitable offensive behavior. You and your footmen will be granted one glass of ale at meals. Drink a drop further at your peril. You may go."

Daisy waited until the butler had made his way out of the room and closed the door behind him. The old fellow had gone very red in the face and she presumed he was outraged that his disgraceful habits were now curtailed.

She took a deep breath to calm herself. She had prevailed over Bellamy in this round and she would see to it that continued to be the case. The housekeeper she hired would be critical—as she knew well enough, the right forceful woman would bring Bellamy and his staff into line.

CHARLES HAD RETURNED to the cottage, if that was what one called it. He had set Tate to doing with it what he could and his valet had not shirked on the matter. He'd found a bolt of canvas and hung it over Charles' bed to stop the rain from falling on his face. He had scrubbed the floors and furniture with vinegar and placed bunches of lavender on every surface, the abode now smelling like a perfumed salad. A washstand had been procured, and Charles presumed Tate had stolen it out of the main house, as well as a tall bookcase that had been commandeered as a makeshift dresser to hold his clothes.

Before he could comment on the improvements, Bellamy burst through the door. "I am insulted to the end of my toes," the butler said. "I do not know how I can stand for it!"

Charles eyed him. Bellamy was certainly in some kind of state, sweat dripped from the old heathen's forehead. "I suppose you are determined to communicate the insult your toes have recently endured," he said drily.

Bellamy began to pace the small room. "As you know, my lord, Miss Danworth wished to have a private interview. Well, she wanted me to understand in no uncertain terms that she is the mistress and you are nothing. Charles Battersea, Earl of Dalton and heir to the Duke of Glastonburg, is nothing!"

Charles folded his arms. It was highly unlikely that Bellamy had worked himself into such a lather over a slight to himself.

"That is all?" he asked. "She said nothing further?"

Bellamy stopped his pacing and stood staring at the lone window at the far end of the room. "She also said that me and the boys are to have no more than a glass of ale at mealtimes. At my *peril*, is what she said."

"I suspect her father may have indulged to excess," Charles said. "There were wine bottles in every corner of the house when I arrived."

"And I should pay for that?" Bellamy said. "*I* do not drink to excess."

"You most certainly do," Charles said, suppressing his laughter.

"I see," Bellamy said petulantly. "Everybody is to drink all they like but the poor butler and his footmen. She says we may have a string of drunken louts arriving at the door and I am to keep them out. Without even a glass of wine to fortify myself against them!"

"Wait a moment," Charles said, "who are the drunken louts she expects to turn up?"

"I do not know," Bellamy said, and Charles could see very well he did not care. "She says her father had engaged in low company."

"I bet he did," Charles said softly. All the wine and brandy bottles strewn everywhere made more sense now. Childress had run his house as if he were a rogue bachelor, with no thought to having a daughter in the house.

"Stop your complainin,' you old reprobate," Tate said to the butler. "You don't hear me complainin' about the impossible working conditions, now do you? We've all just got to get on with it."

"Probably good advice," Charles said, "though I feel rather complaining myself. As for you, Bellamy, it will not do you harm to lay off the wine bottle for a few months."

"We shall see!" Bellamy said. "I fear my body will be shocked and land me in a sickbed."

"If your body is shocked by these new and improved habits, it will be shocked with relief and delight," Charles said. "This may not be how any of us prefer to spend the summer, but we can at least comfort ourselves that I will outwit my father in his ridiculous schemes."

"But my lord," Bellamy said, looking as if a new horror had just occurred to him. "There is to be a housekeeper. A housekeeper! You know what they are like!"

Charles of course *did* know what they were like. Lurking in every corner, pursing lips over the slightest irregularity, and generally making themselves a nuisance. It was precisely the reason he did not have one. He would go back to his comfortable bachelor ways in a few months.

But for now, he would not have it all his own way and neither would Bellamy.

DAISY HAD NOT the first idea what was involved to have a dinner delivered to the house. She did not wish to admit that fact and so sat in the drawing room with Mrs. Jellops and attempted a serene expression.

It seemed to her that Lord Dalton was very well acquainted with the procedure, as he had been directing a long line of boys carrying trays into the dining room. She supposed he did not even bother to keep a cook at his house in town.

Bellamy had made an appearance to announce that dinner was to be served in a quarter hour. Daisy had not missed that he practically spat the words out and neither had Mrs. Jellops.

"He is an unpleasant fellow," Mrs. Jellops said, after Bellamy closed the door.

"He is put out because he proposed that he and his footmen be allocated one or two bottles of wine every night," Daisy said. "One or two bottles *each*."

"Each? He never did," Mrs. Jellops said. "Goodness, what an idea."

"Apparently, it is how he goes on in Lord Dalton's house in London."

"Well," Mrs. Jellops said, patting her hand, "it shan't go on here. There will be no carousing in this house."

"No, there will not," Daisy said resolutely. "We will not allow the past to be recreated under our noses. I should like to go to sleep without pushing furniture in front of my door or listening to shouts and the sound of broken glass below me."

"Those days are over, my dear," Mrs. Jellops said. "You must do your best to leave them in the past else they haunt you forever."

"That would not do at all," Daisy said. "We cannot have survived only to survive unhappily."

"Just so."

"Dinner is served, Miss Danworth," Bellamy said. He had reappeared and stood gravely in the doorframe. He turned on his heel and marched off.

Daisy glanced at Mrs. Jellops. "It does not appear that we are to be led in, so I suppose we must escort ourselves."

"Have my arm, dear," Mrs. Jellops said, "and I will take you in."

Mrs. Jellops showed the way and Daisy was surprised to find the dining table very near what it would have been had she a cook in the kitchens. At least, if the cook had decided to send everything up at once and do the carving while he was at it. The table was laid with sliced beef, a carved roast chicken, a large pork pie, and a fish in a white sauce. There were salads, pickled vegetables, cheeses, and berry tarts. A large soup tureen sat on a sideboard. It became apparent to Daisy that they were not to have courses. They were to have *one* course that included everything.

Bellamy had uncorked the wine and poured it into glasses, though he looked like murder doing it. For that matter, the footmen appeared surly as well. Daisy supposed they were imagining the wine they poured might have been their own under a more lenient mistress.

"I do not know what seating arrangement you prefer," Lord Dalton said, "and so I have put you at the head of the table with Mrs. Jellops on your right, while I will take the bottom end."

"Quite right," Mrs. Jellops said. Daisy did not know if it were right or not, but it seemed satisfactory enough.

"In any case, I presume you will hire a cook on the morrow and we may be done with this arrangement. As I am to have my meals *sent over.*"

Daisy understood perfectly well that Lord Dalton felt himself poorly used over the scheme to keep him to the cottage at meals. Still, what else could she do? She did not trust herself to dine with the gentleman every night of the week. There was no telling how she might fall for his charms, such as they were, and then attempt to convince herself that he was not like the others. Men were all the same, with only rare exceptions, *that* she knew. But how many women had fooled themselves to think otherwise? Her own mother certainly had done.

There were times when she felt society's rules about how a lady was to conduct herself were burdensome, and then other times when she felt protected by them. In this case, she felt rather protected.

"I realize it is an imposition, Lord Dalton," she said, "but I really do not see how else we are to go on. It would not be seemly to do otherwise."

Lord Dalton nodded. "You are, naturally, afraid of any talk that might arise," he said. "I suppose one in the Marriage Mart must be cognizant of such things."

Daisy laid down her soup spoon. "The *Marriage Mart*?" she said.

"It is just a phrase, Miss Danworth," Lord Dalton said. "No need to appear over-delicate about it."

"I am not swooning over the phrase," Daisy said curtly. "I am surprised at the idea. Did you really think that a daughter of Lord Childress, one who has seen what men are, would be so willing to chain herself to one of them?"

Lord Dalton looked up from his soup in surprise.

"I think," Mrs. Jellops said hurriedly, "perhaps that is a subject for another day. Or no day at all."

"So," Lord Dalton said slowly, "you have no intention to marry?"

"Certainly not," Daisy said. "Aside from children, and the money I do not need, what use are men?"

"When Daisy reaches her majority," Mrs. Jellops put in, "we will go to the seaside. Brighton, we think."

"You are already at the seaside," Lord Dalton pointed out. "Why not stay here? I am sure my father would not mind turning over the house to you if you wish it."

Daisy looked around at the four walls and said quietly, "This is the very last place I would stay."

As she had looked about the room, she could not help but notice that the footmen and their butler stared at her wine glass as if they had poisoned it and waited for the effects to show themselves. She'd had enough of their sullenness.

"Further, Lord Dalton," she said, "while it may have been kind of the duke to lend me your servants, I have a mind to give them back. If they cannot manage to hide their disgust at not being allowed to drink themselves into oblivion every night, I will show them to the road before the moon has risen much higher in the night sky."

The shock of her words hit their mark. The footmen straightened themselves and looked off into the distance, as they should have been doing from the beginning. Bellamy's cheeks suffused with an interesting shade of red.

Lord Dalton only laughed. "Hear that, fellows? Do not think I will rescue you if she does throw you out. It will be a long walk back to the London house."

Now it was Daisy's turn to blush, though she worked hard to hide it. There was something flattering about Lord Dalton utterly failing to side with Mr. Bellamy.

Before she was forced to comment, a loud banging came from the front doors. Bellamy nodded at the sound and hurried from the room, no doubt grateful to make his escape.

Daisy presumed it was the tavernkeeper having come with something he forgot, until she heard the raised voice at the door.

"Stand aside, man," the person said. "I was a great friend to Lord Childress and have every right to pay my respects."

Lord Dalton looked to Daisy, who shook her head no. He nodded at the two footmen and they hurried to the scene. Though Daisy had been intent on keeping Lord Dalton from directing servants who were to take their direction from *her*, she was not so intent on it now.

She recognized that loud voice. It was Lieutenant Farthmore. He was one of the very worst of her father's cronies. Even sober, he was not a likable fellow. The one and only encounter she'd ever had with him, he'd leered at her and told her she was pretty enough to be on the stage. He was revolting. How like him to be the first to appear. How like him to attempt an entrance at this time of night.

With relief, Daisy heard the door slam shut. From somewhere on the gravel drive, Farthmore shouted, "Rotters!"

He might shout all he liked; she did not care. He would get on his horse and weave away to whatever low place he went to next. Now that he understood he would be barred at the door, he would not be back.

"Charming," Lord Dalton said.

Daisy dabbed her lips with her napkin and said, "As I informed Mr. Bellamy, my father was not discriminating in those he chose to associate with. None of them are to be admitted."

Behind her, she heard a tap on the window. She turned in her seat and saw that Farthmore had not left at all. He'd gone round the side of the house and now threw pebbles at the glass to gain her attention. He waved, and she turned back round.

"For God's sake," Lord Dalton said, rising and throwing his napkin down. He strode from the room.

Daisy and Mrs. Jellops stared at each other. Mrs. Jellops shrugged and said, "I expect Lord Dalton will manage it."

Daisy peeked back around her chair in time to see Lord Dalton walk up to Lieutenant Farthmore, wallop him in the face, and then throw the staggering gentleman over his shoulder.

Mrs. Jellops, wide-eyed, whispered, "There, you see?"

They were silent for some minutes, Daisy having entirely lost her appetite.

Lord Dalton strolled back into the dining room, brushing off his coat sleeves. "Pardon me," he said. "The gentleman arrived in a carriage, which he has been put back into. His coachman will not dare another trip up this drive."

"Thank you, Lord Dalton," Daisy said.

"Who does the fool imagine himself to be, accosting a house in such a manner? If one is refused entry at the front door, one does not then begin knocking on windows."

Daisy laid down her napkin. "Farthmore was a Lieutenant of the Royal Marines. He thinks very highly of himself, having attended the Siege of Tarragona. According to him, Lord Murray ought to have been hung for his incompetence and the Lieutenant would have made short work of things, had *he* been in command. As it was, he credits himself with an early success of conducting spying missions along the seashore. I know all of this, not because I ever wished to, but because the Lieutenant repeated it, loudly, every time he was drunk in this house."

"Only an idiot would brag about being present at Tarragona. Though, I cannot think he is the only fool who will turn up," Lord Dalton said, taking his seat.

"Possibly not," Daisy said.

"I suppose they will all be sizing up their chances. Your father is out of the way and a dowry is dangling in front of them, and an inheritance from your grandmother too, if I am not mistaken. They will take a run at the place and try their luck."

"I do not doubt it," Daisy said. "Though my father was happy to carouse with them, they all knew very well he would not countenance a more permanent connection. They may think all difficulties have been removed, they are just that odious and vile. What they fail to comprehend is that I would not countenance a one of them if I were starving and penniless. Throwing myself into the sea would be a preferable fate."

"Throwing yourself into the sea? No need to reach *those* heights of drama, Miss Danworth," Lord Dalton said, serving himself a generous portion of beef.

Daisy tightened her hand on her fork. "If you think I am exaggerating, you do not know what I have seen of these men."

"No, perhaps I do not," Lord Dalton admitted. "If you approve, I will hire a few watchmen for the house. They may turn these fellows round at the bottom of the drive. You are welcome to interview them yourself if you like, but men in that line of work are not…"

"Yes, of course, you must see to it, thank you," Daisy said. She had no wish to interview the rough sort of men who would not mind throwing people from a property, nor would she know what to ask them if she did.

"I'm finding the weather unaccountably cool for the season," Mrs. Jellops said loudly.

Daisy suppressed a smile. Lord Dalton's eyebrows only raised slightly. The conversation and the events at this particular dinner had veered far from usual, and Mrs. Jellops had apparently decided it was high time to return to more regular subjects.

CHAPTER FOUR

B ELLE MINKERTON READIED herself to go downstairs. As a usual thing, such an operation did not take overlong. She never could comprehend how some of her friends took an hour deciding on a dress to wear or what bonnet to pair with it. She was generally in a decisive state of mind and did not wobble all over the place in her thinking.

Just now, though, she *did* feel a bit wobbly. She'd harbored some hopes, the sort of hopes one did not dare share with anyone, and those hopes had been dashed.

Dear Harry Dale, or Lord Burke as he was called in wider society, was in love with another.

Oh, she knew she should never have allowed hope to grow in the first place. Harry quite looked upon her as a younger sister. They'd known each other for years and he'd teased her, and shown her how things were done, and even scolded sometimes, just as a brother would.

But still, she had hoped. She had grown an inch this past year and filled out, she thought. She was still on the slight side of things, but she was certain she looked more womanly. She was to be out next season, and did that not mean she was full grown? And then, Harry was to stay with them all summer. Might he not notice this change? Might he not begin to view her in a different light?

What an imagination she had! The true state of things had been forced upon her last evening. Harry had talked endlessly of Miss Daisy Danworth. Miss Danworth was said to have just lost her father. Miss Danworth was a lady anybody might wish to be acquainted with. Miss Danworth would be a fine companion for Miss Minkerton.

Worst of all, Miss Danworth was staying not a mile down the road. Though she was in mourning, they should invite Miss Danworth to a small dinner.

Inviting a lady in mourning to dinner? Did that not suggest some sort of intimacy? Oh, Harry had pressed on with the idea. Miss Danworth's father had been rumored to be unpleasant and so it was likely that Miss Danworth was not terribly grief-stricken.

He seemed to know an awful lot about the lady!

Still not quite wishing to believe the end of her hopes was in sight, Belle had asked Harry what she looked like. Harry had taken his time answering, then said, "She is rather renowned for her blond curls."

Blond curls! Now she was forced to understand that Harry pre-ferred blond curls!

Belle's maid, Peg, had arranged absolutely everything that could be done. Now, she stood staring at her mistress and said, "Shall you go down, Miss?"

Belle rose and shook out her skirts. "Never mind me, Peg. I am just being stupid this morning."

CHARLES SPENT A somewhat more comfortable night in the cottage. He was at least not rained on and the vinegar and lavender that Tate had so liberally doused the place with had driven off a good amount of the insects. Not all of them, though, as he'd woken to a large brown spider leisurely strolling across his bedclothes. No sooner had he noted the spider, than a cat leapt onto the bed and caught it.

The cat took its prey to a windowsill, making short work of the unfortunate spider. It then stared defiantly at him with one spider's leg hanging from its mouth.

"Get out," he said. "Go on, get out of here."

He was not even sure how the cat had got in, other than to surmise that the cottage was so badly built that anything wishing to come indoors might find a way.

The cat chewed up the last of the spider, but remained unmoved by his directive. She was a tabby and clearly not a favored houseguest of anybody's home. Her ribs showed, some of her fur was matted, and she had a look about her of hard living.

Charles sighed, got out of bed, and gave the cat a roll from his last night's tray. The cat was not skittish, she did not run from him until she'd got a firm hold of the bread. She took her breakfast, glared at him as if she suspected he might attempt to take it back, and stole away with it under his bed.

He knew very well he should not have done it, for he'd never rid himself of the thing now. But, he couldn't very well allow an animal to starve. His stable cat in London had been well provided for, in case the rat population proved insufficient.

Now, he sat on a bench out of doors, having coffee before Tate shaved him, while the cat slept under the bench. What an evening! He'd had no idea Miss Danworth had decided she would not marry. She was out two seasons now and had been seen everywhere. Perhaps that should have been a clue, though. She was remarkably pretty, but as far as he knew, nobody had yet asked.

They would not, though, would they? She had kept away all comers with her own cool manner. He had once joked that underneath her laughter was a sheet of ice, and he was not far wrong. He'd just not known why that was. Everybody understood Lord Childress to be an unpleasant sort, but since arriving to Ramsgate he'd begun to get a clearer picture of things. He could not really fault Miss Danworth for not wishing to tie herself if her father had been her primary example of men.

For himself, Charles knew what lay in the hearts of men when they were loosed in war. He had just not supposed a lady would know it. In a drawing room, those qualities were deeply buried under a veneer of civility and that was the veneer most ladies were acquainted with. Miss Danworth had seen the veneer unmasked by her father's unsavory mode of living, and she was repulsed. Perhaps even more so because she was a woman. Not because women were so delicate, he'd never believed that old saw, but because a woman put herself in her husband's power when she married.

Then there was Farthmore to think of. He'd played the whole thing down when he returned to the dining room, but he wondered if he might not encounter the fellow again. What a fuss the rogue had put up as he was being wrestled into his carriage! He'd squealed as if he were being murdered and swore he'd have his satisfaction.

There was always the outside chance that Farthmore might challenge him. It would be idiotic in the extreme, he was a crack shot. But men like Farthmore *could* be stupid when their pride was stung. He could only hope a sore head and the cold light of day would inspire him to close his mouth and move off to a greener pasture.

But if not Farthmore, how many others would he have to contend with? Watchmen or no, what he'd said to Miss Danworth was all too true. Her dowry was respectable and what she would come into from her grandmother was enormous. How many of Lord Childress' loutish friends might think they saw an opportunity? Men of that ilk spent all their time considering what *they* would prefer, with no amount of time wondering if their quarry had any opinion about it.

For a moment, he thought it might be prudent to remove to the estate in Shropshire, run down though it was rumored to be. But what difference would he find there? Loutish soldiers would be replaced by whatever loutish farmers Childress had associated with.

To his surprise, Charles saw Bellamy coming through the garden at an unusually brisk pace. His butler bowed and said, "I've sent word to the agency, my lord, that we require several watchmen. I've thought of how it ought to be done when the candidates turn up. I can head them off at the front door and lead them round and through the terrace door that leads directly into the library. In that way, Miss Danworth and Mrs. Jellops shall not be disturbed in the drawing room."

This was a more energetic speech from Bellamy than Charles had heard in years. Further, he'd seemed to have accomplished the task without the unnecessary foot-dragging that usually accompanied any work to be done.

"I find you in better spirits than I would have imagined, now that your wine holiday has commenced."

Bellamy appeared surprised by the suggestion. "I *am* rather sprightly this morning, but I hardly think…though perhaps…"

"What did you do with yourself last evening, now that you do not carouse with the boys until two in the morning?"

"Well, we were at a loss, at first. I don't mind saying it. But then, Gerald had the idea of reading to us from a book to pass the time, and Tom came upon some cocoa beans in the pantry and had the idea of making some drinking chocolate. It weren't our usual habit, but it went over pretty well, in the end."

Charles did his best to control his urge to laugh over the idea of the three of them drinking chocolate and indulging in literature. "And what, pray, did you choose to read?"

"*The Mysteries of Udolpho*," Bellamy said, staring off into the distance. "What's to be the end of it, I cannot guess. Though, we're all firmly behind Valancourt." The butler suddenly straightened himself and said, "I'm going to have a word with Miss Danworth about the cocoa bean situation. If she does not give us free rein with it, I can't say what might go on."

"Let me guess," Charles said, "you will be insulted down to the end of your shoes."

"To the end of my *toes*, my lord. By the by, did you know there is a cat under your own feet?"

⫸⫷

DAISY WAS IN the drawing room when Bellamy brought in the post. There seemed to be quite a lot of it and she hoped there was not more to do with the estate. As far as she understood it, everything had been settled.

He held the silver tray out and she took the pile and sat it on a table next to her. That would have been the time for the butler to make his departure, and yet he stood there staring at her.

She dearly hoped he was not planning on making another proposition involving the wine cellar.

"Is there something else, Bellamy?" she asked.

"As it happens, Miss," he said gravely. "The boys and me have taken a liking to drinking chocolate and I would just mention that it's a mercy we take a liking to anything after…the wine we do not have."

Daisy could not imagine why she was meant to know anything about it. She waited for him to go on.

"I would only point out that if there was to be some kind of ration of it when a housekeeper darkens our doors… Well, that would sit badly I'm afraid. The beans that are there won't last a fortnight, and then I do not know what we're to do."

"So you are saying you wish to be given leave to drink chocolate each evening over the housekeeper's objections?"

"I do, Miss."

Daisy thought it was a bargain worth taking. She could not care less how many cocoa beans they went through. "Drink away, Bellamy. I cannot imagine a housekeeper will mind what she does not pay for but if she does, I will rectify it. Drink chocolate up to your eyes if you wish."

Though Bellamy only nodded before he hurried from the room, his springing stride gave Daisy the idea that he viewed himself as having won a very great victory. She was perfectly amenable to that idea. As far as she was concerned, she had won a great victory too.

Daisy picked up the pile of letters on the table and thumbed through them. Some had been forwarded from London and some had been sent locally. There was one from Lady Grayson, all the way from Sweden, and she put that aside. She and Kitty had developed a regular correspondence since the remarkable events of Lady Hathaway's themed ball. Daisy knew full well that she'd need tea and concentration to fully take in Kitty's letter—it would be full of delightful tableaus from her wedding trip and the charming things Lord Grayson had said or done, interspersed with interesting conjectures on all manner of sciences. Kitty might be writing quite above Daisy's head when she pondered hemi-parasitic flora, but she was a darling for not knowing it. As well, Kitty would not have been made aware of Daisy's more recent changed circumstances and she would take her time in writing out all the details.

There were seven letters written in distinctly male hands and all sent via penny post. As she had no close acquaintance in this town, she was very afraid of what these letters contained.

Determined to be done with it, rather than sit in dread staring at them all, she opened them one by one.

The first six were as off-putting as she thought they would be. All from her father's unsavory cronies, all purporting to be devastated to hear of his demise, and all proposing to call upon her to pay their respects. Some claimed they understood her at-home day to be Tuesday, some Wednesday, still another Thursday. She had set no at-home day, and if she had she would not be at home to any of them.

The seventh letter was entirely different. It was from Lord Burke, who informed her that he stayed not a mile off with a family named the Minkertons. His note was kind. Though he recognized she was in mourning, he ever so gracefully hinted that she might not be overly distraught and he did not think an intimate family dinner would go amiss. The Minkertons, according to Lord Burke, were anxious to make her acquaintance and Mrs. Minkerton and her daughter would call upon her whenever she found it convenient. He would await her further instructions in case he had overstepped and she was not equipped to see anybody just yet.

It was so like Lord Burke. There was a kind offer, but no pushing in. She would write him back this very day. She was anything but distraught and if *he* judged the Minkertons worth knowing, then they certainly must be.

Daisy heard a soft knock upon the drawing room door and Bellamy came through.

"The candidate for housekeeper, a Mrs. Broadbent, has arrived," he said stiffly.

The butler's tone was distinctly disapproving, which gave Daisy the idea that she was about to like Mrs. Broadbent.

"Do show her in, Bellamy," she said pleasantly.

Though she attempted to look unconcerned, Daisy felt her nerves creeping up on her. She had been determined to do the interview herself with no help from Lord Dalton, or even Mrs. Jellops. She'd felt it vital for anybody who was hired to be in no confusion over who was in charge. Dear Mrs. Jellops would have been a mighty help to her, but Daisy knew that it would appear as if she were not old enough or wise enough to manage her own affairs.

For all that, though, she now wished her companion was by her side.

Daisy had expected the lady to walk through the door, but Mrs. Broadbent rather charged through it. She was, as her name hinted at, rather broad, not just in figure but in features. The *bent* half of her name let her down however, as there was not anything bent about the lady—she comported herself ramrod straight like any soldier. Daisy's grandmother would have called her looks *farm-raised on ample fresh food.*

Aside from her stride, there was a general energy about the lady as she ducked her head and said crisply, "Miss Danworth."

"Mrs. Broadbent," Daisy said. "Do sit down, Bellamy will bring in tea."

Despite telling Lord Dalton that she would do the interviews, Daisy had not the first idea of how they were conducted. As the lady seemed rather surprised that she would get tea, Daisy said, "I will admit to not knowing what is regular in these circumstances, but I do not see how one goes wrong with tea."

Mrs. Broadbent sat herself down and said, "Quite right, Miss Danworth. Just don't go giving tea to a candidate for housemaid else they'll take on airs and prove themselves intractable."

Daisy nodded, though she had no idea what sort of airs a housemaid might take on or what the trouble might be if she did. The housemaids she was used to generally were of a skittish nature, always looking to be well away from wherever her father happened to be.

Bellamy brought in the tea in good time, as Daisy had forewarned him that it would be wanted. He had sniffed at the idea, which had not moved her at all on the subject. She rather thought his complaint was over having to deliver tea to a mere housekeeper.

As he laid the tray, Bellamy eyed Mrs. Broadbent. Mrs. Broadbent eyed Bellamy. The lady did not look the least put off by him.

As Bellamy shut the door, Daisy poured the tea and handed Mrs. Broadbent a cup. "I have your references of course, but perhaps you could tell me of your last employment?"

Mrs. Broadbent nodded as she added an alarming amount of sugar to her tea. "The dear earl and his lady were quite kind, I got on very well there. They ran a tight ship, which any housekeeper must find comfort in. Though, the poor earl was not so tight with his money, gambling you know. Now, they've set off to India to try to rescue his fortunes. I was sad to part with them, but I could not see my way clear to accompany them."

"Ah, I see," Daisy said. "I suppose you would be averse to the heat of the place?"

Mrs. Broadbent shook her head vigorously. "Weather, Miss Danworth, would never have the power to overcome me, of that I can assure you."

Daisy waited to be told the reason, then, that the lady did not go with her employer.

"I see you wonder at it," Mrs. Broadbent said. "I will not prevaricate or shilly-shally round the thing. As much as I like a tight ship, I will never set foot on an *actual* ship. I do not approve of all this traipsing about the world. Englishmen should stick to England and all this marching into other countries does us no more credit than if we were Napoleon himself. It is my view that people, wherever they live, would prefer to be left alone. I am afraid you will find that a daring opinion, but I am an exceedingly direct person!"

Daisy nodded, and heartily agreed that the lady was direct. However, it was not an opinion that concerned in the least as it related to housekeeping duties.

"We have an unusual situation here," Daisy said, "as I imagine you've gathered."

"Oh yes, everybody in town talks about the poor orphaned miss and how the duke ought to have brought you to his estate in Somerset. A shame, everybody thinks it."

Daisy worked not to blush, she'd had no idea her circumstances were spoken of widely. She supposed she should have, there was nothing the *ton* liked so much as gossip. Once a thing was said in a drawing room, it was just as quickly said at the servants' table, and then out the door it went into the wider world.

"Ah," Mrs. Broadbent said, "I should not have been so frank in *this* matter, I see. It's just that, you strike me as a lady who might appreciate directness."

"You are right in thinking it," Daisy said, collecting herself. "Now, I will be direct with *you*. The duke and his son have loaned me some servants—Mr. Bellamy, he is the butler, and Gerald and Tom, the two footmen. I would like to hire a housekeeper who can keep them in order. I know, of course, that the butler is supposed to be the senior servant, but this is an unusual case as he is not my own and he has been used to working for a bachelor."

Mrs. Broadbent set her cup down with a clatter. "I understand you perfectly. You wish to employ a lady who, through sheer force and energy, will cow those fellows into some semblance of a respectable staff."

"Well...yes," Daisy said. She had not put it into precisely those words, but that *was* what she wanted done.

"Look no further, Miss Danworth," Mrs. Broadbent said, "though the earl's butler was nominally in charge, it was *me* everybody came to. And why? Well, I simply over-ran the man with questions and notations and comments until he made a hasty retreat. *That* is what manages men—requiring them to justify themselves day and night. In the end, they are rather weak creatures who cannot bear the onslaught."

Daisy had not the first idea if that were true, but she was delighted that Mrs. Broadbent thought so.

"Also, I have a lady's maid, Betsy," Daisy said, "she has been with me through some difficult times, and I wish to know that she might be made comfortable in the house."

Mrs. Broadbent nodded knowingly. "A favorite. I understand you. We may think servants and masters are standing on the opposite sides of a great divide, but there are times when the two come to depend upon one another. What Betsy will require is a calm atmosphere, a kind and steady hand to guide her, and a formidable housekeeper to stand in front of her, depend upon it."

"I think you will do very well, Mrs. Broadbent," she said.

"I will do better than very well, Miss Danworth," Mrs. Broadbent said. "I always aspire to excellence, nothing else will suffice. Now, might I suggest that I interview the housemaids? We will want pliable girls who know their place and do not dare to attempt any lording it over Betsy—a lady's maid must have her proper place in the rank."

Daisy nodded, exceedingly relieved by the suggestion. "We also need to hire a cook and kitchen maids, may I suppose you might oversee that as well?"

"Naturally," Mrs. Broadbent said. "I happen to know that the earl's cook does not travel with him to India, he informed the earl that he could not cook with foreign ingredients if one were to point the barrel of a gun between his eyes. He's an emotional creature, cooks always are you know, but I can vouch for his skills. He may cry in the kitchen and throw a pot if a sauce curdles, but the food he *does* send up is always first rate. As for the kitchen maids, there are no end of them wanting employment—we will simply hire those that do not mind ducking the occasional pot."

Though Daisy had somewhat dreaded interviewing the servants, it had all come out highly satisfactory. She had full confidence in Mrs. Broadbent. Betsy was sure to get on with the lady and Bellamy…well, he could just fall in line or face her energetic questions, notations, and comments.

A WEEK HAD passed uneventfully, other than Bellamy and Tate grumbling over various circumstances that Charles could not be much bothered to hear about. Bellamy was forever blathering about some contretemps or other with Mrs. Broadbent, Tate was mostly put out about the cat hair that now seemed to be everywhere.

Charles was doing his best to attend to the pile of correspondence that lay on the makeshift desk in the cottage while the cat ate a piece of chicken at his feet. He found he kept losing his train of thought as the sounds of the recently delivered pianoforte being played reached him through the open windows of the main house.

He'd not known that Miss Danworth was particularly skilled on the instrument, she had never been one of those young ladies who pushed forward to play whenever the opportunity presented itself. He'd given her some amount of credit for that—who forced to listen was not painfully bored as one miss after the next showed off her very middling skills? Some of them even sang, to add to the racket. If that were not tedious enough, at the end of it there were the expected compliments to be doled out while the girl blushed and pretended she'd never heard anything so shocking.

The only time he had heard Miss Danworth play had been toward the end of an evening and she'd been practically forced to it. She'd played a quiet Irish air that had in no way indicated the skill he heard just now. It was as if her fingers flew across the keys.

The door swung open and Bellamy came through. "My lord," he said.

"I do not need anything just now," Charles said.

Despite this dismissal, Bellamy stood staring at him. Charles sighed. "What is it?" he asked.

"My lord, you have no idea what goes on in that house!"

"Am I to understand that you wish to tell me, though I have no wish to hear it?"

Charles hardly needed to have asked, as Bellamy was already pacing the floor. "That Mrs. Broadbent! She is a terror! For one thing, she is everywhere. One cannot turn a corner in peace without running into her. For another, she questions everything—why do the boys not sit up straighter at breakfast? Why is there a smudge on one of their neckcloths? How late are the boys up at night and is that really for their good health?"

Charles had not the first idea why he was to know or care in what manner the new housekeeper was harassing his butler.

"Then," Bellamy went on, "we are all to tiptoe round the cook so he doesn't get upset. He's an Irishman! Where did they find an Irishman and why am I to worry about Mr. Flanagan's feelings!"

Charles had no idea where they'd found an Irishman, nor was he particularly outraged. He'd done some shooting there and had found them a remarkably pleasant people, despite what anybody else said about it.

"He is a Catholic! He does not say so, but I know it. He must be."

"See he doesn't make you a convert, then," Charles said.

"Oh, and because *she* hired them all, they all look to *her*!" Bellamy said, ignoring the idea that he might soon be turned into a papist. "The cook, the maids, everybody! I say a thing, and they all look to *her*."

"You have been outfoxed, Bellamy," Charles said drily. "My advice is, get on as best you can."

Bellamy appeared stricken by this idea, as if there were simply no way to get on under these outrageous circumstances.

"Very well, my lord," he said. "Though I may die of shattered nerves one of these days, I will soldier on. I can at least be satisfied that I have won the cocoa bean debate. Mrs. Broadbent may look down her nose all she likes about that, but *I* have won. We *will* have drinking chocolate every night."

"I am delighted for you."

Bellamy turned to exit and then stopped. "I am sorry, I nearly forgot," he said, pulling a folded paper from his waistcoat, "this was just delivered for you."

He handed over the letter and left, sighing loudly all the way across the garden.

Charles could see it was in Burke's hand and tore it open.

Dalton,

I am well settled at the Minkertons and have taken the liberty of suggesting an introduction to Miss Danworth. Miss Danworth has replied favorably and Lady Bartholomew and Miss Minkerton are to call on Miss Danworth this afternoon. They will issue an invitation for a small dinner, just you, Miss Danworth, Mrs. Jellops, and the family. I presume you will welcome the invitation as the word in town is that you are living in a shed and have table scraps delivered for your dinner.

Burke

Dalton crumpled the letter and threw it on the floor. He was incensed over the idea that such a picture had been painted of him!

Perhaps he ought to ingratiate himself to the Minkertons and secure an invitation to stay there. He could, he was certain. A family with a lady ready to be launched always had invitations ready to throw at any highly-placed bachelor. Whatever their accommodations, it must surpass where he currently found himself. As well, he would dine at a dining table, not a tray in his hovel like he was a mistreated governess.

He paused his planning as he glanced at the pile of letters Miss Danworth had handed over. They were from rogues in town who would attempt to push into her company, all after her financial prospects no doubt.

Charles still had not decided what to do about it. Should he write them as her guardian and warn them off? Should he just ignore them and hope they took the hint?

As much as he wished to pack up and be off from this ridiculous place, he could not be entirely comfortable leaving Miss Danworth here on her own. What might be attempted by a man who saw a chance when there were no other chances in his future?

He'd hired a couple of watchmen, but if he were not here what might they be convinced to do for a few pounds. Fall asleep? Look the other way? Pretend they'd seen nothing?

He was still especially wary of Lieutenant Farthmore. So far, it had been silence from that gentleman. Silence, sometimes, was a dangerous thing. Had all of this occurred before the war, he would not have known how far a man would go. He would not have yet seen what desperate depths a man might travel. Now, though, he knew.

It was all well and good to defeat his father and that stupid pact at every turn. It would be another thing, though, for anything to happen to Miss Danworth. Despite her often impossible manner, she did not irritate him like the simpering misses that regularly surrounded him.

Truth be told, he was rather fond of Miss Danworth.

BELLE HAD DRESSED with great care for her visit to Miss Danworth and Mrs. Jellops. She was all but convinced that she could not hold up against Miss Danworth and her famed blond curls. Harry, or Lord Burke, as she must be careful to call him when out in society, had gone on and on about the wonderful Miss Danworth. Belle had avoided any commitment to visit this paragon of beauty for as long as she could, but Harry would not be put off. Finally, it was her mother who arranged it all.

If only her dear mama could see into her daughter's heart, she would not have done it! Belle could not tell her; she could not tell anybody. She could not bear to be seen as ridiculous.

And so, they had gone. There had been some slight hope, as she'd stood on the doorstep, that Harry had exaggerated Miss Danworth's charms. Sadly, he had not.

The lady was exceptionally beautiful, elegantly composed, and so much taller than she was. Then, to add salt into the wound, she'd been so kind. Miss Danworth said she would herself likely not attend the next season, but she would write letters of introduction for Belle to her various acquaintances.

Belle threw aside her sewing. "Really!" she said to the empty draw-ing room. "It is all very inconvenient."

Miss Danworth was to come to dinner, accompanied by Mrs. Jellops, and Lord Dalton, who she had not been introduced to yet. Belle knew very well that she'd end up liking Miss Danworth, though it would have been far more satisfactory to despise her.

She ought to be delighted for Harry. Is that not what one felt when a beloved found happiness?

Belle picked up her sewing and promptly pricked herself with her needle. She ought to be happy for him, but she was not. Her heart felt very like her poor bleeding finger.

CHAPTER FIVE

D<small>AISY HAD BECOME</small> wary of hearing a knock on the front doors, but one knock brought a delightful surprise. She'd nearly forgotten that the London modiste had taken her measurements and promised to send her all manner of dresses, just as the duke had directed.

The trunks had arrived, and Daisy could see now why the duke's wife had claimed this particular modiste as the only one who would do. There were day dresses, tea dresses, and evening dresses, all done in simple and elegant designs. Some were eminently suited to mourning in deep grays and lavenders, though some did seem a bit too cheerful for the state. There was a particularly charming dress in a reddish-orange silk that could not be imagined as mourning clothes—it was divine, but she might wait a few weeks at least before donning it. In all the selection, the modiste had made the most of it with cut, fit, and ingenuity. This night, Daisy had enjoyed donning a light silk gown, dyed a deep gray and decorated with pearl beading on the hem.

As Daisy rode in the carriage beside Mrs. Jellops on the way to dinner at the Minkertons, she could not help but think this was her first venture out into society since her father's death. It was only to be a small dinner, but it was something.

Lady Bartholomew and her daughter, Miss Minkerton, had called upon her and issued the invitation. She'd found both ladies remarkably pleasant, though Miss Minkerton was perhaps a bit subdued. The longer she'd thought upon it, the more she'd wondered if Miss Minkerton were not in some way like herself. Wishing to be carefree and yet not quite as able to as other ladies.

She had always noticed it about herself—she had not the blithe spirits that seemed to come so easily to everybody else she encountered. She had gathered, from hints here and there, especially from Lord Dalton, that she was viewed as rather cold. Miss Minkerton was not cold, not in the least. But there was something in her manner that set her apart. A hesitancy that spoke of private thoughts and a mind not at peace.

"Mrs. Jellops," Daisy said, "how did you find Miss Minkerton?"

"Oh, she seemed a pleasant girl," her companion said.

"But did she seem…a bit sad? Or subdued? Or somehow muted?"

"Sad? I did not think so. Perhaps on the quieter side of things."

"I wonder…"

Mrs. Jellops patted her hand. "My dear, I think you may be more sensitive to variations in temperament than other people. Miss Minkerton was on the quiet side of things because it was likely one of the first calls the girl has made outside of her own little neighborhood. Nerves, you know."

Perhaps that had been the case, though Daisy was not entirely certain. She gazed out the window at the darkness, only the crashing waves in the distance and the salt in the air belying that they were near the sea.

Lord Dalton was on his horse and led the carriage. She could sometimes glimpse him as they made a turn.

She sat back, knowing full well that she should not be trying to glimpse him at all. She had reminded herself of that idea just about every morning. He would come out of the cottage and sit on a bench with his coffee, unshaven and only wearing trousers and a thin shirt with the sleeves rolled up. He was devilishly handsome in his disarray and she would peek round the curtains at him. She had seen him at night sitting out there too. It was very wrong! Now, he had to go and sit a horse so finely.

He did most things very finely, despite his reputation of being difficult.

Daisy supposed the Minkertons would not mind that he was difficult. After all, they had a daughter to settle and he was to be a duke.

Daisy sat up straighter. Of course! This dinner was not meant to cheer Daisy, it was meant to introduce Miss Minkerton to Lord Dalton. How did she not see that before?

How odd that she would not have realized it. When she was her father's daughter, she'd questioned everything and put a cynical eye to every case. Her wits and suspicions were always sharpened and on alert. It seemed that now that his ever-present disapproving eye was gone, she'd softened and become less discerning.

It was not a promising development. If she meant to live without a husband, she must learn not to be taken advantage of. Sharp wits would be necessary. Servants, merchants, unwelcome lotharios—they would all take their chance. She must be prepared to spot any mischief or schemes.

Her thoughts drifted once again to Miss Minkerton and this evening's plan to present her to Lord Dalton. Would he find her pretty? She suspected so. Daisy did not see how anybody could look upon Miss Minkerton and fail to see the depths of her dark eyes or her generous lips always seeming on the edge of a shy smile. Very unlike Daisy herself. She thought, standing next to Miss Minkerton, she must seem rather brittle and frosty.

"But she will not be right for him," Daisy said softly.

"Who will not be right for who?" Mrs. Jellops asked.

"Belle Minkerton for Lord Dalton," Daisy answered. "She is too pliable, I think. He'll be best suited to somebody who can stand up to him."

Mrs. Jellops laughed and said, "By his own reckoning, he is not suited to anybody. Though if he were, I suspect he'd do well with a lady who could cheer him up a bit. No matter, I do not believe Lord Dalton will ever be caught."

No, of course, he would not be caught. Any more than she herself would be caught. He would not go starry-eyed over Miss Minkerton, no matter the lady's attractions.

Daisy was slightly disturbed to notice that the idea sat very well with her.

⇶⫷

CHARLES SAW THE house come into view ahead and turned up the drive. The Minkertons had been sensible enough to line the drive with torches to lead the way. In this neighborhood, one might ride themselves off a cliff and into the sea if one were not careful. Though the coachman swore he'd grown up in these parts and knew the roads like the back of his hand, Charles had ridden ahead of the carriage to avoid such a disaster.

He was rather cheered to be dining out. Mr. Flanagan did indeed produce a good dinner, regardless of how much Bellamy complained about him, but the atmosphere of his crumbling abode rather ruined the effect. When one was employed in driving off daring insects, both flying and crawling, and a cat who had made herself at home and was not afraid to demand her share of beef, one could hardly concentrate on one's plate.

He had supposed Miss Minkerton would be thrown at his feet, as all young misses seemed to be, until he'd considered that Burke would have warned them of his views and disposition. It hardly mattered, he supposed, as many a lady had made a run at him and then abruptly turned the other direction after conversing with him for any length of time.

Charles knew he ought to make himself more congenial. He was perfectly capable of it. It was just that he found these hordes of ladies not so subtly vying for a title so irritating! He had already shouted from the rooftops that he would not marry. He had not shouted *why*, though. As he'd thought more and more about it, he did not see how he was to explain it. Anybody hearing him would think him out of his wits. Or worse, ridiculous.

What was he to say? *Listen here, Burke, I will never marry because I have lost all faith in mankind and do not wish to perpetuate the species. Furthermore, you ought to do the same. Don't you understand that Hampton, Lockwood, Ashworth, Cabot, and Grayson will all send their sons to war someday?*

It sounded ridiculous to his *own* ears and he knew what he meant. Or at least, what he *had* meant. Perhaps the sights and sounds of the war were beginning to fade, or perhaps the unlikely circumstance of all his friends being delighted in marriage had begun to take a toll. He was beginning to lose some little amount of faith in his conclusions at Quatre Bras. Or at least, he was not as certain. His scar was always a reminder, though.

As much as the swirling balls and elaborate dinners worked to convince him that all was well with the world, the scar reminded him of what it could be.

He should not worry over it. It was unlikely that a lady like Miss Minkerton, just preparing for her launch season, would find a gruff and affirmed bachelor interesting. If she happened to, and began to sweetly fan herself, Miss Danworth would be there to bring some rationality to the table. If people were spices, he and Miss Danworth would be on the decidedly salty side and honey would be made very much less cloying in their presence.

Charles shook himself to throw off his thoughts. The house was just ahead and he must put his mind in the present. He was becoming convinced that his incessant brooding did nobody any good, most particularly not himself.

He leapt down from his horse, handed it off, and opened Miss Danworth's carriage door to help her down. He practically knocked a footman out of the way to do it.

⋙⋘

BURKE TOOK SOME amount of pride in introducing Dalton to the Minkertons. Though he could only claim them as friends, and not any other closer relationship he might wish for, he still took pleasure in noting Lord Bartholomew's friendly welcome, and Lady Bartholomew's dignified greetings, and Belle...well Belle was everything wonderful. She was lovely in a pale blue organza and very prettily acknowledged her guests.

He could not help note the contrast as she stood by Miss Danworth. That lady was tall, she had a very fair coloring, and held herself almost rigid. She was, he supposed, what people meant by an English rose. Pretty, dignified, and beware the thorns. He liked the lady, to be sure, and sympathized with her too, as everybody knew what a beast Lord Childress had been to her mother. And perhaps to her, too.

For all that, Miss Danworth could not compare to Belle Minkerton. Miss Danworth was a frosty winter morning, while Belle was a warm summer twilight.

They had gone through and now seated themselves round the dining table. As the party was to be so small, Lady Bartholomew had ordered the leaves taken out of the table and now they were quite the cozy party.

Burke approved very much of the idea, as small dinners were always the most interesting. Of course, any dinner with Belle was interesting.

"If I might inquire, Miss Danworth," Lady Bartholomew said, "and I hope I do not offend, you prior mentioned you would likely not attend the upcoming season. Do you intend to stay in mourning for a full year? I only ask as I think this will be a lonely place in autumn and winter and you are welcome to stay with us, even if you choose to remain out of society."

"You certainly do not offend," Miss Danworth said. "The offer is most kind and therefore I believe I must communicate the real case of it. Though I am dressed in dark colors, I do not particularly mourn my father."

"For good reason," Mrs. Jellops interjected, "though perhaps not reasons that ought to surface at a dinner."

Miss Danworth nodded to her and said, "Surely not. Though, I have made my plans with Mrs. Jellops. When I reach my majority, which is in less than a twelvemonth, we shall purchase a house in Brighton and live there."

"Do you say, then, that you will skip seasons for the foreseeable future?" Lady Bartholomew asked.

"Indeed," Miss Danworth said. "I have no need of them. I will not miss the balls and parties overmuch, I only wish for a quiet existence."

Lord Bartholomew appeared suddenly pensive and said, "You are very young to wish for quiet, Miss Danworth."

Miss Danworth nodded. "I can see how it would appear so, but when one has always longed for quiet and never had it, it does not seem so strange."

"I think I understand you," Lady Bartholomew said. "But you will not wait too long, I hope? Before you rejoin the world?"

"Now I think I understand *you*, Lady Bartholomew," Miss Danworth said, smiling. "You hope I do not closet myself away so long that I am put on a shelf. I cannot say, really. I only know at this moment I am determined to never marry."

Burke could not help but note the surprised looks on the Minkertons' faces. For that matter, he was a little surprised himself.

"Surely, Miss Danworth," he said, "you will not allow your…prior experiences…to color your future?"

"Why ever not?" Miss Danworth countered. "Is not prior experi-ence thought to be a useful guide?"

"Well yes, but in this matter you cannot—"

"I can, though," Miss Danworth said.

"Is it quite right? You might find you regret—"

Burke was cut off by Dalton, who said loudly, "Lord Bartholo-mew, you must compliment your cook on the soup."

BELLE HAD WONDERED if this dinner would further illuminate Harry's feelings for Miss Danworth. And of course, it most certainly had. Miss Danworth, in the natural throes of upset after the death of her father, vowed she would never marry. The lady could not conceive of such a thing at this moment. This wish to retire from society forever was all nonsense, of course, every woman of sense married. What else was one to do with one's life?

However, it was not surprising that poor Miss Danworth should feel her resolve permanent just now. She'd had a shock and must rest her mind from it.

Her dear Harry *had* been surprised by the idea, though. He'd all but railed against it! Miss Danworth must not think such thoughts!

She supposed he was so besotted he could not imagine waiting a year or two to claim her.

Now, he was sitting at the table in the drawing room, partnering Miss Danworth at whist with Belle's parents. She supposed the picture she viewed just now spoke of things to come. Miss Danworth would become Lady Burke and she and her husband would be great friends of Lord and Lady Bartholomew and they would often play at whist.

Where would Belle Minkerton be in all of this? Married off to some fellow who was not Harry. Always comparing the poor fellow to the superior Harry. Who could measure up? Who had his looks, his kind and thoughtful nature, his natural high spirits?

"Miss Minkerton," Lord Dalton said, interrupting her thoughts, "would you terribly mind to show me the sea charts your father mentioned that he has collected?"

Belle forced a smile. Lord Dalton was a weak cup of tea compared to Harry. He was one of those fellows who confused seriousness with dignity and intelligence. Still, she was left to entertain him and must do her best.

As she pulled down one of the heavy books from the shelf and showed him how to use the reference, she said, "I imagine Lord Burke will impatiently wait in the wings until Miss Danworth decides to return to the world."

She could not explain why she said such a thing, other than she wished to have further confirmation of her ideas. She already knew the truth though, so it was silly to hear it told twice.

Lord Dalton looked rather surprised at her boldness, and said, "Will he?"

"I expect so," Belle said. "Certainly, you do not view him an unsteady gentleman?"

"Unsteady? No, I suppose not."

"Then why pretend we do not see what we have clearly seen with our own eyes? He will wait, I am sure of it."

Lord Dalton turned and looked toward the whist table. "I had not thought…"

"In any case, Lord Dalton, allow me to show you the key to the map. Here is the chalk flats and just there are the depths noted."

Belle bent her head over the maps as if she'd never seen anything so interesting in her life. Harry might be across the room besotted by the charming Miss Danworth, but Belle would not be such a ninny as to allow anyone to notice that she cared about it. She would entertain and inform Lord Dalton as if her life depended upon it, though she could not conceive of a more tedious task.

⇛⇚

As THEY MADE their way slowly home from the Minkertons, Lord Dalton ahead of them on horseback and going very carefully as clouds had overshadowed the moon, Mrs. Jellops said, "They give a fine dinner, I would not mind knowing the details of the sauce on the chicken for Mr. Flanagan's edification. Though, my dear, perhaps you might think better of being so forthright about..."

"About my intentions," Daisy said, already knowing she ought to hide them but not being inclined to it.

"Yes, and your feelings toward Lord Childress. It is all well and good for me to know them—I was there and saw the truth of it. They are entirely justified, but for people recently met..."

"They might think me an unfeeling she-devil," Daisy said.

"I do not think they thought that at all," Mrs. Jellops said kindly. "They are a very good sort of people and I imagine they understand your circumstances. Lord Burke would have told them of it, is my guess."

"I do not imagine they think of me at all just now," Daisy said. In a quieter voice, lest her words carry in the still night air, she said, "They have introduced their daughter to Lord Dalton and must see the prospects."

"Lord Dalton?" Mrs. Jellops said. "Oh, I see, they may not have heard of his reputation and so think him a likely catch."

Daisy could not know if they'd heard of Lord Dalton's peculiarities or not, but she did not think it mattered much. She'd watched him over the seasons and this was the first time she'd ever seen him really engaged with a lady.

Oh, how they'd bent their heads together over those silly maps!

Certainly, Miss Minkerton was not at all interested in nautical maps. Certainly, Lord Dalton would have known the same. In fact, she was not at all sure *he* was much interested in them. And yet, they stayed there a very long time while Daisy was at whist.

More telling, Lord Dalton seemed exceedingly awkward afterward. The gentleman was never awkward! What else was to account for it but Miss Minkerton?

Daisy supposed she should not be surprised. Belle Minkerton was everything she was not. She was friendly and warm and had that pretty way of almost shyness, but not the sort of shyness that put one off and made one feel they were forced to do all the work. She was not simpering or fanning, she was simply adorable.

Daisy may have heard, from time to time, that she was herself acclaimed as a beauty. But really, if one were to cut off her hair that was always spoken of, she'd be nothing at all. Further, she could not emulate Belle's warmth. She was cold, and she knew it. *Adorable* was the very last word anybody would use to describe her.

Daisy found herself becoming more and more aggravated, and with nobody other than herself. She should not care a jot how besotted Lord Dalton became with Miss Minkerton. It was only, well it was just that Lord Dalton had not seemed to mind her cold manner. He'd even sometimes seemed to admire her particular temperament. They had jousted and circled round each other and he'd pretended it was nothing, but a man could not hide what he put down on a lady's card, and Lord Dalton had often put down for her supper. It had given her the feeling that she could not be all wrong, if at least one gentleman thought she was right.

Despite not wishing to marry, she supposed it had been a satisfying feeling to be approved of. Especially by one as discerning as Lord Dalton. She must just hope the feeling was not a necessary one.

"You seem to slip into melancholy again, my dear," Mrs. Jellops said. "If it will cheer you, I will dare to venture into a bathing machine with you on the morrow. As long as Mrs. Nash is there to keep me from drowning."

Daisy patted her hand. The illustrious Mrs. Nash was the most renowned dipper in Ramsgate. Daisy had first encountered her when she was just a child and found her delightfully forceful in getting the nervous into the sea.

"It cheers me that you would put yourself into such an uncomfortable situation on my account, even *with* the assistance of Mrs. Nash. I will not let you do it, though. You will comfortably watch from the sand, only daring to get your toes wet, and I will go in with Betsy, as I always do. As you know, she grew up nearby Worthing and has a terrific fondness for swimming."

Mrs. Jellops shivered over the idea of anybody thinking swimming was terrific. "But you will not stray too far away from the machine? There have been times over the years that I have experienced heart palpitations and had visions of you being carried lifeless from the sea. I have said so to Betsy but she only laughs at the idea."

Daisy smiled into the darkness and made no promises. She and Betsy were *both* very good swimmers. It had been the one thing she'd ever enjoyed about her summers. In the cold and salty sea, one could so easily forget what awaited one on land. How much fun she'd had, in past summers, she and Betsy diving down to the sand and returning to the surface or laying on their backs and floating on the swells? In the sea, there was no bad-tempered father made worse by his indulgence the night before, no idiot cronies turning up to insist the only cure was to indulge all over again. The blessed sea would be just the thing to clear her mind just now.

After all, what did she have to be unhappy about? Her father was dead and she would soon enough come into her fortune.

All was as it should be.

"We should perhaps go early," Mrs. Jellops said. "You are technically in mourning and perhaps it will not be the thing to be seen joyfully splashing about."

THE COTTAGE, AS ill-equipped at it was for human habitation, had at least been supplied with a decanter of brandy. Tate had found it in the main house and promptly installed it in his master's abode. Tate was turning out to be an exceedingly resourceful fellow and had removed no end of things he reasoned could not be wanted by the mistress. As he told it, it was a naval operation to slip past the enemy line, otherwise known as the ever-patrolling Mrs. Broadbent.

Now, Charles sat outside on the bench near the door to the cottage, brandy in hand and breathing in the salty night air. What a confounded dinner.

The dinner itself had been up to snuff, but the conversation!

It seemed Miss Danworth was intent on informing all and sundry that she would not marry. She was to live some sort of odd spinster existence at the seaside. Or, so she thought. Meanwhile, Burke was equally intent on overturning those plans and securing her.

How had he not noticed Burke's inclination before Miss Minkerton mentioned it? He supposed it had been there for him to view all along. Did not Burke always secure a dance with Miss Danworth? Did he not sometimes take supper?

Of course, he *had* noticed the supper-taking, and always found himself annoyed by it. But that was only because it would force him to take supper with some other lady of less sense.

Now, he thought he might understand Burke's melancholy at Newmarket, and last season too. Charles had been sure it had been over some lady or other, he had just not guessed it to be Miss Danworth he pined for.

Had Burke asked and been declined? Was that why he'd been so down in the dumps for the past year or more?

He would like to think so. For one, Burke was the last of his acquaintance who had so far escaped the marital noose. For another, Burke was not at all suited to the lady.

Oh, Burke was a fine enough fellow. But Miss Danworth...she

was…well, she was too much woman for him. And Burke, well he was always so damned reasonable. Irritatingly reasonable at times.

Charles paused, a sudden thought occurring to him. If Miss Danworth *did* decide to marry, wouldn't Burke be the most likely fellow? After her father's displays of intemperance, would she not seek out a gentleman who would be reliably sensible? Was that not Burke all over? He was not rash or extravagant in anything. Of all his friends, Burke had always been more settled, more staid, more full of commonsense.

He glanced up to her window, though he'd already told himself a hundred times that it was ungentlemanly to do so. Candles were lit and he sometimes saw a shadow pass behind the thin curtains, though he could not make out if it were Miss Danworth or her maid. It was just as well he could not make out who it was, as it would have been even more ungentlemanly if he could. He'd better throw himself into the cold sea on the morrow to cool any inclinations at looking through windows. He supposed Burke had no similar temptations, Burke was too steady for that.

Charles downed the glass of brandy and rose to go inside. "Stop living so much in your thoughts, Dalton," he said quietly. "It gets you nowhere."

CHAPTER SIX

I T WAS A hot morning with little breeze, just the sort of day that suited jumping into the sea. After a quick breakfast of tea and toast, Daisy, Mrs. Jellops, and Betsy were driven in the carriage and alighted at the cliff stairs to the seaside. Betsy had been exceedingly pleased—a swim was akin to time off—and she'd done the business of hiring a bathing machine expeditiously, though it took some arm-twisting. According to the young fellow who was sweeping out one of the boxes, ladies were not to be on this particular beach so soon in the morning, as it was the gentlemen's time to swim.

Both Daisy and Betsy had heard all about it during other summers, but as young men generally spent the early morning in bed recovering from the festivities of the night before, they did not fear encountering a horde of them, or any at all. After that hurdle was jumped, the fellow claimed that there was not even a dipper available yet. He swore he would not be held responsible if both ladies drowned.

This idea set Mrs. Jellops into a terrible fret, but Daisy only laughed and pointed out that while she and Betsy were excellent swimmers, half the dippers were not so gifted. Last summer, one of them had needed rescue herself when she had apparently advertised herself as far more skilled than she actually was. Betsy had spotted her going under at a distance and swam to the rescue.

Though Betsy had pulled the woman to shore on that particular day, this day she was more interested in having been called *a lady* by this young fellow. After that, and some comment Betsy made that Daisy was grateful not to overhear, there was much winking and blushing between them.

They had finally overcome the youth's objections and been rolled out. She and Betsy had thrown off their clothes down to their shifts and Betsy pushed open the door. There was a ladder set for their convenience so they might elegantly enter the water. Daisy looked at Betsy, Betsy smiled back. They held hands and jumped in.

The water was, at first, a shock. It always was and Daisy knew that it would only be a matter of minutes before she adjusted to it and it only felt pleasantly cool.

As they splashed around, a rowboat passed by. Daisy glanced in its direction and then quickly looked away. Lord Dalton was being rowed to the deeper sea. He wore only a thin shirt over his trousers, just as she'd sometimes seen him sitting out on his bench in the mornings. Though they had supposed no gentleman would be out of bed and making their way into the sea, it seemed Lord Dalton was to be the exception.

She was quite certain the lord had noted them, for it would be hard not to as they were the only other two persons in the water.

"He's a handsome one," Betsy said, "if a little grim for my taste."

"Betsy," Daisy said in as scolding a tone as she could muster, "I am quite sure it is wildly inappropriate for a lady's maid to comment on a lord."

Betsy pushed off the sand and floated on her back. "Aye, I know it. At least, I ought not say it above stairs. Though, all sort of talk does go on between the servants and always has. Nobody likes to think it, but there it is."

"I see," Daisy said, allowing herself to float alongside her maid, "and what is said of Lord Dalton, exactly?"

"Well, let's see, about Lord Dalton," Betsy said, staring up at the clouds, "we've managed to squeeze a word or two out of that old fellow Bellamy. He keeps things rather close, but we've discovered that the lord saw something terrible at Quatre Bras. We was teasing about Lord Dalton's grumpy disposition and now we find out that somehow it's all connected. Bellamy says he used to be a deal more lighthearted."

Daisy was not unaware that some men came back changed from war. Some even came back entirely broken and subject to nightmares. It was hard, though, to imagine that Lord Dalton had ever been other than what he was. And certainly not lighthearted.

"What was it? What was so terrible that he saw?" she asked.

"That's the mystery, Mr. Bellamy won't say. We'll keep workin' on him, though. Mrs. Broadbent scolds us for prying but we do it anyway. Anyhow, one of the kitchen maids said all Lord Dalton needs is a good wife and you would a thought she wished a plague on the fellow, the footmen did take it that hard. They don't ever want a mistress and they say their master ain't never gonna marry anyhow."

"Oh yes, he's quite renowned for saying so," Daisy said.

"As you are, too," Betsy said. "Look at that, two people who won't never marry. P'raps you could marry each other and live in different houses. Though the talk in the servants' hall is you could do better. Lord Burke is said to be a prince—Sissy, one of the maids, has a cousin who knows somebody who works in his house in town, and it's said he's a generous sort of person with days off and duties. He might do, after all."

"And *that*, is quite enough," Daisy said.

Before she could scold her maid any further, which she had a great mind to do, Daisy heard shouting from behind her.

She turned her gaze out to sea and saw the oarsman on the rowboat that Lord Dalton had recently been on. The fellow was shouting and waving wildly. Lord Dalton, however, was nowhere to be seen.

꙰꙰꙰

CHARLES HAD FOUND himself aggravated to find Miss Danworth and her maid in the sea so early in the morning. What was the lady thinking? Surely, she must know this time was only for gentlemen? What lady rose so early anyway?

As it *was* the time for gentlemen, he'd planned to swim as he always did, with not a shred of clothing to weigh him down. Now, though, he'd have to keep his shirt on at least, for propriety's sake. He doubted Miss Danworth would stare at him, nor would he care if she did, but one never knew what sort of nosy Nancy had parked herself at a window with a telescope. If Miss Inquisitive wished to get a glimpse of his person, she was welcome to do so. However, it would not be well for that prying lady to get a glimpse of his person *and* Miss Danworth bathing anywhere nearby at the same time.

For all his outrage at being observed, he could not claim with any honesty that he had avoided his *own* observing. He was rather surprised, as he pulled off his trousers, to find that Miss Danworth did not seem to require the services of a dipper. She and her maid appeared exceedingly comfortable making their own way in the water, as evidenced by the fact that he'd seen them fling themselves into it when he'd got into his boat and now they floated easily on the swells.

Perhaps he had observed the scene for a bit too long, as his rower finally said, "Shall you go in, my lord?"

He nodded and dived into the sea. The cold shocked him and he rose to the surface. As he did every morning, he swam away from the bobbing boat, preferring the feeling of being out in the sea alone. It was not so comfortable as usual, as he'd got his shirt on and the wet fabric exerted no small amount of weight.

Once he had come near to exhausting himself, he stopped. He would tread water for a few minutes to catch his breath and then make his way back.

As he took in a deep breath, he was suddenly grabbed by the ankle and pulled below the surface.

For a moment, as he was pulled down, his mind went blank. But, just as in the war, his wits returned and things began to move as if time had unnaturally slowed.

He could not see what had pulled him down, only a shadowy outline appearing five or six feet in length. The thing had him by one leg and he used the other to kick at it. The strength of the kicks proved ineffectual, the water slowing them too much.

Feeling as if he were close to running out of breath and fighting the inevitable terror that came from realizing one was about to take in water, he used his free foot to angle it against his attacker. He allowed himself to be pulled closer to get leverage, and then pushed off the thing as hard as he could.

He broke free and bolted to the surface. As much as he'd tried to resist the urge to breathe while under water, he had taken in a gulp. He broke the surface and heaved, trying to clear the water out of his lungs. He forced himself to swim toward the boat, each second expecting to be pulled down again. His boat was being rowed toward him at a fast clip.

The rower reached him and hauled him over the side. "There, my lord, that was a close one. P'raps don't swim so far away if you ain't used to it."

"Not me," Charles rasped, attempting to breathe deep. "Pulled under."

Charles could not help but note the look of horror on the fellow's features. He was pretty horrified himself.

"Are you sure?" the rower asked.

Charles ignored the fellow, of course he was sure. He scanned the surface of the water, looking for a telltale fin. Though, as he did so, he knew it could not have been a shark or anything of the sort. His leg was not punctured as it surely would have been.

He saw nothing at first, and then a small something. "There," he said pointing east, "that."

It rather resembled a pole of some sort and did not look like anything that belonged to a sea creature. As quickly as it had appeared, it disappeared below the swells.

Seeing the oarsman's confusion, Charles coughed to clear his lungs. His voice gravelly, he said, "Row. There."

"No, my lord, we don't dare go too close that direction," the young man said, "there's rocks what come up close to the surface and you can't see 'im until you're right on top of 'im. I wouldn't like to get dumped in the sea while something is lurkin' underneath."

Charles nodded between coughs. "Nor I," he whispered.

"You don't have a scratch on you though, 'cept for the red marks round your ankle."

"Yes," Charles said. After a fit of coughing, he said, "Maybe a man."

This sent the oarsman to a shiver. "Don't you say so, my lord. What kind of devil can swim like a fish and is set on drowning people?"

Charles shrugged, pulling on his pants. It hurt to talk, his throat felt on fire.

"Me mum would say it t'weren't no man after you," the oarsman said, rowing with vigor toward the shore. "It were a Kraken or one of them what don't have teeth and wrap their long, slimy arms round and take you down."

Charles would have replied that his mother was to be congratulated on her vivid imagination, had he not still been coughing to clear his lungs of seawater.

As they neared the shore, Charles could see Miss Danworth, Mrs. Jellops, and Miss Danworth's maid standing on shore. Miss Danworth and her maid had exited the sea with alacrity and had not taken the time to thoroughly dry themselves. Both their dresses clung to them damp and Miss Danworth's curls had loosened in the water.

He really should not be noticing Miss Danworth's rather statuesque figure *or* her curls when he'd just been pulled under the waves, and he felt like the bottom half of his lungs were sloshing with seawater.

⇉⟫⟨⟨⟨

DAISY HAD WATCHED as the oarsman rowed and searched the swells for any sign of Lord Dalton.

He could not have drowned. No, he could not have. He was too strong for that. Why would a man go out to the deeper water if he were not an excellent swimmer? He must be an excellent swimmer, Lord Dalton did everything well.

To her relief, she suddenly saw him. It was odd, he seemed to come from nowhere. One moment he was gone and the next he was swimming toward his boat as if he'd been there all along.

She and Betsy had hurried into the bathing machine and thrown on their clothes. Now they stood on the pebbly beach as the boat neared.

The boy pulled his oars up and the boat made a grating sound as the hull scraped the shore.

"Lord Dalton," Daisy said, picking her way across the stony beach, "what on earth happened?"

The lord very determinedly suppressed a cough and said, "Nothing."

"You disappeared," Daisy said. "Your rower was shouting. Then you reappeared."

Lord Dalton did not meet her eye and said hoarsely, "Can one not dive?"

"You said you was pulled under!" the boy said, his outrage evident.

"Nonsense," Lord Dalton said to the boy. He might have said more, but was prevented by a coughing fit.

"Whatever has happened, you have clearly taken in seawater and will need a doctor," Daisy said.

"I need no such—" Again, the lord's words were stopped as he was wracked by heaving coughs.

Daisy well knew he must have a doctor. Taking in water of any sort was damaging to the lungs. She understood that the mechanisms in fresh and seawater were thought to be different, though she had no idea why or what the proposed remedies might be.

A voice behind her startled her. "Dalton," Lord Burke said, "What on earth has happened? We saw you from the cliffs, were you drowning?"

Daisy turned to find Lord Burke, Miss Minkerton, and her lady's maid. "Lord Burke," Daisy said, with no small relief. "Lord Dalton will need to be got back to the house and a doctor fetched."

"I do not require—" Lord Dalton did not get further as the coughing took over again. He leaned against the beached boat and Daisy was sure the endless coughing was beginning to take a toll.

Lord Burke nodded and said, "Come on, put your arm round my shoulders and I'll get you to the carriage."

Despite Lord Dalton insisting he did not need a doctor, he was all too willing to go with Lord Burke. Daisy was sure he was becoming exhausted.

As they left, Miss Minkerton said, "Are you quite all right, Miss Danworth? What has happened?"

Daisy took in a breath to steady herself. "I am perfectly fine, though I am not altogether sure what occurred." She turned to the boy who stood by his boat. "You said Lord Dalton was somehow pulled underneath the water?"

"I said that's what *he* said. *I* thought maybe it was just another high and mighty lord overconfident in himself who goes and practically drowns. Seems like there's one every summer. Last year, one particular lord muckety-muck flailed round trying to impress I don't know who and then blamed me for it."

Daisy had no intention of following this boy down the walks of his memories to complain of every wrong ever done him, which she was equally sure he would not mind doing.

"Lord Dalton told you he was pulled under, but you don't believe it," she said.

The boy rubbed his chin in thought. Then he said, "I don't rightly know. He don't seem a fool and he *was* swimmin' well. Then he disappears. Then he appears and swims well again, 'cept for near drowning. Then he tells me somethin' had him round the ankle and I *did* see the redness on it. On t'other hand, I don't like to think of a creature being out there. No, I don't like to think of that!"

Daisy could not make heads or tails of what had gone on. Miss Minkerton said, "Perhaps the only thing to think about is that Lord Dalton has escaped the situation, whatever it was."

Daisy nodded. "I hope you have not been unduly shocked, Miss Minkerton," she said. That was what she said, but what she meant was she hoped Miss Minkerton would not fall to pieces upon observing the man she admired so recently in peril.

"Goodness, no, Miss Danworth," Miss Minkerton said. "In unexpected situations in which things must be done quickly, I find the best thing is to just get on with it. Now, I will send my maid for Doctor Sheldringham, if you will allow it. My family has known him for years and he is quite the best, I think."

Daisy nodded. She could not help but be thankful for the suggestion. The only doctor her father had ever called for was Doctor Wade, who was a reprobate just like himself and only seemed to have cures for excessive indulgence.

"Now, Miss Danworth, we ought to get you home as well," Miss Minkerton said. "You are beginning to shiver in the breeze."

Mrs. Jellops, who had so far been sitting on the back steps of the bathing machine, said, "Yes, we must all go home and never return to this wretched place again. Nothing good ever comes of flinging oneself into the sea."

Daisy could see poor Mrs. Jellops was shaken by the events of the morning. She was forever predicting disaster in the water and now it had happened.

At least, something had happened, though none of them really knew what.

"Betsy?" Miss Minkerton said. "I have your name correct?"

Betsy bobbed her head and Miss Minkerton said, "Do help Mrs. Jellops and I will help Miss Danworth." She walked to the boy and pulled a coin from her reticule. "And you, young sir, do not go round talking of this and giving yourself nightmares. Best to forget all about it."

The boy nodded, though Daisy did not think he looked convinced.

Daisy felt well able to let Miss Minkerton take charge. She realized she was a bit dazed at the moment. Whatever had taken place out in the deeper water, what she was sure of was that Lord Dalton had come close to losing his life.

His coughing so! It was awful. It was not him. Lord Dalton was never to be weak or hurt.

She did not know why she thought so, she only knew that she did.

〰〰〰〰

DOCTOR SHELDRINGHAM ARRIVED to the house within the hour. He was a late middle-aged fellow with a tanned face and a comforting way about him. He seemed brisk and unruffled and not at all surprised to hear of a mishap in the sea.

Daisy supposed he would not be surprised, he making his practice so near it. She led him through the back garden to Lord Dalton's cottage while Bellamy officiously followed. She would have liked to go in, but for propriety's sake she allowed Bellamy to take him inside and she sat down on the bench just outside. She knew full well she ought to return to the drawing room and await the doctor's conclusions. Miss Minkerton had been left there to tend to Mrs. Jellops' fractured nerves, which the lady had speedily decided could be remedied with tea and biscuits. Mrs. Broadbent appeared in full agreement and bustled off to make up a tray.

Still, Daisy was determined to know more than she knew at this moment. What had happened? Was there any permanent damage done?

She leaned back toward an open window, though she knew very well it was wrong to eavesdrop.

"Lord Dalton," Doctor Sheldringham said, "let's have a look."

Daisy presumed the lord had made some effort to answer, but it got no further than a coughing fit.

"That happens every time he tries to talk," Lord Burke said.

"Swallowed water, I see," the doctor said. "You'll need time to recuperate, I'm sorry to say. Coughing is your lungs' attempt to clear out the salt and whatever other detritus you've taken in, so I will not give you an elixir to calm it. Tea to wet the throat, and a draught to assist your cough's work will be sufficient."

There was a long and silent pause. The doctor broke it by saying, "May I ask, why have you been deposited in this shack?"

"This is where they've put him to live," Bellamy said, his voice full of the indignation he seemed to carry with him everywhere.

"Well he can't live here at the moment," the doctor said. "This will not do at all."

"It's the mistress though," Bellamy went on. "She won't think it proper to have him in the house."

"I see," the doctor said. "Then he must be moved to another house. This place is too damp. There will need to be a small fire laid to take the damp from the air and I have no faith in the chimney I'm looking at just now. It would sooner collapse than provide any benefit."

"I am fine," Lord Dalton said, his normally deep voice thin and raspy.

"He could go to the Minkertons," Lord Burke said.

"Ah yes, the Minkertons. They have a fine house, set back from the sea. That would be just the ticket," the doctor said.

"I will not—" Lord Dalton did not get further than that before being overtaken by another fit of coughing.

"There, you see?" the doctor said. "What do you want to do, my lord? Stay in this God-forsaken shack and get worse? You're already at risk for pneumonia."

As they argued back and forth, Daisy rose to return to the drawing room. Her thoughts were in such a muddle. She could not have Lord Dalton in the house, that would be quite wrong. On the other hand, it had given her some comfort to know that he was nearby.

The letters from her father's friends had continued to arrive and she knew the watchmen had turned back Mr. Gelpsard only the night before. Apparently, he'd turned up after eight, worse for drink and claiming he'd been invited.

Her father's house had been no better than a tavern when he was alive and so they would treat it still. She was grateful for the watchmen, but she would feel more comfortable if Lord Dalton were there to handle any real emergency that might spring up.

As well, she did not relish the idea of the lord ensconcing himself at the Minkertons. Through some late-night self-examination, she had begun to realize that she was fonder of Lord Dalton than she ought to be.

But what was the point of even knowing that? Did she think he would always just keep himself conveniently in her garden? How did one want somebody to stay close but also to stay away?

Regardless of how long the argument went on in the cottage about what was to be done, Daisy was fairly certain that Lord Dalton would be soon enough packed in a carriage and on his way to the Minkertons.

She would be left guarded by the watchmen, Bellamy, and Mrs. Broadbent. Bellamy would be no use whatsoever and she thought Mrs. Broadbent would be her most stalwart defender.

Meanwhile, Lord Dalton would be welcomed into the warm embrace of the Minkertons.

It was all very irritating.

CHAPTER SEVEN

D ESPITE HIS MANY objections, Burke had packed him a bag and
Charles had been deposited at the Minkertons. He could not
string four words together without coughing and had finally commu-
nicated his wish for paper and pen. He'd written a note to Burke,
going some way to explaining that Miss Danworth might be in danger
from ill-conceived lotharios coming knocking. And also, to feed the
cat.

Burke had promised he would go to the house in the evening to
have a word with the guards and assure all was well. And if he really
must, he would feed the cat.

Charles wrote that he really must.

The relentless coughing had exhausted him and the doctor gave
him some sort of awful draught which did nothing to stop it, but
produced a far wetter cough and made his breathing somewhat easier.

As he lay in a bed in the Minkerton's house, he replayed every
moment of what had happened. Had it been a man who had pulled
him down?

It must have been. His ankle had not teeth marks, nor the slime
one might expect from a creature with tentacles. It had not felt like
something otherworldly. It had felt like the grip of a hand.

If it were a man, why? Had it been some sort of joke and now the
prankster failed to come forward on account of it going wrong?

And what about the pole he'd seen so briefly, breaking the surface and disappearing again?

What was the purpose of what had happened?

As he scoured his memory, one thought kept nagging. He'd had to fight hard to break free. There had been no indication that there was a plan to let go of him. No indication that it had been a joke.

If it *were* some sort of prank, he could see how a man might think it hilarious to grab and let go—to surprise and shock with no harm done. But to hold him down for so long…

If someone did mean him serious harm, he had a sinking feeling it might have to do with his guardianship of Miss Danworth. From the letters that continued to arrive, it was plain enough that the last thing these fellows wanted was a guardian on the scene.

Of course there was always Lieutenant Farthmore lurking in the back of his mind. He'd wondered if the fool would challenge him. Perhaps Farthmore had decided that would be too much trouble and had decided to drown him instead.

Charles stopped himself. He was allowing his thoughts to run away from him. There might be scores of fellows who wished to take their chance at Miss Danworth's dowry, but none of them would resort to murder. It was too ridiculous. As for Farthmore, he could not imagine the drunken idiot was up to enacting a scheme so athletic.

Once he had dismissed that idea from his mind, he allowed himself to consider the more pleasant recollection of Miss Danworth's person in a damp dress. It was wrong and ungentlemanly, but she *had* looked rather marvelous. It was not as if he'd spied inside her bathing machine, after all. Further, it was hard not to be gratified that she'd hurried herself in such a manner on his account.

THE AFTERNOON HAD stretched on after Lord Dalton had been

transported to the Minkerton's house and Miss Minkerton had taken her leave. Daisy and Mrs. Jellops sat sewing, though neither of them made much progress. Mrs. Jellops, especially, was unlikely to get much done, as her poor pudgy fingers trembled each time she took up a needle.

As the lady sighed and discontentedly stared at her needle and then sighed again, Daisy said, "You must not allow this accident to discompose you so very much. I am sure Lord Dalton will make a full recovery."

Mrs. Jellops laid down her sewing and said, "I do not doubt it. But something evil has transpired, I feel it in my bones."

"You do not believe in sea creatures?" Daisy said.

"No, certainly not. At least, I hope not. But if Lord Dalton told that boy he was pulled down. Well…"

"I will stay away from bathing, at least for now," Daisy said. "I do not wish you to be upset."

"It is not just that," Mrs. Jellops said. "We've been left to fend for ourselves and I do not like it."

"The watchmen will come at sunset," Daisy said hopefully.

"Yes, I suppose so. I only feel so uneasy!" Mrs. Jellops said. "There was something calming about knowing Lord Dalton was just across the lawn. He is so strong and well I thought…dependable. I know I am being a ninny."

"No," Daisy said, "you are not. I feel it too. I think the best we can do is have an early dinner and we can sleep together, just as we have done in the past when we had need of comfort."

Finally, Mrs. Jellops seemed to calm. "Of course, that is precisely what we will do. We will close the curtains and lock the bedchamber door. We will have each other for company and that will ease us both."

"And perhaps we might have Mrs. Broadbent sleep in your room as it is next to mine?" Daisy asked. "I know it would be unusual, but the lady is, well she is so very…"

"Indomitable," Mrs. Jellops finished. "I heartily agree to that idea. In truth, the lady gives me more comfort than any watchman at the bottom of the drive."

ALL MATTERS IN Daisy's household having been arranged, dinner had been served early and Mrs. Broadbent had been ensconced in the chamber next door. According to Betsy, this arrangement had caused a near uproar below stairs, as none of them had ever known a servant, housekeeper though she might be, to stay in the family's wing.

Mr. Bellamy seemed most opposed on the theory that Mrs. Broadbent would take to crowing over it and reminding everybody that she'd done it. Gerald and Tom were put out because they'd grown used to Mrs. Broadbent's fussing over them at night, making sure they'd had enough to eat and ordering water heated when they needed a bath. As for the maids, it further cemented in their minds that Mrs. Broadbent was a mysterious creature with unlimited powers.

Daisy could not much bother herself over the upset downstairs, as she was certain she'd made the correct arrangements. With Mrs. Jellops gently snoring next to her and Mrs. Broadbent snoring like thunder next door, she drifted off to sleep.

When she was awoken, she could not say how long she had slept or even what had disturbed her sleep. She sat up cautiously and listened.

Faintly, she heard the creak of a door below her. After years of frightened listening to noises below, she knew the house's every sound. She was certain it was the door leading into the library.

She felt a wave of fear grip her, until it suddenly occurred to her what it must be that she'd heard. There were decanters of liquor in the library and she was certain Bellamy or the footmen had decided to slip in and steal a drink. Of course they would think of it, with Mrs. Broadbent safely out of the way above stairs.

Daisy leapt out of bed and silently opened the door. She intended to spot them and then shout at them. That ought to scare the wits out of them, which would be quite right for scaring *her*.

She moved softly down the corridor, avoiding all the floor planks that were loose and made a sound.

At the top of the staircase, she crouched down. She listened to rustlings and footsteps and then saw the figure of a man pass by the open library door. She could not make out who it was, but the person was dressed as if he'd been to a party. It was no servant.

She turned and hurried away, entirely forgetting to skip over the floor planks that creaked.

"Mrs. Broadbent!" she cried, knocking on the lady's door. She knew she'd said it far too loud, but panic had overcome her. Someone had broken into the house!

The lady opened the door, her nightcap askew.

"There is someone downstairs," Daisy whispered.

Though Daisy was certain there could only be terror writ on her features, Mrs. Broadbent was of a different nature. She pulled a wood bat from behind the door and said, "Go in and lock the door behind you. I will deal with the scoundrel."

"Do be careful, though," Daisy whispered. "He may be armed."

"As am I," Mrs. Broadbent said, charging down the hall. As she neared the top of the stairs, the lady rang the bell pull for fire and the ringing sounded throughout the house.

Though Mrs. Broadbent had told her to lock herself in, Daisy could not in good conscience leave the lady to her fate.

She tentatively followed as the housekeeper bounded down the stairs. From her perch at the top of the stairs, she watched the lady chase after the dark figure, who had made for the front door. He disappeared through it and into the night.

As fast as footmen in nightshirts ran carrying buckets of sand in answer to the ring for fire, Mrs. Jellops staggered down the hall behind

Daisy. "Are we on fire?" she cried.

"No, no such thing," Daisy said. "There was an intruder and Mrs. Broadbent has chased him out."

"An intruder! This place is well and truly cursed!"

Daisy knew this circumstance was unlikely to do anything good for poor Mrs. Jellops' nerves, but she could not attend the lady this moment. She must discover what had been meddled with in the library.

"Do go back to bed and I'll have Betsy bring you up a hot drink, a toddy will do you good."

"Are there enough toddies in the world to settle me, I wonder," Mrs. Jellops said, wandering back to her room.

Daisy hurried down the stairs and into the commotion that had since taken over the front hall. The footmen bravely stood at the doors, daring the scoundrel to come back and try his luck with their fists. Bellamy looked equally ready to take on all comers, though he remained safe behind them. The maids stood to the side, admiring the bravery before their eyes and perhaps admiring the bottoms of legs seen below nightshirts. Mr. Flanagan had taken one look at the situation and run back to the kitchens to retrieve heavy pots and pans, those articles of his profession being his preferred weapons. It was only Mrs. Broadbent who was all equanimity and sense.

Daisy hurried to her and the housekeeper pointed at the boys and their butler at the door. "Observe our heroes," she said.

"Indeed," Daisy said. "Though you and I know the truth of it. Let us go into the library and discover if anything has been disturbed."

Betsy was the last to arrive to the scene and was somewhat less in awe to find the footmen and butler standing at the doors and loudly proclaiming they'd give somebody a pounding. She hurried to her mistress.

"Betsy," Daisy said, "Mrs. Jellops is in a state, do be so good as to whip up some sort of toddy for her and stay with her until I return."

Betsy bobbed her head. Mrs. Broadbent said, "Be generous with the rum, dove, and make one for yourself while you're at it. And do be a dear and tell Mr. Flanagan we have no need of his pots and pans."

Betsy hurried toward the stairs to the kitchens and Mrs. Broadbent said, "Let us proceed."

Daisy had expected to find some small clue or other that would hint toward why somebody had broken into the house—a fine figurine gone or the desk rifled for money. What met them was astonishing. It seemed every book had been taken off its shelf, every drawer opened. Most alarmingly, paneling on the walls had been pried off, as if someone looked for a secret safe or a hidey-hole. The intruder had clearly been in the house for quite some time.

"Good gracious," Mrs. Broadbent said.

"This must have taken hours," Daisy said softly, the horror of the idea coming upon her.

"I suspect, based on the state of the room," Mrs. Broadbent said, "that whoever this scoundrel is, he did not find what he was looking for."

"Then he will come back another night," Daisy said.

"No, miss," Mrs. Broadbent said, her voice full of efficiency. "He will *try* to come back. In the morning, I will send a note to the company that supplies the watchmen and demand an audience. I will give them a stern what-for. Then, I will demand they send twice the men, and they will send their very best. These new men will not just stand around at the bottom of the drive, we will have them surround the house. The boys can sleep in the drawing room as an extra precaution."

Daisy was comforted by these ideas, and comforted that Mrs. Broadbent seemed well capable of managing things and giving the watchmen service a severe dressing-down.

"But what could this man be after?" she said. "What was he looking for?"

"That I cannot say, miss. But no sort of carryings-on such as this will take place a second time under Maggie Broadbent's watch. I won't stand for it!"

CHARLES FELT BETTER in the morning and had begun to think it had been the doctor's wise idea to move him to the Minkerton household. It was a pleasant room, not one which would have awed him in the past, but one that was so superior to his recent accommodations that he could help but appreciate its arrangements. His dinner had been good and, though he was periodically woken by his own coughing, he had spent an entire night without needing to brush an insect off of his face or finding a flea-ridden cat stretched out on his legs.

There was still the mystery of what had happened to him, but with time and distance he'd begun to think it was either a prank, or someone had mistaken him for somebody else. Whatever the circumstance, it was not likely to happen again, the foremost reason being he had quite given up swimming for this season. In truth, he might never look at the sea the same way again. What once had seemed a friendly place had now transformed into something mysterious and untrustworthy.

A footman came in and brought him a tray of eggs and sausage and steaming hot coffee. Also on the tray lay a letter just delivered and Charles recognized the hand easily enough. It was a missive from Bellamy, and he was certain it was filled with all the insults he currently endured at the hands of Mrs. Broadbent.

Had Bellamy not known him since he was child, he would not dare take the liberty of disturbing his rest in such a manner. But the fact was, Bellamy *had* known him since he was a boy. When Bellamy acted as his father's butler, he'd extricated Charles from no end of scrapes. The butler was the keeper of his boyish secrets and was still the only person who knew that it had been Charles who'd set the drawing room on fire. He'd been in pursuit of a silver snuffbox on the tall mantle of the fireplace, thinking to try out the habit. A wobbly stool, a fall, a candle knocked over on the woven Barbary mat his mother favored in summer, and flames within minutes.

Bellamy had got the fire out and claimed a strong wind had come in an open window. He'd later handed the snuffbox to a shaken Charles and told him that nobody in the house liked the Barbary mats anyway.

As he'd grown into an adult, Bellamy kept other kinds of secrets. A gaggle of actresses at the London house late at night did not raise eyebrows or elicit talk.

He supposed there was bound to be a price to pay for the old fellow's loyalty. Bellamy's particular price was free access to his wine cellar and the leave to voice endless complaints.

Charles finished his breakfast and put aside the tray, his coughing hardly interrupting him as it had done the day before.

"I suppose I'd better discover what has insulted him down to his toes this time," he said to himself, tearing open the letter.

My lord,

The past evening has been most irregular! An intruder broke into the house and ravaged the library. He was bravely pursued by me and the boys, though we could not catch him. We would have given him a severe pounding if we had. Mrs. Broadbent, as highhanded as ever, has called for Mr. Deer, the gentleman who supplies our watchmen. She intends on giving him the what-for, whatever that is, and demanding more and better men.

I knew all along that this would be a rum situation. (Not that we get any rum.) Me and the boys will be spending most of the day attempting to put this library back in order while Mrs. B goes round giving people the what-for. On top of that, she has directed my boys to sleep in the drawing room tonight. SHE has directed THEM. Who am I, I wonder? Am I not the butler? Never have I been so treated.

It will come as no surprise to understand that my lowest append-ages are gravely affronted.

Bellamy

Charles dropped the letter. A man had entered the house and searched the library? What would he have done if he were not interrupted? What was going on here?

It did not seem likely that it would be one of Miss Danworth's hopeless lotharios, else they would not have spent all their time in the library. In any case, he did not really think any of them had the nerve for a kidnapping or some other ludicrous scheme. Knocking on the door was one thing, breaking in during the dead of night was another.

It could not be a coincidence, though, that he'd been nearly drowned yesterday, and then last night while he was conveniently out of the way, someone dared enter the house.

There was danger lurking in the shadows, he just could not fathom from what direction it came.

There was a soft knock on the door, and Burke let himself in. "How do you get on? You look better than you did yesterday."

"I don't doubt it," Charles said. His voice was still raspy, but he was not gripped with coughing when he tried to speak. "I must get my clothes, I must return to Miss Danworth at once."

"Certainly not," Burke said. "The doctor will come this morning and he will be the judge of what must be done at once, which I suspect will be nothing but rest."

Charles handed Burke the letter and said, "Ignore all the complaining and just take in the facts."

As Burke read through the note, Charles threw his covers off and sat up. He felt a bit woozy doing so, but it was impossible for him to lie there after Miss Danworth's doors had been breached.

Burke laid down the letter. "But who—"

"I do not know, that's the problem. However, I am to act as her guardian so I cannot very well lounge about here."

Burke was thoughtful for a moment. He said, "Very well. I was to take Belle, I mean Miss Minkerton, to walk the pier this morning, but I am sure she will not mind a change of plans. We will all go together to Miss Danworth's aid."

Charles only nodded, but he could not help but be a little irritated that Burke should wish to run to the rescue. The fellow had been told clear enough that Miss Danworth did not care to marry and that should be sufficient. There was no need to charge in and present himself as a knight answering a call of distress.

CHAPTER EIGHT

THOUGH THE SUMMER had so far provided very few entertainments, Daisy and Mrs. Jellops found themselves unexpectedly delighted at this moment. They sat in the drawing room with the door open to listen to Mrs. Broadbent's interview with the proprietor of the watchmen's services. The indomitable lady had just led Mr. Deer into the dining room and did not waste a moment before launching into the *what for* she had promised he would receive.

Mr. Deer was to understand that the men he'd sent as watchmen had proved woefully inadequate—a gaggle of children might have protected them better. While Mrs. Broadbent thought herself exceedingly liberal regarding what sort of duties she was willing to take on, chasing housebreakers was beyond the limit. She pointed out that it was hardly a recommendation for his business that such a thing had occurred, and she darkly hinted that *something would be done* if the situation were not rectified. Daisy had not the first idea of the something that would be done and doubted poor Mr. Deer knew either.

Mr. Deer made some feeble attempts at explaining or promising but was just as quickly run over by Mrs. Broadbent's boundless fortitude. As Daisy listened to her housekeeper's tirade, she came to two conclusions—she must learn some of Mrs. Broadbent's arts and she must keep the lady always in her employment.

The end of it was: they were to have six men for the price of three, and Mrs. Broadbent was to hold off on the threatening and mysterious *something would be done*. Mrs. Broadbent then added the final stipulation that if these men were to encounter a tabby cat prowling the garden, they were not to chase it off. It was Lord Dalton's particular cat and he would be most put out.

Mr. Deer very unconvincingly put forth that, down to a man, his fellows possessed a general love of cats. Then he fled the house.

After the door shut behind him and Mrs. Broadbent charged off to manage some other matter, Mrs. Jellops said, "I hadn't the first idea that Lord Dalton kept a cat."

"Nor I," Daisy said. "How odd." In truth, it was more than odd. Where had the cat come from? How on earth did a gentleman like Lord Dalton come into possession of a cat? He seemed more the type that would have dogs for hunting that he laid eyes on only during the season. How strange to think of him caring for an animal other than a horse.

"Our Mrs. Broadbent is very determined. I quite take comfort in it."

"As do I," Daisy said. "I do not know how we would have hoped to sleep a wink this coming night if we did not have that good lady nearby."

There was a knock on the door and a footman hurried to answer it.

"Dear me," Mrs. Jellops said quietly, "it cannot be Mr. Deer coming back for a second round. If it is, he is very foolish."

"Maybe it is the cat," Daisy said. She and Mrs. Jellops suppressed their laughter as the doors swung open.

It was not Mr. Deer or the elusive cat. Lord Burke and Miss Minkerton, and then Lord Dalton, were shown into the drawing room.

Bellamy led them in and then closed the door behind them.

"Goodness," Daisy said, certain she was blushing from the surprise of it, "I had not expected you to be risen from a sickbed so soon, Lord Dalton."

"I could hardly stay in it after Bellamy informed me of the house-breaker," Lord Dalton said.

Daisy was pleased by the sentiment, but did not wish to appear pleased. It was the stupidest thing in the world, but it was so. She did not wish Miss Minkerton to think there was any competition in her admiration of Lord Dalton. She did not wish Lord Dalton to have any hint that she might admire him too much. Sometimes one's feelings were not pointed in the direction of one's own good. In this instance, they certainly were not.

The convenient thing about feelings, though, was they could be put down and dismissed with the proper determination.

"Are you quite recovered from your ordeal, Miss Danworth?" Lord Burke asked.

"Yes, I suppose," Daisy said. "Mrs. Broadbent chased the man off."

"Mrs. Broadbent?" Lord Dalton said.

"Oh yes," Mrs. Jellops said, "she's a terrifically brave and stalwart lady. We've just listened to her give the proprietor of the watchmen the *what for* and it was striking. It sent shivers down my spine for poor Mr. Deer."

Lord Dalton nodded and said, "I might have thought my butler and footmen would have been of some use in the situation."

Daisy pressed her lips together and would not for the world give away Bellamy's pointless bluster in front of his master. Mrs. Jellops, however, was not of that mind.

The lady sniffed and said, "Talking about pounding somebody to bits when the somebody is long gone is rather closing the barn door after the horse is out. At least Mrs. Broadbent had the good sense to charge after the fellow with a wood bat."

"You must have been so frightened!" Miss Minkerton said, sitting down beside Mrs. Jellops.

Mrs. Jellops patted her hand. "I was, my dear, just about out of my wits. Mrs. Broadbent was kind enough to send me up a strong toddy and that settled me quite nicely."

The drawing room door swung open, and Bellamy led the footmen in with a tea tray and a second tray of cakes and biscuits. As they laid the tea things, Lord Dalton said, "Have you any idea what the man could have been after?"

Daisy shook her head. "None. Nothing obvious, anyway. It was not a usual robbery, everything of value was left behind. Some of the paneling on the walls was pried loose, as if the person looked for something that was hidden. My only thought was it might be a gambling debt a gentleman did not want found?"

"Perhaps," Lord Dalton said, "though breaking in and tearing the house apart seems rather extreme for a debt that cannot be legally enforced. My father would hardly bother trying to collect on it."

"May I ask, Miss Danworth," Lord Burke said, "have you gone through all of your father's personal papers in case there is a hint of some unsavory matter or something yet to be resolved?"

Bellamy had set the teapot down and Daisy had just raised it to pour the first cup. She quickly set it down again, her hands shaking. She had not gone through any of her father's papers. Mr. Crackwilder had done it for her in London, and had removed to Shropshire anything of note for the duke to determine what to do with. He'd set aside a stack of personal letters to discover if Daisy was interested in keeping them and she'd refused. Mr. Crackwilder had seemed relieved and said that most of them were probably not suitable for a lady's eyes anyway. They'd gone into the fire.

She did not wish to handle anything her father had handled, she did not wish to see his handwriting, she did not wish to smell the scent of his soap on the paper. She wished to forget he'd ever lived, not drown herself in his memories.

Lord Dalton broke the silence. "I believe the task of sorting through Lord Childress' correspondence may prove unpalatable to Miss Danworth. Might I suggest I tackle it. Perhaps I can find some clue as to the cause of...recent events. I am supposed to rest and there can be nothing more dull than reading through papers and letters."

Daisy nodded and willed her hands to steady so she could get on with the tea. It was a welcome suggestion. There might be relevant information in her father's papers, she just could not bear to touch them.

"His room has been locked," Daisy said. "Though the man who broke in has seemed to thoroughly examine the library, I suppose there must be papers in his bedchamber too."

"I will be happy to assist," Lord Burke said. "I do not mind reading through papers."

Though Daisy thought Lord Dalton must be gratified by the offer, he did not seem so.

For that matter, Miss Minkerton did not seem so either. Rather sullenly, she said, "Our walking of the pier must be pushed to another day."

Lord Burke appeared rather stricken by the lady's comment and said, "I am sorry, I ought not upset your plans so often."

Now it was Miss Minkerton's turn to appear stricken. "Of course you must! Miss Danworth needs your assistance."

Daisy was looking back and forth at everybody and wondering why they all looked so unhappy. It was only a walk, after all.

Had Lord Dalton promised *he* would walk on the pier and now Miss Minkerton was disappointed that the scheme was called off?

"You ought to go," Lord Burke said to Miss Minkerton, "and Miss Danworth too. The air coming off the sea is beneficial and you can take Mrs. Jellops, if she agrees, and some footmen. There can be nothing dangerous in broad daylight with a proper escort."

"I do not mind going," Mrs. Jellops said. "I quite like the sea, as long as nobody leaps into it. Though, we'll need Mrs. Broadbent, rather than the footmen."

Bellamy, who had been straightening a cloth on a side table, said, "Please excuse me, perhaps it would be more suitable were I to go in Mrs. Broadbent's place."

Mrs. Jellops waved her hands and said, "Dear me, no. We would wish to have somebody who would pound a person to bits while they were there, not after they've departed."

Bellamy flushed. He glared at Lord Dalton, bent forward, looked at his shoes, and dramatically pointed at them. Then, he stalked out of the room.

Daisy had no idea what any of it meant. For that matter, she was certain she did not understand half the significance of the past few minutes' conversation.

For all that, she was not opposed to a walk on the pier. It would be well to leave the house, for she had no wish to be nearby while her father's papers were examined.

⋙✦⋘

CHARLES HAD GOT the key to Lord Childress' bedchamber from Bellamy. His butler had seemed annoyed that Burke trailed their every step and Charles was certain the old fellow had a laundry list of complaints he wished to air. His toes had been so recently insulted by Mrs. Jellops, and then Mrs. Broadbent seemed to make a career out of offending him. Now, it seemed Mrs. Broadbent had set herself up as the heroine of the break-in, while Bellamy came off as an idiot shouting at the wind.

Though Charles was not sorry to miss whatever tirade Bellamy had in store, he was annoyed at Burke's following as well. What was the purpose of the fellow pushing in? Did he suppose Miss Danworth would swoon over the idea that he'd put himself forward to thumb through some papers? Did he think she would throw over all of her ideas just because he'd indicated he wished to be helpful? He would go and say he did not mind reading through papers? What a bit of nonsense, absolutely everybody minded reading a pile of papers.

They had reached the top of the landing and made their way down the east wing. Charles found the door and unlocked it, pushing it open.

Childress' room was as dark as his temperament had always been. Charles crossed the room and opened the heavy curtains to let in the light.

There was not much remarkable about the room, other than the general disorderliness of the place. Empty wine bottles sat on the mantle, the bed was barely made, even the bedstead itself was not in order. At the head of it, one of the bedposts was missing, the other an odd bit of metalwork depicting a man atop an eagle. There was a rumpled shirt on the floor, as if the lord's valet could not be bothered to attend to it, and the grate had not been swept out. Charles supposed the maids he'd hired had taken one look at the room, closed the door, and pretended they'd never seen it at all. It appeared that on Childress' last visit, he'd decided to leave suddenly, without giving his servants the time to do things properly.

Witnessing the disarray might have been pointless, but for the desk pushed in the far corner of the room.

"I suppose we'd better start there," Burke said, pointing at the desk.

"I don't suppose we would start anywhere else," Charles said.

"What's put you more out of sorts than usual?" Burke asked. "Please tell me it is not because the housekeeper has bested Bellamy."

"*You* are far more ridiculous than my old butler," Charles said, rummaging through the desk and pulling out papers. "That whole, *I don't mind reading papers* business. She won't marry you, you know."

Burke had gone a deep shade of pink and Charles knew he'd hit the mark. Burke was not inclined to embarrassment, but just now he looked as if he'd gone to a ball and suddenly realized he'd forgot to wear pants. Miss Minkerton had been correct, Burke *was* mooning over Miss Danworth.

"I am well aware of my own situation, thank you," Burke said.

"Then why do you hang around?" Charles said.

"Never mind what *I* choose to do," Burke said sharply. "Look to yourself for once. If you are not serious in your pursuit you ought not to appear so. Especially not to a lady so innocent."

"I am not in any pursuit!" Charles said.

Though, Burke's words did give him pause. Had his fondness for Miss Danworth been noted? If it had, that would be a mistake. Yes, he admired the lady, but that was only because she was so much elevated above the rest. Nothing more.

But why would Burke make such a point of Miss Danworth being so innocent, as if she were a newborn fawn? Miss Danworth was proper in every way, but she was no foolish ingenue.

Of course, the fellow was in love with her and so he viewed her through his own particular lens. This was precisely why Burke was not the man for Miss Danworth. He did not even understand her.

"Let's just get on with it," Burke said.

"Yes," Charles said, shoving a stack of letters into his hands.

THIS WAS DAISY'S first time walking the pier. Though it was the usual place for a promenade, her father had never allowed it. He was of the opinion that all sorts might be met at such a place, and Daisy was only to go to places where one might be sure of who was in attendance. Balls and such in London were perfectly fine, the hostess would keep out the undesirables, but a public pier was altogether different. Daisy had always been perfectly aware that these edicts were not meant to protect her, they were to make sure that her father could suitably crow over a lofty connection gained through her marriage.

Every summer, Daisy and Mrs. Jellops were mostly confined to their own garden, with occasional outings for sea bathing, surrounded by a bevy of footmen. It had taken Daisy some time to realize her father suspected everyone of having the same preference for low company that he did himself. She was also certain the only reason he would ever be opposed to her making a disastrous match was that men of rank would laugh at him.

She had donned a light gray silk day dress and once more found appreciation for Mrs. Belle's clever designs. The lady had written that this one was particularly meant for walking about on windy days and she had sewn light weights into the hem so that there was no danger of exposing a leg in a sudden gust.

It was a clear day, and Daisy could see the outlines of the coast of France in the distance, and the towns of Deal and Sandwich to the south.

Daisy walked along with Miss Minkerton at her side, while Mrs. Jellops and Mrs. Broadbent had fallen behind. The two older ladies had been talking since the excursion began and Daisy thought they were both enlivened by a conversation with a lady close to their own age.

"It must gratify you, Miss Danworth, to have Lord Dalton investigating the break in. He seems very competent."

Daisy supposed it should be no surprise that Miss Minkerton wished to direct the conversation to Lord Dalton. Really, she would never have guessed they would have been suited. She would have thought the lord would go for a more worldly and experienced lady, if he ever went for anybody at all. Nevertheless, it was impossible to ignore that something was between them.

She could not deny that the idea still irked. Daisy had been sure that Lord Dalton admired her own sort of temperament, and Miss Minkerton was so entirely different.

"Competent?" she said. "Yes, I suppose he is that. I expect you'll see quite a lot of him in the upcoming season."

"Shall I?" Miss Minkerton asked.

Daisy did not know if the lady were being coy. It seemed strange, as Miss Minkerton had not struck her as a lady prone to those sorts of arts.

"Oh yes," she said. "He will turn up at balls and put himself on your card for supper."

To Daisy's surprise, Miss Minkerton appeared a bit distressed over this idea. "I suppose you will come for the season after all," Miss Minkerton said, "and have a great deal of suppers with Lord Burke."

"I have dined with Lord Burke in the past," Daisy said. "Though I would not claim it had ever been a *great deal* of the time. In any case, I shall sit out this season and dine with nobody. You shall have them both to yourself, your friend and your…whatever he is to be."

"I could hardly call Lord Dalton a particular friend!" Miss Minkerton said. "And as for any other person, well, he is to be nothing I'm afraid. He will bide his time, surely, you must know it."

Daisy was entirely confused. She had meant Lord Burke as Miss Minkerton's friend. How on earth had the lady thought she meant Lord Dalton?

She paused, the confusion beginning to clear. "Miss Minkerton," she said slowly, "I had presumed, and I am sorry if I have been wrong, that you were developing some feelings of attachment for Lord Dalton."

Miss Minkerton nearly staggered at the suggestion. "Lord Dalton? Why ever would you think it?"

"Well, the two of you were ever so engaged with one another at the dinner at your house. I had never seen him so engaged. Over nautical maps, of all things. It did seem quite obvious."

Miss Minkerton touched her palms to her cheeks as if to cool them. "I was only trying to pretend I did not care about…"

"About what?"

"Not about what, about who!" Miss Minkerton said, rather vehemently. "I can see very well that Lord Burke is in love with you. Oh, I know you are retired from society, but he will wait. He is a loyal fellow, so there is no doubt of that."

"Lord Burke?" Daisy said, incredulous. "That is preposterous. We are brother and sister, if we are anything at all."

"No, you see," Miss Minkerton said, "it is *I* who am viewed as the sister."

Now Daisy began to understand the real case.

"I think I do see," she said. "You are in love with Lord Burke and had somehow convinced yourself that he and I had developed an attachment. And *I* had supposed you had developed an attachment to Lord Dalton."

Miss Minkerton shook her head. "I am only a sister to Harry, though, so it is entirely unrequited."

"But that might change, might it not?"

Miss Minkerton gazed at the sea. "I did wonder, I hoped, but then when I supposed he was in love with you…"

"Which is a bit of nonsense," Daisy said.

"If I have been that mixed up," Miss Minkerton said, "does that mean you have an attachment to Lord Dalton?"

"Certainly not!" Daisy said. "You must dismiss that idea at once. Instead, you must think of how you might subtly communicate that you are no sister to Lord Burke."

Miss Minkerton sighed, long and deep. "That is a difficulty. You see, we have gone on so many years one way, and now to go another way…"

"But when did you realize your feelings had changed?" Daisy asked. "What was the moment that made you think you'd rather *not* be as a sister?"

"Oh, my feelings have never changed a jot," Miss Minkerton said. "I loved him the moment I set eyes on him. I was only thirteen and he was a dashing older boy and well, now, I'll have to go and marry somebody else!"

"Do not give up so easily," Daisy counseled.

"Daisy? Miss Minkerton?" Mrs. Jellops called in the distance. "Stop a moment, you leave us quite behind."

Daisy and Miss Minkerton stopped to allow the other two ladies to catch up to them. It had been a remarkable conversation, so rarely did one ever hear of real feelings or candor from another lady.

As well, she could not help but feel remarkably cheerful over Miss Minkerton's apparent distaste over the idea of Lord Dalton. As for the lord's own feelings, that of course was another matter. It was a mystery, really.

CHAPTER NINE

W HEN DAISY HAD returned to the house, she'd thought she would rest and then change her clothes for a quiet dinner with only Mrs. Jellops as her company. As it turned out, Lord Dalton had been as highhanded as ever and arranged for guests. He'd left her a note that said there were things to discuss regarding discoveries in her father's rooms and the most sensible thing to do was to put all heads together. He had taken the liberty of speaking to Flanagan in the kitchens and Lord Burke would inform Miss Minkerton that they were to come to supper. Mrs. Jellops would act as chaperone and so there could be no impropriety.

She had, for a moment, thought to charge over to the cottage and demand that he undo his invitations immediately. She changed her mind when she considered that she might as well hear what had been found, and she would be most interested to observe Lord Burke and Miss Minkerton, and Lord Dalton for that matter, through the glass of the information she now knew.

She put on one of her best dresses, a pale lavender that hinted even the modiste knew she was not too broken up over her father's demise, and descended the stairs.

Daisy had not much to say to Lord Dalton as they awaited their guests in the drawing room. The only subject that came to mind was decidedly off-limits—*are you swooning over Miss Minkerton, and have you noticed that she is swooning over Lord Burke?*

Mrs. Jellops helpfully filled in the silences with endless praises of Mrs. Broadbent, which reliably put Mr. Bellamy in a grim state of mind. Then, as if to ensure Lord Dalton would be equally grim, she pointed out that he seemed to have some sort of animal hair on his trousers and suggested Tate use a ball of damp bread dough to pull them off without too much trouble.

Lord Burke and Miss Minkerton arrived in good time, the lady prettily dressed in a fine white lawn that set off her complexion wonderfully. Her maid had accompanied them in the carriage and was sent below stairs to the kitchens where Mr. Flanagan would supply her with a supper. Daisy only hoped the poor girl could keep her appetite amidst the various complaints from her butler and footmen about how badly they were treated.

They had gone through to the dining room without further delay, Daisy taking the head of the table and Lord Dalton taking the bottom. As was custom, Lord Burke was seated to her right and Miss Minkerton to Lord Dalton's right, while Mrs. Jellops was to her left.

As the first course was brought round, the party was oddly silent. This would have been the moment to speak of the weather, a very reliable topic at every table, and yet all seemed to be waiting for the real subject to be raised.

Once the soup had been delivered and the footmen stepped out to look for the next course, Lord Dalton said, "I believe Burke and I have discovered something, but we are not certain what it is."

"That is very mysterious," Daisy said, fiddling with her napkin and attempting to appear composed. She was leery of hearing anything at all of her father's business. Had there not been a break-in, his bedchamber door would have remained closed forever.

"Miss Danworth," Lord Burke said, "are you at all familiar with the name Dagobert?"

"No, not at all," Daisy said, "though if it were one of my father's cronies I might not be. So many of them were unsavory and if they were not often about the house, I might never know their names."

"Mrs. Jellops?" Lord Burke asked. "Does this name sound familiar?"

"Not at all," Mrs. Jellops said. "An odd name, though. It does not sound particularly lyrical."

Daisy suppressed a smile, remembering that the staff in the London house used to refer to Mrs. Jellops as Mrs. Jellies, which they thought suited her ample frame far better than Jellops.

"We do not actually know that it is the name of a man," Lord Dalton said. "It was never referred to as 'Mr.' or 'sir,' or any rank of service, only on its own or with the in front of it. As in, the Dagobert."

"What was the nature of the discussion about Dagobert?" Miss Minkerton asked. "Was it an argument?"

"Not an argument, so much as a questioning," Lord Dalton said. "There were very many letters between Lord Childress and Lieutenant Farthmore about where Dagobert was or who might know."

Daisy shivered at the mention of the lieutenant. Of all people, why must he be brought into this?

"Is the lieutenant known?" Miss Minkerton asked.

"Unfortunately, he is," Daisy said. "He was one of the worst people my father ever associated with and we have seen him since."

"Wait," Lord Burke said, "was he the fellow that…"

"That was thrown from the premises," Daisy finished for him.

"A nasty piece of work, that one," Mrs. Jellops said.

"He seems to be involved in this conversation with Lord Childress," Lord Dalton said, "because Dagobert, whoever or whatever it is, returned to England on a boat coming back from the disastrous siege of Tarragona."

"Perhaps Dagobert owed them a deal of money," Miss Minkerton said.

"Perhaps," Lord Burke said. "But there were some references that did seem to imply that Dagobert is a thing, not a person. Things like, *whoever has possession of the Dagobert*, and *get the Dagobert back.*"

"Well," Mrs. Jellops said, "if it is some artwork or other, I cannot think what it might be. Lord Childress was never much of a collector, aside from those books he bragged of to all and sundry."

"Books," Lord Burke said. "Could that be why the library was sacked? Did not your father purchase the Palaskar collection?"

"Indeed he did," Daisy said, "and talked about it everywhere. Though I never heard mention of a Dagobert book or collection. Had he acquired it, he would have advertised it had it the least amount of value. He liked people to know what he had."

"If he acquired it through usual means he might advertise it," Lord Burke said. "But if he did not…"

Lord Dalton sighed. "If we looked for a person, inquiries might be made with the navy. But if it is a thing, a thing we do not even know the sort of, I have no idea how we would identify it."

"Though," Daisy said, an idea having just come to her, "if it is a thing, it must be of some great value or there would not have been so many questions about it. Or someone to come looking for it in the dead of night, if that is what they were after."

Lord Dalton nodded in a way that said she had just stated the obvious.

"Something of great value usually has a history and is known. And so, Lord Dalton, we must consult with a person likely to know of such things," Daisy said, to alert him that she had more ideas than what he deemed obvious. "I must write to Lady Grayson."

"Lady Grayson!" Lord Burke said. "Capital idea. I have always felt there was nothing she did not know something about, or could not find out about, and she has a plethora of learned connections. But must the letter travel all the way to Sweden and chase her from place to place? I do not recall when they were set to return from their wedding trip."

"They have returned," Daisy said, "Kitty wrote me of their expected arrival back to England some weeks ago. They have bought a house in town and are there overseeing renovations of some sort. Or, at least, Kitty is overseeing the library and Lord Grayson is overseeing everything else. I shall write her—she is a diligent sort of person, I doubt we will wait long for an answer."

"Ah, she manages the renovation of the library," Miss Minkerton said to Lord Burke. "Is she the lady you spoke of, the improbable match between the lady librarian and the dandy?"

"Most improbable," Lord Dalton said. "I am *still* trying to work it out."

"There is nothing under the sun that is not made probable by affection," Mrs. Jellops said.

This idea seemed to strike the party strongly, as all looked in different directions. Daisy looked over Lord Dalton's head, Lord Dalton stared at the window behind her, Miss Minkerton peered into her soup, and Lord Burke gazed at the picture on the far wall.

It was only Mrs. Jellops who seemed to find her idea at all comfortable. "Well then," she said, "there is the solution. Daisy will write to Lady Grayson."

WHEN THEY HAD retired to the drawing room, Miss Minkerton played the pianoforte while Lord Burke turned the pages for her. As Daisy wrote her letter to Kitty, now Lady Grayson, about the mysterious Dagobert, she paused from time to time to glance at the couple. She was not so sure that Miss Minkerton was entirely correct in her assumptions—Lord Burke seemed as any man paying his attentions to a lady in a drawing room, and so perhaps he did not view her as a sister after all.

As for Lord Dalton, Daisy did not detect any jealousy on his part by Lord Burke's attentions to Miss Minkerton; he was far too busy telling her of this thing or that thing that she must include in her letter.

That circumstance could not say anything conclusive, though.

Lord Dalton was not the type to wear his heart on his sleeve, if he had such a heart to wear. If he suspected Miss Minkerton's feelings lay elsewhere and was affected by it, he would never reveal it.

Before she could finish her letter, there was a sound heard, growing louder, of a carriage barreling down the drive. Miss Minkerton's carriage stood outside, so it could not be hers. Whoever it was, they came at a furious pace.

Lord Dalton and Lord Burke looked at each other. Lord Burke left Miss Minkerton at the instrument.

"My pistols are in the cottage," Lord Dalton said.

"Mine in the carriage," Lord Burke said.

"We are idiots," Lord Dalton said.

Both men looked round the room as the sound grew ever louder. Their eyes both settled on the fire pokers and they grabbed one each.

Miss Minkerton had stopped her playing and rose in alarm. "What is it?" she asked, just then becoming cognizant of the approaching hoofbeats.

"We ought to go above stairs," Mrs. Jellops said, her face gone white.

"There's no time," Lord Dalton said, "lock the doors behind us."

Daisy hurried to the doors as the men strode out to the hall. As she locked them, with a rather flimsy lock, she thought, she heard Lord Dalton say to Bellamy, "Stand aside, we'll answer it."

Mrs. Jellops and Miss Minkerton had moved to the very back of the drawing room. Daisy thought she ought to do the same, but she must know—was it Lieutenant Farthmore returning? Was it someone else? Was it the same person who'd broken into the house?

She pulled the curtain aside just in time to see a coach clatter to a stop. It was as well-made as any she had seen and had a coat of arms on the door, though she could not see the details in the darkness, only the glinting of gold paint.

A finely-dressed servant leapt out of the carriage and said, "A communication for Miss Danworth, daughter of the late Lord Childress, and Charles Battersea, Earl of Dalton, from His Royal Highness, The Prince Regent."

"What?" Lord Dalton said from the front steps. Daisy pressed her cheek against the window to get a better view and saw that he stood there with Lord Burke, both of them with fire pokers raised.

The servant, who appeared slightly bored, as if he'd seen everything in his career and two lords threatening him with fire pokers was hardly enough to discompose him, repeated, "A communication for Miss Danworth, daughter of the late Lord Childress, and Charles Battersea, Earl of Dalton, from His Royal Highness, the Prince Regent."

"Good God, man," Lord Dalton said, lowering his weapon, "why are you coming up the drive as if the hounds of hell were on your heels?"

"I am in a hurry, my lord, as I usually am," the man said with aspersion. "Will you take the invitation? I have more stops to make."

"Invitation?" Lord Dalton went down the steps and took the paper from the man's hands. The fellow bowed, hopped back in the carriage, and rapped on the roof. They were off as fast as they had come.

Daisy hurried to unlock the doors and Lord Dalton and Lord Burke came back in. Lord Dalton had unfolded the paper, which in fact was two papers. He folded it back up and said, "Good Lord," before handing it to Daisy.

The first was addressed to both she and Lord Dalton and was a formal invitation to an assembly at Ramsgate for Tuesday next. The second was a handwritten note to Daisy. She read it as Mrs. Jellops peered over her shoulder.

Dear Miss Danworth – I am well aware you are meant to be in mourning, however, the more one knew Lord Childress, the less one actually mourns him. As I am to be in this town for a week to survey the harbor and give my considered opinion, which of course would take a quarter hour but for the ceremonial displays I must also witness, I require amusements of my own making. Do attend my assembly and blast whoever says you ought to be at home weeping—I cannot abide false sadness. Bring your lady companion if you like—if I remember rightly, she is a jolly enough personage.

Daisy showed the note to Miss Minkerton and Lord Burke. Miss Minkerton said, "Goodness, that is a familiar sort of sentiment."

Daisy smiled. "I have met the prince on a few occasions, on the last he told me he found me charming because I was not overawed by him."

"His mistake was in thinking Miss Danworth is overawed by *anybody*," Lord Dalton said.

"But shall you go?" Miss Minkerton asked.

"I suppose I must," Daisy said, "as he's added the personal note."

"He may not be the cleverest soul alive," Mrs. Jellops said, "but he read Lord Childress right enough. Though, am I jolly? I suppose I can be on occasion. Well, it's nice to be remembered."

"You must tell me all about it," Miss Minkerton said. "Who was there, what they wore, what did the prince say to you…"

"I suspect you'll receive your own invitation," Daisy said, "I doubt the prince will care if you were out a few months ago or coming out a few months from now. Ramsgate is a small society and he will leave no stone unturned."

"I should not know what to say," Miss Minkerton said.

"Do not fear that particular problem, Miss Minkerton," Lord Dalton said drily, "he will do all the talking. Just pretend at deep interest while he tells you of the building of his pavilion, which never seems to end."

Miss Minkerton looked to Lord Burke and he nodded reluctantly, as if to indicate that it was entirely true, though he was loath to admit it.

Behind Lord Burke, Daisy saw a shadow move past the window.

She clutched at Lord Dalton's sleeve.

"It is only a watchman," he said quietly.

She let go and felt herself a fool. Of course it was a watchman—they had been ordered to prowl the perimeter around the house. Still, she was grateful that the lord would be back in the cottage and Mrs. Broadbent would continue her reign in the bedchamber next door.

News of an assembly held by the Prince of Wales did nothing to solve the mystery of who had broken into the house, what they were looking for, or if they would try again. There was also no explanation for why Lord Dalton was convinced he'd been pulled under water. She could only hope that dear Kitty could shed some light on what on earth a Dagobert was.

MRS. JELLOPS HAD fallen asleep as soon as her head had touched her pillow, that lady perhaps taking two extra glasses of Madeira to settle her nerves after the excitement of hooves clattering on the drive and the gentlemen going out to meet the danger only armed with fire pokers.

Daisy was not tired, though. She blew out the candle and curled up on the window seat, allowing the night breeze to cool her. Lord Dalton's cottage was well lit, Bellamy no doubt making free with baskets of candles for his use. The lord was not in the cottage, though. He was out of doors, sitting on the bench that seemed to be his usual place, his dark outline illuminated by the light shining through his windows.

He held a glass and Daisy assumed it was from the brandy decanter that had gone missing from the library. She had at first wondered if it had been Bellamy and the footmen who'd made off with it, but discarded the idea when she considered that Mrs. Broadbent was all-seeing and all-knowing. She would have noted it and given them the *what for.*

She did not begrudge Lord Dalton his brandy, or the other things his butler and valet had swiped from the house. She was more amused than anything, sometimes seeing one of them furtively cross the lawn with something under his arm.

Daisy bit her lip as she watched a thin and scraggly-looking tabby cat hop up on the bench and Lord Dalton pat its head. It appeared a rangy creature and no doubt riddled with fleas. She had not been entirely sure that news of the cat had been real. She had begun to think it might have only been Mrs. Broadbent amusing herself at Mr. Deer's expense.

She could not help thinking what would have happened to the creature if her father was still in residence. He would have ordered it poisoned or grabbed it by the tail and swung it over the garden wall. He had always been cruel toward animals, even his own, and Daisy had early come to the conclusion that it was a hallmark of a bad nature.

Long ago, when she'd been eight or so, she had been out for a walk with a maid when she encountered her father on the road, speaking to the Duke of Somerston. In an attempt to appear the indulgent father, he'd reminded her that he'd said she could buy herself a puppy. He'd never said it and she never did—she was too afraid of what might happen to any poor creature she dared bring into the house.

The cat made itself at home on Lord Dalton's lap. Daisy peered down, certain the lord would instantly shoo the creature off.

He did not. He only patted its head again.

How strange.

Lord Dalton rose, and rather than the cat falling to the ground as she would expect, he swept it up under one arm and carried it into the cottage.

Daisy leaned back and sighed. He certainly was an enigmatic sort of person. What kind of gentleman went about so grim and then was kind to a cat? A rather unpleasant-looking cat, as far as she could tell.

Enigmatic he might be, but she felt safer that Lord Dalton was there.

⯈⯈⯈⯇⯇⯇

THE NEXT DAYS passed quietly. Nobody had any idea of who or what Dagobert might be, and only waited to discover if Lady Grayson would write to shed some light on it. Nobody knew what the purpose of the break-in had been, or if it would be tried again. Nobody was much interested in sea bathing after Lord Dalton's misadventure.

Daisy did not mind how quietly they went on. It became a habit for Lord Burke and Miss Minkerton to arrive in the afternoon and for them all to gather in the garden. A large wood table had been set up with chairs round it and a tea was served. Were the breeze insufficient or coming off the land, Mrs. Broadbent would march out carrying one of her own inventions. She had made a series of basket frames and covered them with netting to sit over the cakes and biscuits to protect them from flies and bees.

These contraptions were enormously effective, and only over-thrown occasionally by the cat when nobody was looking. The cat's nature, as far as Daisy could divine it, was bold and inscrutable. It would use a claw to flick over a net basket, swipe at whatever was found there, knock it to the ground, examine it, and then stroll off if it was not deemed suitably tempting. It appeared to have a fondness for ham and an abhorrence of cucumber.

The cat was not interested in any other person aside from Lord Dalton, and sometimes Daisy laughed as she watched the incorrigible feline follow him when he walked the paths. If he chose to notice her stalking, she promptly dove into the shrubbery.

The garden itself was well laid out for opportunities to walk round it and have a private conversation, and yet remain under Mrs. Jellops' watchful gaze. At least, watchful when the lady's eyes were actually open.

Which they were very often not. The sound of the waves crashing in the distance seemed to lull Mrs. Jellops to sleep with regularity.

Daisy was determined to help Miss Minkerton in her effort to alert Lord Burke that she was in no way his sister, and she sent them off whenever she found the opportunity, usually to examine a particular flower in bloom in some far corner. She did not know if her suggestions were having any effect, but both parties seemed eager enough to follow them.

Just now, Miss Minkerton and Lord Burke were engrossed in examining a patch of recently bloomed sea pink. There was nothing at all extraordinary about it, though the couple appeared to be having an animated conversation nonetheless.

Lord Dalton sat at the table, his ever-present feline companion asleep under his chair. Mrs. Jellops had joined the cat in that activity and was gently snoring from a settee that had been carried out for her convenience.

"If you do not wish to attend the prince's assembly," Lord Dalton said, "I can easily make your excuses."

"Why should I not wish to?" Daisy asked. The fact was, since she'd been thinking about it, she *did* wish to attend. The distraction would do her good and she did always find the prince's parties amusing. At least, those were the reasons she attempted to convince herself of. There were perhaps other reasons that it did not suit to examine so closely. She had always enjoyed dancing with Lord Dalton and she would much rather be doing that than staying home alone with Mrs. Jellops, wondering if someone might break into the house while her protector was out frittering the night away with the regent.

"I only say, there might be talk because you are in mourning. The prince may not condemn it, but others might."

"And what can disapproving talk do to *me*?" Daisy asked. As she asked it, she realized that she was indeed past the time when talk could do much of anything. After all, what did gossip ever do but ruin a lady's chances of marriage or cause invitations to dry up? She was in no need of either of those two things.

It was a cheering idea, really. The *ton* no longer held any power over her.

Lord Dalton had only nodded and said, "I have hired a few more men for that evening in particular. If someone is intent on returning, they might choose the evening when we are likely not at home."

"Excellent idea," Daisy said.

"Why do you send them away so often?" Lord Dalton said, nodding toward Miss Minkerton and Lord Burke.

Daisy had not realized the habit had been noted. She supposed she ought to have known. While she was all for Miss Minkerton communicating her real feelings to Lord Burke, she had somehow managed to forget that Lord Dalton might have his own feelings for Miss Minkerton to contend with.

"Would you rather I did not send her away?" she asked, though she was not certain she wished to hear the answer.

"Her?" Lord Dalton asked, seeming confused. "I was rather thinking of *him*."

"Him?" Daisy asked, completely lost.

Lord Dalton did not immediately answer. He played with a biscuit, crumbling it onto a saucer. "I suppose it's too soon, in any event."

"Soon for what?" Daisy asked.

Mrs. Jellops suddenly sat up and rubbed her eyes. "Soon? Are we late?"

"Not at all," Lord Dalton said, rising. He walked away with the cat at his heels.

What had he meant by it? Why would he wonder about Lord Burke being sent away?

Daisy did not know, but could not ignore that she was rather happy that he did not seem to mind finding Miss Minkerton sent away.

CHAPTER TEN

DAISY HAD DEBATED what she would wear to the regent's assembly. She was most inclined to choose the pale blue crepe silk that had been so skillfully made by the London modiste. Intricate patterns of periwinkle flowers had been embroidered across the whole and it had a cheerful summer feel to it. However, she also knew perfectly well that particular dress was more suited to one coming *out* of mourning, so little did it hint of sadness. In the end, she reminded herself that she was not at all afraid of talk and put on the dress.

The assembly rooms were by the harbor and while Daisy had passed the building many times on her way to a shop, she had never been inside. She did not know if her father had regularly attended the assemblies, particularly since the building was rumored to have a billiard room, but he had never escorted her there.

Lord Dalton, though he was usually inclined to be on horseback, had ridden in the carriage with them. As Mrs. Jellops unobtrusively picked a cat hair from the edge of his coat, he said, "I suppose it would be best if I took supper."

Daisy knew perfectly well that he meant he ought to put himself down for her supper, and was rather thrilled by it, but somehow ended saying, "It *is* usually best that people take supper."

Mrs. Jellops, delightfully oblivious, said, "Even if you are not in-clined to it, you ought to pretend you are. The prince is very fond of his food and won't like to see you starve if he's arranged something."

"Miss Danworth understands me, I think," Lord Dalton said. "It will be proper that I take the lady's supper as I am her guardian. It would not be seemly for her to dine with some unknown gentleman at this moment in her history."

"Would it not?" Daisy said.

"Well, I see what you say, Lord Dalton," Mrs. Jellops said. "But then, Lord Burke is well known by us so I suppose he would do just as well."

"No," Daisy and Lord Dalton said at the same time.

They both looked to opposite sides of the carriage.

"Ah," Mrs. Jellops said, gazing out the window at the passing scenery, "I understand you. Lord Burke will be set on taking Miss Minkerton in. He seems fond of the lady."

"Yes, of course," Daisy said hurriedly. "He does seem fond of Miss Minkerton."

"Does that bother you?" Lord Dalton asked, staring at Daisy.

Before Daisy could answer, Mrs. Jellops said, "Not in the slightest. Why ever should it?"

Thankfully, the carriage stopped and there was no more time for circular and very confusing conversations.

CHARLES HAD ESCORTED Miss Danworth and the confounded Mrs. Jellops into the assembly rooms. As they waited their turn to be greeted by the prince, he cursed himself for his heavy-handedness. He might have just asked the lady for her supper without the speech about it being proper, and he being the guardian and whatever else he'd gone on about.

Or, he might have been even more clever and not asked at all.

What was he doing, anyway? Was this only some silly competition with Burke?

If it was, they were both fools, as Miss Danworth was not inclined to entertain any gentleman's interest.

Perhaps that was why he was so interested in Miss Danworth. It was pleasant to engage with a lady who was not set on dragging him up the church steps.

That was likely it. As for Burke's interest in the lady, he could not understand how the fellow was going about it. He seemed to spend far more time speaking to Miss Minkerton than he did Miss Danworth.

Well, if Burke thought he would move in and take supper, he was about to find out he was mistaken.

The prince had taken his time greeting Miss Danworth and Charles was not surprised by it—he had noted at other events that the regent had a particular regard for the lady. Miss Danworth, if she were anything, was a composed creature and Prinny admired it. The regent was also not opposed to a fine set of fair curls.

"Dalton," the prince said, "how do you do these days? We expected to see you at Brighton this summer before we heard the duke had sent you off to squire Miss Danworth here. A rascal of a father, eh?"

Dalton nodded, despite the fact that *rascal* was not the word he'd use for his patriarch. Though, any words he *would* use he had rarely said aloud.

Far behind him somewhere, he heard an unmistakable voice. It was noisy, it was pushy, and it was grating on the nerves.

It was unpleasantly unmistakable. Lady Montague.

Charles was not at all eager to see that particular lady. Not only was she vile and intent on causing trouble wherever she went, but he did harbor some amount of guilt over having connived with her to keep Lockwood away from Lady Sybil. He'd even helped the creature back into society after Hampton had helped her out of it and sent her packing to Yorkshire.

It had seemed an unfortunately necessary bargain at the time. Now, she reminded him of his less than honorable actions in attempting to keep his friends from the altar. She reminded him that he had been in the wrong more than once, though he'd justified himself at the time. He did not like it, and he did not like her.

Charles stared at the prince. The regent had winced at the sound of Lady Montague's voice, then glanced at Charles and shrugged. "She made a point of informing all and sundry that she was in town," the prince said. "What could I do?"

"Pretend you did not hear?"

The regent laughed and said quietly, "She will spend her time stirring things up in the card room—keep yourself on the ballroom floor and you will hardly know she's present. In any case, you will not be her target. I understand she is put out that I did not invite some cousin or other. She will not dare mention it to me, but I am sure she will plague anybody else within hearing."

Charles nodded and moved on, not at all surprised to hear of the lady's latest contretemps. If she was not busy offending others, she was offended over something herself. The prince had suggested staying in the ballroom and that was precisely what he would do. He'd never had any intention of going into the card room anyway. He was a guardian and had responsibilities. It was all well and good that Mrs. Jellops acted as companion to Miss Danworth, but that lady did not know men as he did. It was left to him to keep any unsavory characters at bay who may have weaseled their way onto the regent's guest list. Even if Lady Montague's cousin had not been admitted, there were sure to be others not quite up to snuff. The prince often valued amusement over respectability and the vying for invitations would have been fierce.

DAISY FELT MORE alive than she had in the past weeks. It was something to be dressed in finery and out at a ball. It seemed she had begun to take such evenings for granted during the season, but having gone nowhere since her father died had brought back all the wonder of it.

She certainly noticed that she was stared at from time to time, but she could not say it bothered her overmuch. The prince had sanctioned her appearance and she doubted anybody would challenge it. What she had been most worried about, that one of her father's cronies might make a showing, seemed to have been a needless fear. There were some officers, to be sure, but they were senior and circumspect. Not the type her father had ever gathered round him.

The only person in attendance that she would wish to have nothing to do with was Lady Montague. That particular lady had caused no end of trouble for Cassandra Knightsbridge before she married Lord Hampton, and Daisy had heard she'd been unpleasant to Lady Sybil too, though the details were rather fuzzy.

She could not even understand why Lady Montague had turned up in Ramsgate. She did not ever remember hearing her name spoken in prior summers.

Daisy suppressed a smile. For all she knew, Lady Montague was quite a regular in local society. Her father would not have tolerated her for a moment and Daisy herself had never been introduced into the society of Ramsgate, penned in the garden as she had been.

None of it mattered much, as Lady Montague had taken herself off to the card room and was no doubt harassing people there.

Despite anybody's surprise, or even shock, to see Daisy out so soon after her father's passing, her card had filled rapidly enough. Most of the young men who claimed a dance were as they had been in London. She had taken to thinking of their general mien as callow-yet-gallant. They seem to have a rehearsed set of phrases to throw out, followed by a series of inane questions. It was all pleasant enough, though it endlessly surprised her that any lady would willingly place her fortune into one of these young fool's hands. It did *not* surprise her, however, whenever she heard one of these fellows had decamped to the continent after betting his family's fortunes on cards or a horse. It had occurred to her more than once that it was a mistake to assume men knew best—it was proved again and again that they did not.

Lord Dalton came to collect her for the dance before supper and she must admit to herself that *he* was wholly different from the other gentlemen. There was nothing callow about him, and little overtly gallant for that matter. Though, it had perhaps been gallant to claim her supper before they'd even left the carriage.

She began to think that he could not like Miss Minkerton very much if he were willing to throw over the opportunity to claim *her* supper.

It was a cheering notion, though she understood it should very much *not* be a cheering notion.

The fact was, she liked Lord Dalton better than anybody else, and she always had. Their relatively close quarters and his near-drowning had perhaps made that liking more pronounced.

She really did not think she would mind if he stayed in her back garden forever.

Just no closer than that.

As he led her through the changes, he said, "I expect the regent will have arranged the seating according to rank, and we may well find ourselves nearby Lady Montague."

Daisy had not thought of that, she had only thought of Lady Montague being safely away in the card room. Most suppers at balls were a more casual affair, though she should have realized that the regent, of all people, would insist on some sort of ranking.

What ranking though? Lord Dalton was an earl, someday to be a duke. She was only the daughter of a viscount.

"That is all well and good for married people who choose to go in together," Daisy said, "but what shall he do with unmarried couples? If he goes by the man's title we will be near the top, if he goes by the lady's we will be further down."

Lord Dalton smiled. "I expect he will go by the men's rank, as he is himself a man and a higher rank than anybody else. I expect Lord Home to take in Lady Montague and so we will be in her range, I think."

Daisy sighed. "Well, she may say what she likes about my mourning habits."

"She certainly may not," Lord Dalton said.

Daisy suppressed a shiver. There was something in Lord Dalton's protective tone that struck her. She supposed it was that it was so foreign to her. Whatever her father had ever been, he'd not been protective. Her mother had been too weak and gone too soon for it. Mrs. Jellops, the dear lady, was stalwart in her defenses, but not exactly built for leading daring charges. Daisy had been so used, all her life, to depending upon only herself. It was entirely novel to hear somebody raise a verbal sword in her defense.

There had been some silence between them, and Lord Dalton said, "Do you enjoy these sorts of things?"

Daisy smiled. "If you mean balls? Yes, I suppose I do, though you have ever looked pained in your attendance."

"Yes, well, there are a lot of fluttering eyelashes, claims of delicateness, and gentle fanning to contend with. I just got done with Miss Martel claiming my arm was shockingly strong. Twice. I thought she might pretend a faint as a dramatic finale to her playacting."

Daisy could not stop herself from laughing. She supposed the lord was endlessly beset with young ladies who would work very hard to like him in case they might be destined to be a duchess.

"Poor Miss Martel," Daisy said.

"Poor Miss Martel nothing," Lord Dalton said. "She will go to her mama and say I seemed very taken with her and they will scheme together to force another encounter. One day soon, I will walk down some avenue and a handkerchief will fly at my face and gently flutter to my feet. They will have discovered where to find me by paying off a servant and then they will look deeply shocked to encounter me."

"And then they will hear, eventually, of your vow to never marry," Daisy said. "That will be the end of it."

"I'm sure they've heard it already," Lord Dalton said. "The problem is, nobody ever believes it."

"I believe it," Daisy said softly.

"Do you?" the lord said, his voice just as low.

Daisy nodded. "Just as I have said that I will never—"

"You are certain you will not?"

The set ended before Daisy was forced to answer. She was sure she would have answered affirmative. She was not some silly girl who changed her mind with the weather. And yet, she was glad she had not been pressed to answer.

JUST AS LORD Dalton had predicted, Lady Montague was in range. In fact, she was seated directly across the not over-wide table. Daisy was further perturbed to note that Lord Dalton had been right, her husband did not accompany her. It had always been her opinion that Lord Montague was a more pleasant sort and it had been her guess that he went some way to controlling the lady's worst instincts. Rather, Lady Montague was seated by Lord Home, a middle-aged gentleman Daisy did not know well.

At least Lord Burke and Miss Minkerton were in range of Daisy too, Lord Burke to Lady Montague's right. Daisy could not help but note that they seemed anything but brother and sister. Miss Minkerton certainly must be wrong in her opinions—after all, what brother took a sister into supper?

Whether she was wrong or no, Miss Minkerton seemed delighted with him and he with her.

As there were a few persons who outranked even Lord Dalton or who were otherwise given precedence as being a senior military officer, the regent was just a bit too far away to be in their conversation. That was well, Daisy thought, as she'd already heard some very detailed stories of the building of the pavilion. Apparently, Mr. Nash was a stickler for quality and had even once sent back a box of nails he did not feel was up to snuff. The regent, if she understood him at all, had a fondness for people who deemed things not good enough for him.

Poor Mrs. Jellops, having partnered at whist with Mr. Kelleher, was somewhere near the bottom of the table. Daisy supposed the lady would not mind it, though. When it came to supper, she was far more interested in what was *on* the table than who was seated at it.

Daisy had noticed for some minutes that Lady Montague was staring at her. She pretended she did not notice and hoped the lady would find something else to engage her attention. Lord Dalton had no doubt marked it as he had engaged Daisy in a very nonsensical conversation about the tides.

"Miss Danworth," Lady Montague said. "I say, Miss Danworth."

She was impossible to ignore. Daisy looked over and smiled sweetly. "Lady Montague. How lovely to see you."

Lady Montague sniffed at the sentiment and said, "And so we see each other. Though, I had been under the impression, Miss Danworth, that you were seeing nobody at all. At least, that is what my cousin said."

Daisy had braced herself for some comment on her attendance at the assembly or the light color of her dress. She had no idea what the lady was talking about.

"My cousin, Miss Danworth, or I suppose I should say distant cousin as he is three times removed. A very pleasant fellow who was a dear friend of your father's. Lieutenant Farthmore. He stays at my house, you know."

Daisy was dumbstruck. Of course, she had not known any of it. Not that Lady Montague kept a house nearby, not that she was related to the lieutenant, and certainly not that he stayed at her house.

"Your cousin," Lord Dalton said to Lady Montague, "however distant, arrived at an unseemly hour and did not gain admittance."

"Oh, don't bother dripping honey on it, Dalton," Lady Montague said. "I know all about it."

"If you knew *all* about it," Lord Dalton said, "you would not have brought it up."

Lady Montague's thin lips pressed together in a sharp line and her eyes narrowed at Lord Dalton. She looked as if she were confirming the location of her prey before she pounced.

"I *know* that the Lieutenant arrived to pay respects to the daughter of a dear departed friend and was summarily thrown from the property," Lady Montague said. "I *know* Lieutenant Farthmore, who is a renowned member of the military, is celebrated for his amphibious operations at Tarragona. I *know* that one might have been generous and assumed that Lord Childress' daughter was too broken up over her father's death to see anybody. But then, I also *know* that same daughter is out at a ball wearing a dress that does not hint at such devastation. That, Lord Dalton, is what I *know*."

Lady Montague had been loud enough to attract attention up and down the table. The rest of the diners had gone silent, almost as if they'd had their ears primed all night in anticipation of what the lady would stir up.

Daisy had a great urge to run from the room, but at the same time felt frozen in her seat. She could feel Lord Dalton's fury coming off him like a heat.

Lord Dalton laid down his fork very deliberately and said, "I see you are now to be the arbiter of mourning. But I wonder…who will mourn when *you* depart, Lady Montague? Who will don the black and pretend at weeping? I think the best you might expect is your husband wears an armband for a while, because it is not much trouble. Otherwise, it will be more a time for jubilation than not. *That* is how villains may expect to be sent off to meet their maker."

It seemed to Daisy that Lady Montague had never experienced such a vigorous defense upon one of her attacks. She so often cowed people that she was in the habit of gaining her victory and most certainly *not* in the habit of being crossed. Especially not in such a manner or so publicly. Her face had paled to such a degree that Daisy wondered how she stayed upright.

"You will answer to my husband, Lord Dalton," she said, breathing heavily.

"I certainly will not," Lord Dalton said, "he has too much sense than to get himself killed over one of your arguments. Else, he would have been dead long ago."

The prince laughed at the head of the table. "Hah! That's right, eh?"

Lady Montague turned to Lord Home. "My lord, how do you answer this?"

Lord Home looked very surprised to be asked to come to the lady's rescue. "How do I? My dear lady, I only offered my arm into supper, not my blood at dawn. I do not know what argument you have with this young lady, nor do I wish to."

Lady Montague rose. "Dalton," she said, "you will pay for this. You will see that my husband comes to my defense."

"I put a stop to this right now," the regent said, seeming to lose his humor over the outburst. "There are to be no duels over something *I* sanctioned. *I* personally invited Miss Danworth. If there is to be any consequences from this ridiculous argument, I will take steps that everybody involved will find unpleasant. Lady Montague, do stop stirring pots all over my realm—I grow weary of it, madam."

Lady Montague, though she might have been willing to go toe to toe with nearly anybody, could not carry it off with the prince. Though he had not outlined the unpleasant steps he might take, all within hearing knew it would involve a banishment from society. Of all things, that was the threat Lady Montague could not bear to see realized. She curtsied and swept out of the dining room.

Lord Home looked for a moment as if he might follow her, then shrugged his shoulders and went back to his plate.

As if Lord Home had signaled to everyone what they ought to be doing, the rest of the party went back to their conversations. Though, Daisy was certain, the conversation for the rest of the evening would be solely focused on Lady Montague.

"I am afraid you have made an enemy, Lord Dalton," Daisy said.

Lord Dalton only waved his hand in a dismissal of the idea. "Lady Montague has too many enemies to count," he said. "I know Lord Montague, she will rant and rave and he will take a book and find some quiet corner until she runs out of steam. In any case, she will be careful, she has garnered the irritation of the prince and will not take that lightly."

Daisy hoped Lord Dalton was right, though she was not certain of it. "Might she not, though, rant and rave to Lieutenant Farthmore? Might not he think he ought to challenge you in defense of his cousin?"

"Leave Farthmore to me," Lord Dalton said, "and eat your dinner. I think you do not eat enough and have thought to speak to Flanagan about it."

Daisy did put her attention on her dinner. Not because she was particularly hungry, but because she was taken aback by the lord's words. There was something about him noticing what she ate as being…what? Very personal?

She did not know what it was, though it seemed somehow intimate that he should notice and even more so that he had come to a conclusion about it and decided to mention it.

She stabbed at a piece of beef and refused to think on it further.

CHAPTER ELEVEN

C HARLES SAT OUT on his bench in the moonlight. Despite waving off Miss Danworth's fears about Lady Montague and her threats, he could not dismiss them completely. He supposed he should not be surprised that the lady was related to Lieutenant Farthmore, distant though the connection might be. Despite its apparent distance, the fellow stayed in her house and had evidently told a very sad story about his treatment in attempting to pay his respects to Miss Danworth.

Charles could make a guess that Farthmore was favored by Lady Montague because they had the same low standards and he no doubt allowed her to ramble on about her enemies, of which there was never a shortage. He further assumed that Lady Montague had been intrigued to hear of Farthmore's ill-treatment at Miss Danworth's house, outrage being the woman's life-giving drink.

He could not imagine what *Lord* Montague made of Farthmore. Lord Montague was a reasonable man, and not likely to be particularly enthused by his wife's relation ensconcing himself in the house. But then, if Charles knew that lord at all, he might not even be in town. He might very well be enjoying the quiet of Yorkshire without the racket and din that always accompanied the presence of his dear wife.

If ever there were an advertisement against marriage, poor Lord Montague was it.

He had almost inquired of Lady Montague if she knew of anybody called Dagobert. He had decided against it, lest he put Lieutenant Farthmore on his guard or provoke him into action. After reading Lord Childress' letters, there was little doubt that Farthmore was somehow involved and he may have shared something of the matter to his hostess. Charles had begun to suspect that it had been Farthmore himself that had broken into the house. Coupled with the idea that it might have been Farthmore who had pulled him down in the sea and then Lady Montague mentioning something about his amphibious operations at Tarragona, he could only think…what did he think? Nothing firm, nothing known as a fact, but a feeling that things were adding up on the side of Farthmore and that he'd not seen the last of the rogue.

Daisy must be protected…

No, he must not think of her as *Daisy*. He'd heard her called so by Mrs. Jellops so often that he'd begun to think of her using her given name, but it was not right to do so. *Miss Danworth* had kept remarkable composure in the face of the dragon-lady. To be sure, she'd been shaken, but she had not fanned herself or called for a vinaigrette. She had remained elegant and unruffled, at least she would have seemed so to an observer. He had noticed her hands shaking in her lap, but she did not allow her nerves to show on her features. She was quite a lady, after all.

That idea somehow led to him reviewing the earlier part of the evening. When they'd danced, why had he insisted on questioning her, again, about whether she was really determined to never marry? It could not matter to him in the least, as he himself would never marry.

And yet, if he ever changed his mind, because after all people did sometimes change minds, would she not be his first choice?

Would she not be his only choice?

He knew that she would.

If he ever changed his mind. Who else was as marvelous as Daisy?

He did not *think* he would change his mind. But then, he'd begun to notice that his views developed after Quatre Bras had seemed to somehow soften. He'd also noticed that, despite the shabby living conditions of the cottage, the insects, and the troublesome cat, he did not wake as often from a nightmare. Did he still have them and not remember? Perhaps they still came but did not wake him in a cold sweat because he was too exhausted from the endless inconveniences of the abode. Perhaps, though he really did not know.

Well, it was better that he held to his convictions. There was no point in throwing them over unless she threw her own over as well.

Would she? He did not know. What if she did and he did not see the change until something was announced? Burke might swoop in. Well, if she were going to marry, it could not be Burke. He was a safe choice, but he was not a right choice. Once she became used to Burke's endless good humor, evenhandedness, generosity, indulgence of his friends, kindness to his servants and tenants, affection for his neighbors, and all-around reasonableness, she would...what? Become bored?

That was likely it.

He remained firm in his opinion that they would not suit.

Perhaps he would just wait and see. Was not time often the great solver of mysteries? Had not his grandmother, wily as a fox but wise too, often counseled him to do nothing about some matter? Simply wait and allow time to pass. Time would often make clear what direction one ought to take, or if one needed to take a direction at all.

There was the shooting season not too far off and he'd thought he might accept invitations with a note to the hostess that Miss Danworth and her companion would also arrive. Inconvenient to the hostess, to be sure, but he doubted any of them would say anything of it.

But then, there were so many men at a shooting party. He was her guardian and he ought to ensure she was not harassed by those fops' unwanted attentions. As well, Daisy would not like to be dragged from house to house, having to smile at dinner every damn night.

No, she would rather stay here, he thought, until she reached her majority and had the funds for a house in Brighton.

Perhaps he would suggest it. Perhaps he would propose that they just go on as they were.

He glanced behind him at the decrepit cottage and wondered exactly how cold it would get when autumn rolled in. The doctor had expressed little faith in the chimney and he suspected the doctor was right.

The cat jumped on his lap, a large grasshopper hanging from her mouth.

"You are a revolting wretch," he said.

The cat stared at him defiantly. Charles had not been at home for dinner, a meal she had become accustomed to sharing, and he supposed this was her way of protest. If she could not have fish or beef or fowl, she would cater to herself from the garden.

It was all well and good to ponder how he would manage Miss Danworth, but what on earth was he to do with this cat?

He sighed and carried her inside. There was probably a cup of milk or a wedge of cheese to be had somewhere.

DAISY HAD BEEN busy with Mrs. Broadbent and Mr. Flanagan for most of the day. She was to have Lord and Lady Bartholomew, Miss Minkerton and Lord Burke to dinner. And Lord Dalton, of course.

Somehow, each time she thought of food and Lord Dalton at the same time, she found her cheeks burning. She must not be so silly over one remark about how much she ate, or did not eat, or a suggestion that she eat more. He may well have said it only to end the conversation about the danger of Lady Montague and Lieutenant Farthmore.

Still, Mr. Flanagan had just left, having suggested including a particular beef dish as one Lord Dalton favored and she was certain her face looked as if she'd spent the day in the sun without a bonnet. She'd practically jumped when he'd suggested the lord's fondness for it and her cook had looked at her in alarm.

She felt jumpy in general, though she did not relay *that* to Mr. Flanagan.

Something was happening to her, though she was not sure what. It was as if she were coming alive after being half asleep all her life. The things she looked at seemed brighter, the sea seemed bluer, the sun blazing. She felt filled with an energy she'd never had before—as if she hardly had need of sleep.

Where once she might have satisfied herself to pass an afternoon quietly sewing with Mrs. Jellops, gratified that nothing frightening or untoward was happening around them, now she was restless. Now, she often paced the room or fiddled with a book she had no intention of reading or gazed out the window, only to go to another window.

She had not guessed that her father's death would produce such a change, but it seemed that it had. She supposed she'd been living some sort of half-life all along, and she was coming to full life. Now, her mind was finally convinced that Lord Childress could never again reappear. All the energy that had once been spent on staying out of the way, guessing at his moods, and avoiding trouble had nowhere to go.

Her restlessness had begun to prompt her to think about how going on in Brighton as a spinster might be. All along, she'd looked forward to the peace of it, especially during the winter months when barely a soul would be in town. Early and quiet dinners in a hushed house had been her dream. Rainstorms when nobody was about and reading by soft candlelight on a chill and cloudy afternoon seemed as if it would be heaven. The more closed in she could be, the more comfortable she would be.

Would it really suit, though? Might not she become bored? And what of Mrs. Jellops? She'd assumed the lady would like the quiet just as much as she looked forward to it, but was that true? Of course, Mrs. Jellops would claim it was true, if she thought it was what Daisy preferred.

Though, if she did not go forward with her plan to live an isolated life, what then?

Perhaps she might return to London and set herself up as a lady eccentric and host salons for amusing people?

Daisy sighed, knowing she would be more bored with that than being alone in Brighton. There were endless amounts of people who considered themselves amusing, but very few who actually were. She would be plagued by every young gentleman-poser come to town, determined to throw around carefully composed bon mots. It would be tedious.

Daisy sighed. It seemed no place she could think of seemed exactly right. Perhaps she ought to simply wait to decide what to do. Her feelings had changed quite a bit since the day her father died, they might change more still.

The right course would no doubt present itself. For now, though she might not have set her *own* course, she'd at least set the courses for dinner and it was time to go above stairs and change.

THE FIRST COURSES were out and, so far, the dinner had come off well. Mr. Flanagan, always a talented cook, seemed to take the idea of guests as a very personal and serious challenge. The dishes were composed so skillfully that Lady Bartholomew commented they must employ an artist in the kitchens.

Each dish, whether it be mackerels resting on delicate fronds of fennel dotted with capers, or a round of beef festively sat on large green slabs of cabbage from the garden, or a cod shoulder settled amidst thin-sliced lemons, was a delight. The fish was the most spectacular of Mr. Flanagan's efforts and Daisy knew from Mrs. Broadbent that he'd spent the early morning haranguing fishermen to acquire just what he wanted.

Daisy had ordered the extra leaves taken out of the table so they were not talking across great distances. This seemed to suit everybody, but it perhaps suited Lord Burke and Miss Minkerton the most. It had given Lord Burke the opportunity of extolling one of Miss Minkerton's recent efforts at painting the seashore. According to Lord Burke, she had a remarkable ability to capture the landscape, and in particular the lighting, that was near equal in skill to a Claude-Joseph Vernet.

According to the pressed lips and sudden concentration on plates seen round the table, the only person who did not find the notion ridiculous was Lord Burke.

And, Daisy supposed, Mrs. Jellops, who said, "Are they as good as that?"

Miss Minkerton did make a valiant effort to demur, telling Mrs. Jellops that they certainly were not as good as that.

Miss Minkerton probably wished she did not say so, as that only led to Mrs. Jellops saying, "Beauty *is* in the eye of the beholder, though."

Lord Burke nodded sagely, as if to say that this beholder was quite sure of his opinion.

Daisy was now certain that Miss Minkerton's fears of being viewed as a sister were wholly unwarranted. Lord Burke was sensible through and through, yet only a besotted fool could compare one of Miss Minkerton's paintings to a Vernet. Her efforts were pleasant enough, as Daisy had seen for herself when the lady painted in her garden, but they were not out of the usual way.

Dear Lord Burke had been blinded and made insensible and it was delightful to witness.

Lord Dalton, not appearing as delighted to see his friend in such a befuddled state, said, "Lord Bartholomew, I understand you served directly under Wellington. Had you ever heard anything of amphibious operations at the siege of Tarragona?"

Daisy was surprised by the question, as it was no doubt about Lady Montague's comments regarding Lieutenant Farthmore's history at Tarragona. She had not expected that to be a topic of conversation. Lord Bartholomew, however, appeared vastly amused.

"Good heavens," he said laughing, "what a travesty! I had not thought the circumstance was common knowledge—Wellington was irate over it. I must admit I was surprised to hear Lady Montague hint of it at the prince's assembly. If I were involved in such nonsense, I might keep it very quietly under my hat."

Lord Dalton looked at Daisy in surprise, then he said, "But what did she hint of, exactly?"

Lord Bartholomew took a sip of wine and put his glass on the table. "Well, you know how things went at Tarragona—if there was a wrong way to go it was taken. Apparently, unknown to Murray or Admiral Carew, one of his men devised some sort of snorkel—a tube one could breathe through underwater. The plan, as we eventually heard it, was to launch a bunch of seamen, swimming around with weights tied round their waists to keep them just below the surface, to spy on the coast."

Daisy began to get a sinking feeling, just as she supposed the seamen had.

Lord Bartholomew went on. "Well, you can imagine how that went wrong. Murray was told of this remarkable plan when five of the men did not return after their first try at the thing. Drowned, the lot of them, as it was supposed that their weights were secured so tightly they could not throw them off when they needed to. Poor souls."

"But they did not *all* drown," Daisy said.

"No, I suppose not," Lord Bartholomew said. "I understood there were fifteen or so involved though we never did receive the list of names we requested. No surprise, really, considering what came afterward."

Daisy nodded. The siege had been wildly unsuccessful. Major-

General Murray had been court-martialed, though in the end he received only a scolding.

She glanced at Lord Dalton and knew they were both coming to the same conclusion. Lieutenant Farthmore must have been one of the men who'd survived. Had he not always bragged he could do better than Murray? Had he not always claimed that he had better ideas?

It would not surprise Daisy to learn that the lieutenant had not just been among the men, but had been the one to come up with the idea. And that meant Lieutenant Farthmore was the person who'd pulled Lord Dalton underwater. It really could not be otherwise. Who else might have the skill to approach a person underwater, without being seen?

The idea sent a chill down Daisy's spine. Why would Farthmore attempt to kill Lord Dalton? He'd been thrown from the house and of course he'd been insulted by it, but to enact such a scheme? A murderous scheme?

In the distance, Daisy heard the unmistakable clip-clop of a horse's hooves approaching. She gripped her fork, having the irrational feeling that it might be the lieutenant approaching.

Lord Dalton rose and said, "I will go with Bellamy to see who calls at this hour. Another invitation from the prince, no doubt."

Daisy felt that reassurance was given to her alone, to ease her mind. It did not particularly ease it, as she well knew the prince's emissaries would arrive in a carriage and not a lone rider on horseback.

But if it were Farthmore, surely the watchmen would not have let him through the gates?

The table was silent as they all listened for what might be heard in the front hall. There was nothing intelligible, except for muffled voices and then the door closing.

Lord Dalton came back into the dining room and said, "It was only a letter, delivered by messenger. It is from Lady Grayson."

There were some at the table who understood the significance of the letter and others who did not.

Miss Minkerton said to her parents, "We have been awaiting a reply from Lady Grayson to see if she had any idea of who or what a Dagobert is."

Lady Bartholomew nodded. "Ah, the mystery of the letters between Lord Childress and Lieutenant Farthmore," she said.

Daisy had not known if Miss Minkerton had told her parents all that was understood of the break-in or the mystery of Dagobert that was noted in her father's letters, but she found she was glad she did not need to explain it now.

"I propose," Lady Bartholomew said, "that we have dessert in the drawing room and dispense with the gentlemen hanging behind with their port, if Miss Danworth would not deem it too irregular. The men might have their port in the drawing room if they like it. That way, the reading of the letter might not be delayed as I am sure Miss Danworth is eager to understand its contents."

Daisy was vastly approving of the idea and nodded her head.

"No smoking though," Lady Bartholomew chided the men. "I personally cannot abide the smell of smoke and it makes my daughter cough."

"Does it make you cough?" Lord Burke said solicitously to Miss Minkerton.

The lady nodded and Daisy rose before the lord began comparing Miss Minkerton's coughs to a Vernet.

THE LETTER LAY on the side table in the drawing room, next to the sofa. Daisy picked it up and tore it open.

"Do read it aloud," Miss Minkerton said, "we are all on tenterhooks over it."

Daisy smiled and nodded in acquiescence.

My dear Daisy,

I was just beginning a response to the letter you sent me recently when a second arrived of the most unusual kind! Upon reading the name Dagobert, I instantly surmised it must be reference to the last and greatest of the Frankish Kings, now long buried in St. Denis Basilica in Paris. Oh, there is so much I could tell you about his fascinating history! Alas, I fear it would not interest you at this moment in time.

What puzzles me is why anybody would refer to King Dagobert as THE Dagobert or wonder where he is? Or, why would it even be important to know that he is in the Basilica? And then, there was a question of who had possession of him? It is all very odd.

I discussed the matter thoroughly with Lord Grayson and, while he had never heard of King Dagobert, he did have a clever suggestion. He posited that I should put it to the learned men and women it has been my pleasure to become acquainted with, and I have since sent letters all over England. I delayed my reply to you in the hopes that I would have received a response that might shed light on the subject, but so far none have been received. The only promising lead has been from Mr. Croydon, who writes me that he has a friend who is expert on French history and who he has written to on this matter.

Please be assured that the moment I hear something I will send the fastest messenger with the information. Further, I will conduct my own research and have already arranged to meet with Mr. Lackington to see if we can discover something at Lackington and Allen.

How darling of you to send me a mystery to consider!

Now, I must run, my friend. Lord Grayson has taken my free hand and tells me the sun is shining and we must go out and take in the day. As always, he looks entirely dashing and I cannot deny him.

Kitty Dermot

Daisy laid the letter down. "I do not suppose we are much further in our understanding, but I am grateful Lady Grayson will make inquiries."

"What on earth could involve anybody with a long-dead Frankish king, I wonder?" Lady Bartholomew mused.

"There is something we are missing," Lord Dalton said, "and I hope Lady Grayson can find it out, perhaps with Mr. Lackington's assistance. The fellow has a shop with thousands of books in it, certainly there must be something they could discover if they put their minds to it. That is, assuming Grayson does not keep dragging his wife out of doors."

Daisy found she must bite her lip to stop herself from laughing. Lord Dalton had little idea of how true that was. Daisy knew from Kitty's letters that her friend was always buried in books somewhere, and Lord Grayson was always pulling her away from them. One moment she was delving into a paper recently published by the Royal Society, and the next she was picnicking under an old oak while her lord read her Shakespeare.

"So, the mystery continues," Lord Bartholomew said.

Bellamy led the footmen in with trays of desserts—berries, jellies, cream tarts and a savarin cake. He sniffed as he laid it out on the card table that would usually see a game of whist. Daisy watched him, having some pity on the fellow, as Bellamy was never very approving of veering away from what would be usual. But then, Bellamy was never very approving of anything.

She supposed he was right in some respects, as a card game would be *very* usual and now there was nowhere to play.

In lieu of cards, Daisy urged Miss Minkerton to the pianoforte. As she had suspected, Lord Burke was all too happy to turn the pages for her. After a few airs, Miss Minkerton claimed that Daisy ought to have a chance, but Daisy had already an excuse prepared by way of a supposed sore finger.

She loved playing, and she thought herself skilled, but she would not for the world upstage Miss Minkerton's moment or interrupt any progress she might be making with Lord Burke.

This, happily, left everybody free to admire Miss Minkerton. Lord Burke was very taken with her playing, as he always seemed to be, and her parents were suitably proud. It was perhaps not quite as delightful for Lord Dalton, as Daisy caught him stifling yawns and re-reading Kitty's letter.

As for Daisy, she could not help her mind drifting to Lieutenant Farthmore and Lady Montague. She did not know what danger those two people were, but she feared they were dangerous indeed. Perhaps even more dangerous than her father had been. With him, she had at least known what she could expect.

BURKE SAT ON the Minkerton's wide veranda overlooking the sea and pretended to read a book, though he was far more engaged in watching Belle at her embroidery. He was certain nobody was so pert with a needle. Each stitch was an attack on the fabric, and then so often the stitch seemed to go wrong and she would adorably sigh, pull out the thread, and attack once more. It seemed everything she did was in some charming fashion.

It had been some days since the dinner at Miss Danworth's house. He felt that night was the moment when he'd begun to dip his toe in the water. All along he'd convinced himself that Belle would never look upon him as a brother, but then they'd had so many walks round the garden where she seemed so interested in anything he said…well, he decided he must try. Subtly, of course. He would not wish to embarrass the lady with any feelings that were unwelcome.

He'd praised her painting as good enough to be confused for a Vernet. Certainly, it must be taken as a high compliment. She *was* skilled with a brush in a pleasant sort of way, but not exactly a master. It had been a flirtatious gambit, it really could not be seen otherwise.

It had seemed to go over well and that had given him some little bit of hope. It could be that Belle's view of him was changing, that he was not so much a brother. Or it could be only his hopeful imagination.

The Minkertons' butler, a thin and forlorn-looking fellow who always seemed as if he'd just heard bad news, came onto the veranda with a note on a silver tray and took it to Belle.

"Oh good, Branway," she said, "you cannot know how grateful I am to have an interruption from this diabolical piece of needlework. It is torturing me, or I am torturing it, I hardly know which."

Branway, seeming to be quite used to Miss Minkerton's struggles in that department, only nodded sadly and held out the tray.

Belle opened the note and then laid it down on her lap. "We are invited to a card party at Miss Danworth's house. It is to be a buffet. How lovely!"

Harry nodded, though he was not that enthusiastic over putting Belle and Dalton in the same room. He was not altogether clear whether Dalton had any designs on the lady. He'd once thought so, but he'd since seen no sign of it.

"Miss Danworth is very like a sister to you," Belle said. "Is she not?"

"Oh, yes," Harry said. After a long pause, he plowed on. "Though I would not like every lady I know to consider themselves my sister. Some may know me longer and still not be as a sister."

"That is true," Belle said. "Length of time cannot have anything to do with it."

"No, it really cannot. And then, one may seem a sister at one early moment, and then not a sister at some later moment."

"Yes, of course, things do change. I have often noted it."

"Change, yes," he said. "It is the nature of things."

"Indeed," Belle said, "things are always changing."

"Often for the better."

"Usually for the better, I think."

"One must only recognize the change."

"Yes, even when it is right in front of a person, they might not see it. At first."

Belle had gone back to stabbing at her fabric. Harry could not tell if they were talking of the same idea or not. Was she saying she was not his sister? That their relationship was changing? Or was she only politely answering his roundabout conversation?

He suppressed a sigh and went back to the book he wasn't reading. He hoped nobody would ever ask him about it, as he had been turning pages without reading for over a week.

CHAPTER TWELVE

B ETSY WAS BRUSHING Daisy's hair, or at least that was what she was supposed to be doing. Daisy watched her maid fiddle with the brush and finally said, "What is it, Betsy? You are completely distracted."

Betsy laid down the brush and said, "Mightily distracted. You see, I cannot decide if I ought to tell you of what I heard in the servants' quarters, or whether I ought to leave it alone."

"Now that you have mentioned it, I think you must tell me," Daisy said, preparing herself to hear of Bellamy's latest complaints. "I cannot go forward, forever wondering what it was."

Betsy nodded enthusiastically. "That is very true. Well, it is just this—Mrs. Broadbent was in town yesterday and she heard from the grocer that Lady Montague has been telling all and sundry that Miss Danworth isn't mourning as a dutiful daughter should."

Daisy only nodded, though she would have liked to have hit Lady Montague over the head with her hairbrush at that moment.

"She is tellin' people that it's almost like you are *glad* Lord Childress is dead," Betsy said.

"And so I am," Daisy said. "Though I ought not advertise it."

"But here's the best part," Betsy said, hurrying on, "it seems nobody does care. The grocer said nobody in town likes Lady Montague, what with her sneering down her nose and complaining all the time.

When her cook came in the other day, he sent over the worst of his produce and he don't care if he loses the business. Lady Montague can eat old potatoes for all he cares of it."

Daisy stifled her laughter. She did not know what else Lady Montague was up to, and was rather afraid to find out, but it tickled her that the lady had been given old potatoes for her trouble.

"Then," Betsy said, "our Mrs. Broadbent told the grocer if he was to hear of any more talk like that, he was to give the talker the what-for. She told him how to do it and he says he's at the ready."

"No, truly not," Daisy said, laughing.

"Oh yes," Betsy said. "Mrs. Broadbent calls it the laundry list speech. You just get in your mind all of your complaints, and then you say them all together with hardly a breath. It's overpowering, she says."

"I suppose it would be," Daisy said, thinking back to Mrs. Broadbent's what-for to poor Mr. Deer.

"And last night, the staff was all so moved at hearing the story that they swore they'd give any talkers the what-for too. Even Mr. Bellamy claimed he wasn't above giving a good what-for when necessary. Though, he put his foot down at getting one."

"Goodness," Daisy said, catching her breath from laughing, "What else did you talk about?"

"Oh, after that it was mostly about the cat. Our Peggy said she spied Lord Dalton giving it a bath in the garden and talking to it about fleas and how it was a disgusting wretch, though she swears he said it fondly. Mr. Bellamy tried to claim the cat was a noble creature, or would be when it was not quite as mangy and had filled out a bit, and so it was worthy of the lord's notice. Nobody could help but fall to pieces laughing over it and Mr. Bellamy got up and ordered his boys to make cocoa to settle his feelings."

Daisy had not had any idea so much was discussed in the servants' hall. She supposed she should have realized it. Her ideas of their table being filled with a vague silence never made any sense, now that she was considering it. As it happened, it was rather lively.

But how extraordinary. Her housekeeper had harangued a grocer in her defense and the staff were ready to give out Mrs. Broadbent's particular style of what-fors.

And then, of course, Lord Dalton had washed a cat.

⇢⇢⇢⇚⇚⇚

CHARLES HAD NOT set foot in the rudimentary kitchen of the cottage, except to retrieve a tray of cured meats or cheeses and rolls that Flanagan had sent over. Irish papist or no, the fellow understood that a gentleman might want to eat at any time of day and had supplied him accordingly.

However, he'd finally admitted to himself after one too many flea bites around his ankles, that somebody was going to have to bathe the wretched cat. He could not see his way clear to asking anybody lest he be viewed as favoring the cat, and so he'd determined to do it himself.

As he'd searched the cupboards for rags and soap, he came upon a bundle of letters tied up in ribbon and stuck far back in the silver drawer. After he'd wrestled with the cat and water and soap with only a few scratches for his trouble, he'd taken the letters to his decrepit drawing room and laid them out on a table.

As he read through them, one by one, a picture of Lord Childress' activities began to emerge. At first, all he could make out was that it appeared the lord was using this location by the sea to move goods in some kind of smuggling operation. As he read on, he understood that it was not cases of brandy or bolts of silk that Childress was interested in. No, the lord shot far higher than that.

He was interested in works of art and one-of-a-kind items that might fetch an exorbitant price.

No wonder Childress had allowed his estates to fall into disrepair—

it was not from them his income had been derived. It seemed this run-down cottage was the real base of his operations. It was a likely location—with a good telescope one might view any boats lurking offshore, and there were cement steps leading down to a lonely expanse of rocky beach not particularly suited to bathing.

In fact, the steps were behind a locked gate, were very obviously in disrepair, and he had yet to see anybody go near them. And why would anybody go near them, unless they were unloading a boat under cover of darkness?

He found several letters regarding the Palaskar collection of books. It seemed that the lord had, in the end, found they would be too much of a risk to steal, and so tricked the old man who had possession of them to give them up for a paltry sum. He had planned on keeping them, advertising his possession of them to likely people, and then selling them to the highest bidder. He had died before he could do so, and now they were the property of Charles' father. Charles supposed he'd have to make an effort to track down the old man who'd been swindled and return them.

Though most of the letters were from Farthmore, they often men-tioned another person named Jenkins. Little was said of him other than *he was aware of the plan* or he was *ready for the next step.*

It was the last few letters in the pile, though, that gave him real pause. While he could only see what was sent to Childress and not what Childress himself had written to anybody else, the idea was clear enough.

The Dagobert was most definitely a thing, and not a person. It had been acquired from some unknown individual crossing into Spain from France. Whispers of it had made the rounds of the camps, and Farthmore made it his business to find the fellow, dispense with him, and make off with it. Its value was inestimable if the right sort of collector were approached, and Napoleon might even pay a ransom for it.

It seemed Childress had made vague promises to Farthmore of trading Miss Danworth's hand for the Dagobert, then had reneged. Childress had written that he never did receive the Dagobert, and therefore, their agreement was nullified. The item was considered lost at sea.

Farthmore was irate about it and swore the Dagobert had been delivered by Jenkins.

Though he still did not know what a Dagobert was, Charles had a better understanding of what it *might* be. Some piece of stolen artwork that would fetch a good price. He assumed whatever it was had long been sold off, perhaps even to Napoleon, while Childress pocketed the money and claimed he'd never got it.

Farthmore had been a fool in so many ways. Not the least of which was thinking that Childress would connect himself to such a low branch of Lady Montague's family tree by marrying off his daughter to him. Childress was far too conscious of rank to ever have considered it. He had only promised it as a swindle.

Charles picked up the letter and examined the date on it. August of 1814, just months after the failed siege of Tarragona. Just months after Farthmore would have returned from Spain.

The last letter was in a different tone and far more recent. Farthmore wrote that he agreed to wait until Miss Danworth's twenty-first birthday to claim his prize. Charles could not make out what the prize was—Lord Childress would have no ability to force Miss Danworth to marry Farthmore. If he were intent on forcing her, he would hardly wait until she had the maturity to fight him off—he would have tried it when she was sixteen. Further, at her twenty-first she would also have the funds to support herself and would have no need of her father's house. At her majority, Childress would have lost all power to pressure her into anything.

Charles paused. Perhaps there had been some scheme in the works about the money she was to come into. Or, more likely, perhaps

Childress just sought to put Farthmore off for another few years.

While Farthmore served General Murray in Spain, he'd got his hands on something valuable called the Dagobert and he'd gone to his reliably criminal partner with it. But, like most criminals, it looked like that partner turned out to be a double-dealer.

At least, that was how it seemed. He dared not discount that Farthmore might have some scheme still in mind that involved Daisy.

Not Daisy, *you idiot!*

Miss Danworth.

THE CARD PARTY had been arranged and Daisy was quite looking forward to it. It would break up the sameness of the days, pleasant as they had been. Most had been taken up with tea in the garden, usually with the company of Lord Burke and Miss Minkerton. Lord Dalton would bring out a book and Daisy often observed him when she pretended at some embroidery work. He seemed to lose himself when reading and his features softened quite a bit—it was as if a mask he wore publicly dropped away. Even his scar seemed to recede and fade. She found it both fascinating and unnerving.

While she was being fascinated and unnerved, Lord Burke and Miss Minkerton seemed to be progressing nicely. Miss Minkerton had, at some point in her travels round the garden, managed to twist her ankle. This of course necessitated leaning heavily on Lord Burke's arm, and the occasional offer from the gentleman to carry the lady if she deemed it necessary. So far, she had not deemed it necessary, but Lord Burke seemed to hold out hope that she would. Daisy did not know to what extent Miss Minkerton suffered, or whether she suffered at all, but it was a fortuitous condition the lady found herself in. Lord Burke appeared delighted with her injury.

The days were a quiet sort of happy, aside from wondering about the Dagobert, Lieutenant Farthmore, and Lady Montague. The four young people who occupied the garden had fallen into a very comfortable and familiar friendship. Daisy realized she'd never experienced anything like it. She had developed some amount of intimacy with other ladies, perhaps more so through letters than anything else, and particularly with Kitty, now Lady Grayson. But she'd never had the opportunity to live day to day with anybody but Mrs. Jellops.

Dear Mrs. Jellops spent most of her time in the garden sleeping, only to wake with a start, certain she was late for something. Discovering she was not, she would soothe herself with a few biscuits or sandwiches and drift off again. At the end of the day, as the sun dropped below the horizon, Daisy and Mrs. Jellops would have a quiet dinner together and retire early. Her companion had moved back to her own bedchamber and Mrs. Broadbent had relocated back to her own quarters, much to Mr. Bellamy's approval. Daisy could not help but admit that she approved of the arrangement too. After blowing out the last candle, Daisy was free to peek out the window unobserved to spy Lord Dalton, his brandy, and his cat on their usual bench.

All the while, there was a constant watch on the post while they waited for any news from Lady Grayson regarding the Dagobert. There had been some alarms from the watchmen, who felt they needed to report to either Bellamy or Lord Dalton anything unusual they had spotted. Daisy attributed this to Mrs. Broadbent's scathing what-for to poor Mr. Deer and his hope to never experience the like again.

At first, the watchmen's racing to report everything they'd seen had startled Daisy, but she'd grown more used to it, as it seemed always to be something verging on the ridiculous. One evening, they had spotted a male cat on the premises and chased it off, lest it put Lord Dalton's cat in an unwanted motherly condition. They had then promptly second-guessed themselves and inquired over whether Lord Dalton might indeed wish to have kittens about.

Another time, they'd harassed a grocer who was only attempting to bring Mr. Flanagan the radishes he'd been waiting for. Just an hour ago, they'd told the tale of a peddler who was turned back and noted there was a boat sailing off the coast. Daisy had listened, amused, as Bellamy gave them the what-for by way of noting there were peddlers everywhere on God's green earth—and the boat was in the water because it would not do very well if it attempted to sail on land.

Now, though, the watchmen were back at their posts and had been told to expect the Minkertons so there was no danger of them driving her guests off like the poor peddler.

Two extra tables had been brought into the drawing room and a sofa moved out to accommodate it. Lord and Lady Bartholomew were to bring Mrs. Phelps, a lady visiting from their own neighborhood in Somerset, to make an even eight. They might pair off in fours for whist, or one table of whist and two tables for piquet.

As the activity swirled round her, Daisy could not help but notice the unusual spring in the servants' steps. Betsy said it was due to everybody having perfected the skill of giving the what-for and feeling like they'd armed themselves against all comers. Daisy only hoped they would not be too liberal with it and start giving what-fors to anybody they might encounter.

The last platter for the buffet had been laid, a fanning of perfectly sliced ham with Mr. Flanagan's secret recipe mustard cream in a crystal bowl in the center. Betsy had reported that they'd all been chased out of the kitchen while he prepared the mustard and all he would say about it was he used very cold water and liberal vinegar. However he prepared it, Daisy had found it was as hot-tempered as Mr. Flanagan himself. Mrs. Jellops had just taken a small spoon to taste it and appeared rather red in the face and teary-eyed.

Daisy gazed round the transformed drawing room with satisfaction just as the Minkertons' carriage rolled up to the doors.

Lord Dalton came in not long after, and Daisy wondered if he'd been waiting for them to arrive before coming himself. The idea irked her, though she could not say exactly why. He was as handsome as he ever was though, perhaps more so with his tanned face, despite the usual scowl on it and the more recent addition of telltale cat hairs liberally decorating the bottom of his trousers.

Mrs. Phelps had been introduced round and Mrs. Jellops had taken an instant liking to her, the ladies being of similar age. She'd already warned Mrs. Phelps about the heat of the mustard cream as if this were a usual subject between middle-aged ladies. Mrs. Phelps had nodded knowingly and they went together to the sideboard to examine it more closely.

"Miss Danworth," Lady Bartholomew said, "we have just had a lively exchange in the carriage. Lord Burke claims that he and Belle can easily trounce Lord Bartholomew and myself at whist. My lord says it is terrible nonsense."

"So it is. Though I also mentioned," Lord Bartholomew said, "that as much as we'd like to find out, it must be the hostesses' purview to pair us up."

"If it is my purview," Daisy said, "then I say let the battle commence." She could see they were all keen on the idea and she was rather delighted with Lord Burke for coming up with the notion. It was precisely the sort of gambit a lovesick gentleman might be counted on for. She was further gratified to see Miss Minkerton's eagerness for the scheme. This satisfaction was capped off by Lord Burke insisting that Miss Minkerton's ankle must still be sore and lending his arm to escort her to a chair. Really, the two of them were fooling themselves if they did not see they were exceedingly admiring of one another.

Mrs. Jellops and Mrs. Phelps returned from viewing Mr. Flanagan's mustard at the sideboard. Mrs. Phelps said, "I was just telling Mrs. Jellops that I really do not understand piquet as well as I'd like, and she has graciously consented to be my instructress."

Daisy hardly knew what to do with that information. For one, Mrs. Jellops was ghastly at piquet. They occasionally played together, as she did have a fondness for the game, but Daisy was forever making bad moves just to stay apace of Mrs. Jellops' bad moves to keep the game going. For another, that would only leave herself and Lord Dalton un-paired, and therefore paired.

Still, there was not much she could do about it. It seemed everybody had decided what they would be playing, and with who. Was she even sorry over it? She supposed she was not.

Daisy said, "It seems, Lord Dalton, that it is left to you and I for a game of piquet."

The lord nodded, but as usual it was impossible to determine if he viewed it a good thing or bad.

After everyone had seated themselves, Bellamy brought round his own particular selection from the wine cellar. Earlier in the day, Daisy had discussed what would be best and been somewhat relieved that he did not seem to still shoulder his sullenness over not being able to drink a few bottles a night himself. Having been so liberal in his past consumptions though, he was extremely knowledgeable. He'd suggested a white German wine from the Riesling region. It was a young vintage and would have the light crispness of a tart apple, exceedingly appropriate for the summer season. He would leave it in the cellar to remain cool until the last moment to enhance its refreshing qualities.

Daisy had trusted him and, in a moment, seen that he was correct. Lord Bartholomew had taken one sip before asking Bellamy more about it.

As Bellamy delivered his speech about the region, the type, the acidity, the finish, the vintner, and the year, Lord Dalton unwrapped a new pack of cards.

Daisy did her best to keep her concentration on her own table, but it was near impossible to avoid overhearing Mrs. Jellops and Mrs.

Phelps. Dear Mrs. Jellops was communicating all sorts of wrong information, including what sounded like a completely made-up scoring system.

Mrs. Phelps nodded eagerly over each bit of misinformation and said things like, "Ah, I see! I hadn't known."

As Lord Dalton dealt the cards, he raised his eyebrows, no doubt also listening to this fascinating and very wrong conversation.

Daisy shrugged and pressed her lips together hard to stop herself from laughing.

"Perhaps we might play by the more usual rules?" Lord Dalton asked drily.

Daisy nodded. "Indeed, we'd better," she said softly, "as I hardly understand how they have arranged their game."

This elicited a very rare laugh from Lord Dalton and Daisy felt herself inexplicably gratified. She supposed when something was rare, its value was all the greater.

Daisy studied her hand. After discarding two and picking up, she found herself with a pair of aces. She decided to sink them, a trick she'd learned from Lady Ashworth, a rather renowned card player. They called the points, sequences, triplets and fours and Daisy thought her hand measured up very well against Lord Dalton's. Particularly since he would go forward unaware of the aces she held back. As a further deception, she allowed him to take the first trick with a low card. He would be convinced to play his high cards at the end, and then he would lose them to her aces.

As they played on and Daisy noted down the running score, it was impossible to avoid understanding how the other piquet game was going. Mrs. Phelps was near-drowning in a sea of bad advice while Mrs. Jellops said comforting things like, "Do not scold yourself, Mrs. Phelps, you *will* catch on."

Daisy did not know if it was the wine, or the idea that poor Mrs. Phelps would one day soon find herself at another card party attempting to explain Mrs. Jellops' rules to an unsuspecting stranger. She could not help laughing.

She held her fan of cards over the lower half of her face but it was not enough. Lord Dalton's shoulders heaved as Mrs. Jellops informed Mrs. Phelps that she'd just scored forty points for producing two eights in a row, an idea so far removed from piquet as to be from here to heaven.

Mrs. Jellops suddenly called over, "What is it, Daisy? Has Lord Dalton told a good joke?"

"Oh do tell us," Mrs. Phelps said. "I do love a joke."

"No, no," Daisy exclaimed, knowing how impossible it would be for Lord Dalton to be forced to tell a joke, if anybody had ever dared tell him one. "I was just laughing at the awfulness of my hand. It is so bad as to be ridiculous."

"Oh dear," Mrs. Phelps said. "And here I am racking up forty points for a double run of eights. Sometimes it's just down to luck, you know."

Daisy bit down on her lip lest she fall off her chair in heaves of laughter. Lord Dalton leaned his forehead against one hand as if rubbing a headache, though Daisy saw perfectly well enough that he was attempting to control his own laughter.

She took in a deep breath and said, "I think we shall get on better if we do everything we can to concentrate on this game. And *this* game only."

Lord Dalton nodded. "As far as I understand it, this is the only game of piquet being played in the room."

Daisy did her best to ignore the wit of the statement, as that would only lead to more laughter. Lord Dalton could be witty when he liked, a very dry sort of wit that she'd always found amusing. Now, though, she must not continue laughing over Mrs. Jellops' instruction or they were bound to be found out.

However bad Mrs. Jellops' memory of the actual game was, Daisy would not point it out for the world. It would be for Mrs. Phelps to discover on her own at some future moment.

They had finally come to the last two plays. As she had expected, Lord Dalton was looking very satisfied with himself as he laid down the queen of hearts.

Daisy laid down her ace of clubs and took the trick.

Lord Dalton looked up in surprise. "You sank an ace?"

Daisy smiled. "Or two," she said.

The lord reluctantly laid down the king of diamonds and Daisy took the last trick too. The extra points for taking the last trick would put her ahead.

"Where did you learn that little piece of deception?" Lord Dalton asked.

"Lady Ashworth," Daisy said, "and it is perfectly within the rules."

"You are a wretch."

"I thought that was what you called your cat."

"What cat?" Lord Dalton said, pulling the score pad toward him. "See here, what about this? I played a ten and then another ten—is that not an extra forty points you have not added in? Must I consult your intrepid companion about the rules?"

His playfulness in imitating Mrs. Jellops' unique scoring system caught Daisy so by surprise that she began to laugh again. She took deep breaths to stop herself and thought she'd never laughed so much in her life. Others may not have found the state at all unusual, they were those who'd had a childhood filled with games and jokes. She had not, however. It felt somehow liberating, as if a great weight of seriousness had flown from her shoulders. As if it were not always necessary to be entirely serious.

When she thought about it, she realized she had laughed quite a lot this summer. It was meant to be a summer of quiet mourning and had somehow brought danger with it. Nevertheless, she'd found herself often amused by Mrs. Broadbent's indomitable what-fors and

Betsy's interesting stories from the servants' hall and of course, Lord Dalton's cat. Now, here was darling Mrs. Jellops' excellence at inventing an entirely new game and calling it piquet.

Just as these pleasant thoughts were rolling through her mind, she heard a distant knock on the front doors.

CHAPTER THIRTEEN

THE KNOCK ON the door instantly chased away any lighthearted-ness Daisy had felt, and she looked up in alarm.

Lord Dalton rose and said, "I will go. Don't forget about my run of tens and the forty points."

She smiled at his joking, though inside she felt a sort of terror. She could not even say why. After all, it was not every time somebody knocked that had turned out unpleasant. But there had been *some* times. The time Lieutenant Farthmore had turned up. The other times when Bellamy had refused entry to one of her father's cronies. Those unpleasant times were always at night.

She must not let a knock affect her so!

Certainly, if it were someone who should not be arriving, the careful watchmen would have chased them off. They could not chase off a peddler and stand in the way of the grocer and then let the likes of Farthmore through. In any case, whoever it was, if they were not wanted Lord Dalton would send them packing.

Lord Dalton returned to the room and gave her a reassuring nod. Loudly, he said, "A letter has just arrived by fast messenger. From Lady Grayson."

Daisy let out a long sigh she'd not even realized she'd been hold-ing. Dear Kitty had written again. They had waited and waited, and now they might finally hear something definitive about Dagobert.

The parties all stopped their games and Mrs. Jellops whispered to Mrs. Phelps what all the fuss was about.

"A mystery!" Mrs. Phelps said. "How diverting! What a pleasant card party this is."

Lord Dalton strode across the room and handed Daisy the letter. The Minkertons and Lord Burke had laid down their cards and risen to join her, with Lord Burke carefully transporting Miss Minkerton via a strong hand on her delicate elbow. Mrs. Jellops and Mrs. Phelps were not far behind.

Daisy tore open the letter.

My dear Daisy,

What a time I have had writing back and forth to all my learned acquaintances! Just as it seemed I was to get nowhere with it, as I was forever receiving histories of King Dagobert I was already perfectly well aware of, I finally received the information I believe you have been looking for.

Mr. Croydon sent my request on to a fellow expert on France, and in fact the man is in Paris as we speak. Monsieur Benoit has written back to Mr. Croydon and he has faithfully made a copy and sent it on to me. The information is both exciting and alarming.

M. Benoit explains that the Dagobert is certain to be the Dagobert Scepter. It is part of the French crown jewels and had been housed in St. Denis Basilica. It was discovered stolen a few years ago, though it is not at all clear when precisely it was taken. It may have been missing for some time before it was even noticed gone.

Surely, this must be the answer to your mystery. Though, I am on tenterhooks to discover if you know where this item is located or who has possession of it or how it came to your attention at all. Needless to say, Mr. Croydon and Monsieur Benoit are interested too.

I enclose a drawing done by M. Benoit to show what the scepter looks like.

Please do send me news when you have it, as I will do too.

Kitty

Daisy unfolded the enclosed picture. It was a drawing of a rod, and Kitty had helpfully noted that it was two feet in length and the whole was enameled in gold. At the top, a man rode some sort of bird. It was an ugly-looking thing, and not one that Daisy would have thought would prompt a thief to make off with. But then, as it was part of the French crown jewels, somebody had understood its value. Somebody had secreted it out of the basilica. How it had ever become associated with her father and Lieutenant Farthmore, Daisy could not fathom.

Lord Burke peered over Daisy's shoulder and pointed at the scepter. "Wait a moment," he said, "I have seen that somewhere before, I am certain I have."

Lord Dalton took the paper from her hand. He stared at it in silence as Mrs. Jellops and Mrs. Phelps confirmed to one another that it was not the sort of thing *they* would display in a drawing room. According to the ladies, the scepter lacked a sense of delicacy and refinement.

"It's the bedpost," Lord Dalton said.

Nobody save Lord Burke seemed to understand this interesting speculation.

"My God," Lord Burke said to Dalton, "I believe you're right."

"What bedpost?" Daisy said. She was certain it was not any bedpost in this house. The thing was horrid-looking and would haunt a person's dreams.

"The day we went into your father's room to search for letters," Lord Dalton said, "we found it in complete disarray. Not searched, as your library had been, but just unkempt. I noted at the time that even a bedpost was missing."

He pointed at the picture. "*That* was the one that remained."

"So the Dagobert is a scepter, and it has been here all along," Daisy said softly.

Lord Bartholomew said, "But why should Childress have got himself involved with stolen crown jewels?"

"I cannot answer *why*," Lord Dalton said, "but I know that he had. I found letters in the cottage that indicated that smuggling was his primary business. I did not say anything of it because I did not wish to frighten Miss Danworth, as there has been some contention, and some dirty-dealing, over it."

"What do you mean by contention?" Mrs. Jellops said. "What was there in it to frighten Daisy? Certainly, nobody can hold Daisy responsible for anything Lord Childress had ever done."

"The lady lands right on the point," Mrs. Phelps whispered approvingly to her new friend. "A daughter cannot control a father, it is very well known."

"Farthmore claimed the Dagobert had been delivered," Lord Dalton said, looking not very eager to convey the details. "Lord Childress claimed it had not. The lord had initially, at least from what I can gather...Farthmore thought he was to marry Miss Danworth in exchange for the Dagobert. Later on, there was some kind of altered agreement that they would wait until she had reached her majority, though I do not understand what could have been promised."

"Hateful man," Lady Bartholomew said softly. "There is no soul in a father who would bargain his daughter."

Lord Bartholomew nodded and he and his lady looked fondly at Miss Minkerton.

Daisy felt a little pang at noting their affection for their daughter. It was clear that Miss Minkerton had grown up protected and loved. Daisy could hardly imagine how it had been. Her own house had always given her the feeling of being an intruder in enemy territory.

"Of course," Lord Burke said to Lord Bartholomew, "any right-thinking father would only wish that his daughter marry someone who can give her a good life, and treat her well, and honor her in every way."

Miss Minkerton gazed up at the lord admiringly.

"My father," Daisy said, "was many things. He was not, however, *right-thinking*. But, for all his penchant toward lowness of all sorts, he did have an almost obsession with rank. He would have never connected himself to Farthmore through marriage. Not even to punish me in some fashion."

"I agree," Lord Dalton said. "And that is why I cannot imagine what he promised to fend Farthmore off for a few years. That must have been his purpose, to delay him for a period of time. I had assumed, not knowing what a Dagobert was but concluding it was some piece of art, that it had been long ago sold. I don't know what Lord Childress' plan was to deal with Farthmore, but he was just buying himself time. Perhaps he would have sold it and paid some of the money to his conspirator. It was Farthmore who got his hands on it in Spain. I do not know who originally stole it, because it likely changed hands a few times over the years. But I believe that the man who arrived to Tarragona with it was murdered by Farthmore."

A cold began to run through Daisy's veins, as if her blood were turning to ice. She was not particularly shocked to hear of the lieutenant as a murderer. She was not even surprised that her father had been involved in such a scheme or that he had dangled her as bait. But a terrible truth, far worse than any she could have imagined, had stolen over her. If her father had made a deal with Farthmore to wait until her majority, he could only have had one thing in mind—he wished to wait until she had her money. He would not, however, have waited until she'd composed a will. She would have conveniently died intestate, and then the money would go to him.

That was how he planned to pay off Farthmore, and they had both agreed to it. He would pay off Farthmore with part of her inheritance and then sell the scepter at his leisure. He was a high stakes gambler to the end. All his claims that she must marry high, and at the same time being sure to show her what men could be, exposing her to the lowest forms, keeping her as locked in as possible…it was all a delay tactic to be certain she was still unmarried when she came into her money.

Had her father lived one more year, it was not very likely that *she* would have lived much longer after that.

Daisy gripped the arm of her chair to steady herself as Lord Dalton went on with his speculations.

"There was some other fellow mentioned in the letters, a man named Jenkins," Lord Dalton said, "though I am not sure what part he's played in it. He seemed to be some sort of middleman. I also do not know why Childress should have left such a valuable piece posing as a bedpost."

Daisy decided she would not reveal what she'd guessed of her father's real plans. The company was already horrified by him and she somehow felt responsible for being related to such a man, as if the taint was upon her.

"I cannot be certain," she said slowly, "but knowing my father, it would have amused him to use crown jewels as a bedpost. He would have felt superior to them, as he liked to feel about all things and all people. He would have felt powerful, hiding it in plain sight."

"Though, perhaps he accidentally left it behind?" Mrs. Jellops said. "Remember Daisy, that very strange year when we were sent back to Shropshire quite suddenly, we were only given a day to pack. Then, your father was to remain here for another month, but arrived a week later with a black eye."

Daisy nodded. "Yes, of course I remember, though I just chalked it up to his general capriciousness and assumed he'd been in a brawl in town. And that does not account for the other years. He left the bedchamber in disarray and left it behind *last* year."

"We may never know what prompted his hasty exit last summer," Lord Dalton said, "but from the state of his room it was indeed done at a run."

"Those poor watchmen outside just now would be shaken right out of their boots if they knew they were guarding part of the French crown jewels," Mrs. Jellops said.

"Indeed," Daisy said, "they would be." She paused, a sudden new idea filling her with dread.

Lord Dalton, instantly noting her distress, said, "What? What is it?"

"The watchmen," Daisy said. "It may be nothing, but only a few hours ago they reported to Mr. Bellamy that they'd turned away a peddler and also…that they'd spotted a boat off the coast that struck them as suspicious. I am sure it does not mean anything…"

"But it might," Lord Dalton said. His voice had taken on a harsher, crisper tone than Daisy had heard in some weeks. "The distraction of a party and my cottage unoccupied might be just the time somebody might choose to slip in and slip out. After all, Farthmore knows what he is looking for, while we did not."

"Is he here? In the house?" Daisy asked, her voice sounding too high to her ears.

Lord Dalton did not answer, but turned to Lord Bartholomew and said, "Will you care for the ladies?"

Lord Bartholomew nodded. Lord Dalton turned to Lord Burke and said, "Let's go."

Burke gently placed Miss Minkerton in a chair. The lady wrung her hands and said, "Oh, do be careful, whatever it is you are planning!"

Lord Dalton and Lord Burke raced from the room and Daisy heard them bounding up the stairs.

Over Lord Bartholomew's objections, Daisy ran from the drawing room to the bottom of the stairs. She could hear the pounding of feet overhead, a door thrown open, and then Lord Dalton shout, "The window!"

Daisy hurried back into the drawing room, to the far side that housed the windows overlooking the garden. They were the windows that sat directly below her father's bedchamber and whatever now occurred there.

"What do you look for, Daisy?" Mrs. Jellops asked tremulously from the other side of the room.

Daisy hardly knew what she looked for, she'd heard Lord Dalton yell something about the window and so she'd run to it.

The garden was softly lit with a full moon and punctuated with shadowy outlines—the shrubbery lining the garden's walls, the well-worn paths in the scrubby coastal grass, worn down from trodding feet, the gate in the distance that led to the old cement stairs. The cat stretched out on the bench in its usual spot, illuminated by the lone candle burning in the window of the cottage.

It seemed peaceful as it ever did, but for the pounding of feet and shouting overhead.

A rope dropped into her view and a man's legs dangled in front of the window. At first, she'd only seen shoes and trousers. The shoes were worn and the trousers dirty and frayed. Then came the rest of the man.

It was Lieutenant Farthmore. His eyes met hers and Daisy recoiled from the hate she saw in them. She instinctively grasped at the window sash to ensure it was locked, lest he leap in and murder her, as he had no doubt planned with her father.

She was certain that he'd dressed himself as a peddler earlier in the day to gain entrance—he was dressed as a peddler still. After he'd been turned away at the front gate, he'd found another way in.

He clutched the scepter and raced toward the back of the garden. He skirted the bench that sat outside the cottage, the cat since disappeared.

Lord Dalton came down the rope next. Daisy was horrified that he would pursue the lieutenant.

"Do not follow him," she cried through the glass. "There may be others with him!"

Her words fell on deaf ears. Lord Dalton had set off in a run and now Lord Burke had landed on the ground and was fast on his heels.

"Please, please do not let anything happen to him," Daisy whispered, her palms against the glass. "Nothing must happen to him."

As soon as Charles had heard of the suspicious boat offshore that had been reported by the watchmen and dismissed by Miss Danworth and his butler, he'd known Farthmore was making another run at the scepter.

Of course he would choose this night. Somehow, Farthmore had discovered the card party—easy enough to hear of it from a grocer or a maid chattering about it in a shop. Since none of household often left the premises, the second-best thing was to ensure that everybody was in the same room, engaged in an activity together.

It was his own fault for discovering it at the last moment. He'd said nothing to anybody about the letters he'd discovered in the cottage. Nobody but himself had known that Lord Childress had been a smuggler.

He'd told Daisy, *Miss Farnworth*, that he had not informed her of it because he did not wish her to be frightened. That was true, though he had also not wished her to be damaged. News that one's father had engaged in criminal activities was a quick way to find doors shut in one's face across England. That sort of news would be picked up and carried everywhere by the likes of Lady Montague. That her cousin, three times removed, was also involved would have been conveniently glossed over or she would have simply cut the connection.

He'd bounded up the stairs, Burke coming behind him, and raced to Childress' bedchamber. In his hurry, he'd been stupid enough to forget a candle and at first, he could not see much when he threw open the door. He could feel, though, and what he felt was a distinct breeze from an open window.

His eyes quickly adjusted to the gloom with the help of the light from the full moon. The scepter that had stood in for a bedpost was gone, and a man climbed out the window.

Charles had run to the window and found a rope tied round a stone gargoyle that sat just below it. The man, who he was certain was Farthmore, had reached the end of the rope and leapt to the ground. Charles followed him out the window and he'd heard Burke coming down after him as he set off across the lawn. Farthmore was making for the back gate and Charles wondered if that was how he'd gained entrance in the first place. Beyond the gate was only the dilapidated cement steps leading down to a rocky beach. It was not a place for swimming, or even strolling. It was a hemmed in cove and so had never been particularly guarded. After all, nobody could reach that beach unless they came by boat.

Before he'd known that Childress was a smuggler, he'd wondered why the steps were there at all and had assumed that the lord had some plan or other to clear the beach of all the rocks and somehow make it pleasant. Once he *had* known about the smuggling, he surmised that this was where the goods had come and gone.

Farthmore blasted through the gate, and it had been clearly left unlocked for him to do so. Certainly, that was how the scoundrel had come in.

Charles gained on him, though he was not certain he would catch him. He was also not certain of who else he might run into. He'd heard Daisy's warning to him that there might be others, though he'd pretended he hadn't. He remembered well enough that some fellow named Jenkins had been involved all along. As well, if Farthmore had come by boat, which seemed likely, he could not have come alone.

Burke caught up with him as he reached the gate. There was a sloop offshore, big enough to do a safe channel crossing, and a rowboat with a man standing next to it beached on the shore.

Farthmore raced down the winding steps, the scepter in one hand, and a burlap bag that came from he knew not where in the other.

As Charles burst through the gate, he suddenly saw the cat appear on the steps in front of Farthmore. *He* saw her, but Farthmore did not.

The lieutenant tripped over her and crashed headfirst down the last of the steps.

As the cat scampered into the scrub bushes that lined the rocky cliff, the man who stood by the rowboat ran to Farthmore, who lay motionless among the rocks. He leaned over, grabbed the scepter and the burlap bag, and made for his boat.

Charles scrambled down the steps, which felt like they were nearly crumbling underneath his feet. He kept his eye on Farthmore, who had remained motionless.

"He's getting away," Burke said of the man with the rowboat.

Indeed, the man had already thrown the scepter and the bag into the boat and pushed it back into the water. He leapt on and grabbed his oars just as Charles and Burke reached Farthmore.

"We won't catch him," Burke said, as the man rowed furiously out to sea. The larger boat which sat in deeper water signaled with a lamp to guide the rowboat toward it.

Charles reached down to feel Farthmore's neck for a pulse. There was nothing, the man was dead. As far as he could tell from the angle of Farthmore's head, his neck had been broken on the impact.

He stood up and looked out to sea as the rowboat reached the larger sailing ship and the man and his goods were hauled up over the side.

"I will assume that is Jenkins," Charles said. "The middleman who has outlived both his partners."

"We'd better send for the magistrate," Burke said, "though I hardly dare imagine what he will make of this tale. Should we carry the body back to the house?"

Charles considered it, then shook his head. "The tide is out, and will be for some hours. We'd best let the fellow see the scene of the accident as it is."

"Will he even believe it, I wonder," Burke said. "A stolen scepter, climbing out a window, a boat waiting offshore, and all that only to be done in by a cat?"

"She is an exceedingly clever cat," Charles said, "but perhaps we might just mention that Farthmore fell of his own accord."

Burke nodded and they began making their way back up the steps.

As they climbed back up, careful on the crumbling edifice lest they meet the same fate as the lieutenant, faces began to appear over the back wall of the garden.

Charles was at once aggravated that Miss Danworth had not stayed in the drawing room as she should have, flattered that she'd been concerned for his safety, and admiring that she did not wail in the face of a dead body as Miss Minkerton was just now doing.

Charles called up to Bellamy, who had joined them in looking down upon the gruesome scene. "Send for the magistrate and tell them if there are any naval ships at the docks, they ought to set sail and be on the lookout for a sloop that is just now making off with some French crown jewels."

Bellamy nodded at the unusual request, a testament to his years serving a master who might be counted on to involve himself in all sorts of odd matters.

Burke was through the garden gate first and Charles was surprised to see Miss Minkerton throwing herself at him. Just a moment ago, he'd been certain she was on the verge of a swoon. Now, he was not so certain that the lady had been wailing over the dead body at all, as it seemed she was now wailing over Burke.

"Don't you ever, ever put yourself in such danger again!" she cried, beating her little fists against his chest.

Burke took her in his arms and said, "I was never in any real danger."

"You were, I know it," Miss Minkerton said sobbing. "And well, I could never, what I mean is how could I go on…"

"Could you truly not go on?" Burke said.

Charles heaved a sigh of disgust, as he could see perfectly well where this was going.

"Now, Belle," Lord Bartholomew said, "it's all come right in the end. Do release poor Burke."

"But with your permission, Lord Bartholomew," Lord Burke said, "that is, with Belle's permission too of course, well what I wonder is, am I really suited to being *only* a brother to Belle? That is what I have been wondering."

Charles could see that neither Lord nor Lady Bartholomew had the least idea of what Burke was trying to say.

"It seems that Miss Minkerton," Daisy said, "has been afraid that Lord Burke views her as a sister."

"I do not!" Lord Burke said. "Not ever!"

"And," Daisy continued, "I suspect Lord Burke has been afraid that Miss Minkerton views *him* as only a brother."

"But I do not!" Miss Minkerton cried.

"I believe," Daisy said, "they are quite taken with each other."

Both Miss Minkerton and Lord Burke nodded vigorously. Lord Burke said, "Belle has been the love of my life, well...as long as I've been old enough to think of a life. From the very moment I set eyes on her."

"Ah," Lady Bartholomew said, "*now* I see. Well! How wonderful, do not you agree, Husband?"

"Yes, of course, couldn't be more delighted," Lord Bartholomew said, though he looked more befuddled than anything else.

"But you never said..." Miss Minkerton whispered, gazing up at Lord Burke.

"I say it now, Belle," Lord Burke said.

"I say it now, too, Harry," Belle said.

"Perhaps," Charles said drily, "we might take this romantic wonderment indoors to await the magistrate."

Daisy nodded. "Quite right. Two people on their way to an engagement ought not to be gazing down at a dead body."

Charles was rather surprised by the sentiment, though he supposed it was full of good sense.

Lord Burke, seemingly convinced more than ever that Miss Minkerton should not dare put weight on her injured ankle, swept her up and strode toward the house. Daisy ran ahead of them, and Lord and Lady Bartholomew strolled back at a more sedate pace as Lady Bartholomew explained to her lord what precisely had happened.

Charles watched Burke. There went the last of his friends on his way to the altar, though not to the lady Charles thought he had in mind. He should have seen it coming, how many times had Burke spent a full hour with Miss Minkerton, examining a non-descript flower? How ridiculous Burke had been, comparing Miss Minkerton's painting to Vernet.

He could not be sorry that he'd been mistaken about the direction Burke would take. After all, he had always been convinced Burke was not suited to Miss Danworth.

The cat suddenly appeared and wound its way round his ankles.

As everybody else had gone ahead of him and could not see it, he swept her up. "Look what you have done now, you wretched cat," he said quietly. "You have turned yourself into a murderess."

The cat yawned in his face, appearing entirely unconcerned over the accusation.

CHAPTER FOURTEEN

D AISY WAS SUCH a whirl of emotions that she hardly knew how she felt. Farthmore was dead and that was a great relief. She ought to feel at least a little sad over the loss of a life, or frightened over seeing him lying on the rocks, or even downhearted that the Scepter of Dagobert had sailed off, but she did not. She did not feel any worse over Farthmore's demise than she'd felt for her own father. She supposed her arduous upbringing had left her a rather hardened individual. Though, it would have been difficult to avoid the state, particularly when she'd only recently surmised that her own father had likely planned her murder to gain her inheritance.

Hardened or no, she *did* rather quake when she considered what Lady Montague would make of Lieutenant Farthmore's death—the manner in which it had happened, and that it had happened at Daisy's own house. She had a sinking feeling that Lady Montague would never believe her lieutenant had stolen anything, nor turned up here to retrieve it. Daisy sighed. She would depend upon Lord Dalton to handle the woman, just as he'd done at the prince's assembly.

The notion made her realize how very grateful she was that Lord Dalton had come through unscathed. Her heart had nearly stopped as she'd run across the garden. She'd heard a cry, and then a crash, and she'd known someone had fallen. She'd thought of how crumbling those stairs were and how she and Mrs. Jellops had once thought to go down them and then turned back at the third or fourth step, it being clear how easy it might be to lose one's footing. Somebody *had* lost their footing, though she had not known who until she reached the garden gate.

What a relief it had been to see Lord Dalton standing on a step, upright and alive.

And then, she must consider that the race to the cliff's edge had not turned out *all* bad. The shock of the situation had caused Lord Burke and Miss Minkerton to finally see their way clear to admitting their true feelings. They were just now in a cozy corner, no doubt exchanging all the wrong things they had believed of one another. Miss Minkerton's parents sat together, staring at the happy couple. Lord Bartholomew still seemed dazed while Lady Bartholomew patted his hand and whispered encouragingly to him. She also fetched him a rather large glass of wine, which might have helped along the effect of her words.

When Mrs. Jellops heard the news of what had occurred on the beach, she'd fainted dead away. She'd since recovered with the help of a strong-scented vinaigrette, two generous glasses of Riesling wine, and Mrs. Phelps' vigorous fanning. Daisy took it as a positive sign that her companion was becoming more interested in the recent engagement than she was the news of a man dead on the rocky beach. She claimed she'd always seen it coming between Miss Minkerton and Lord Burke.

As time passed, Daisy's roiling thoughts and feelings began to settle. Farthmore was dead, he could not hurt her. The Dagobert had sailed away and whoever else was looking for it would follow. She was safe.

The magistrate arrived and Lord Dalton took him and his men down to the beach to examine the body before it was moved.

They were gone for a good half hour and then the magistrate was shown into the drawing room. Sir Matthew was a well-dressed gentleman and Daisy guessed he'd been called out of some party or dinner he'd been attending. She felt some amount of pity for him as he was told the story of what occurred that evening. Everybody had something to add and statements came shooting at him like arrows from all directions.

Sir Matthew held up his hand to silence the room. "While I can only appreciate everybody's willingness toward candor in this matter, I have not heard anything that Lord Dalton has not already informed me of so it may be what I know is sufficient for the time being. Lieutenant Farthmore was caught exiting the premises with a valuable item, a scepter that has been stolen from France, he fell upon the rocks, and his conspirators made off with the good."

Sir Matthew paused, then said, "I would ask though, was that *all* that the lieutenant carried? Just the scepter?"

"No, as a matter of fact," Lord Dalton said. "I was so intent upon the scepter that I forgot he also had a burlap bag. I have no idea what was in it—it might have been clothes he intended to change into once he'd safely boarded the boat."

Sir Matthew, who had been handed a glass of the Riesling by Bellamy and looked very grateful to have it, shook his head. "Oh no, my lord, I know what was in that burlap bag and it was not clothes."

The party leaned forward with bated breath, even Lord Burke and Miss Minkerton stopping their own conversation to listen.

"You see," Sir Matthew said, "before I was fetched here, I was already looking for Lieutenant Farthmore. It seems he'd made off with Lady Montague's jewels. Now, it all comes together."

"He stole from Lady Montague?" Mrs. Jellops asked in wonder. "That seems...rather daring."

Mrs. Phelps patted her friend's hand. "Even after a shock, you fly right to the point, my friend."

"As a matter of fact," Sir Matthew said, "Mrs. Jellops *does* fly right to the point. All this evening, as I had my men out searching the roads and trying to determine his route of escape, I kept wondering how he thought he'd get away with such a crime. Where would he live? Who would he sell the jewels to? Now, I understand his gambit was far more complicated than I had imagined. He was off to a different shore, confident that the scepter he stole from this house would finance him for all his days. I suspect the jewels he took were more for an amusing revenge than anything else. According to Lady Montague, they'd had some sort of argument over his rather constant drunkenness. Taking her jewels was his final adieu to the lady."

"I do not suppose," Daisy said, "there will be any way to find the scepter."

Sir Matthew had taken a long and satisfying draught of wine and nodded to Bellamy in approval of its quality. He said, "Unlikely. I've sent a few boats out, but we won't catch them. They'll be running without lights and on their way to France or hugging the coast north or south, and we'll not know which. The sea is vast and one's best chance of catching a smuggler is to happen upon them by accident."

"Well, that scepter was a horrid-looking thing," Mrs. Jellops said. "Mrs. Phelps and I were in total agreement on that point. I wonder, can the French really miss it so much?"

Sir Matthew declined to comment on whether the French would miss part of their crown jewels. He said, "There will be an inquest of course, but with so many witnesses to what occurred, I suspect it will be dealt with promptly and will trouble you no more. The stickier problem will be what our government will ever decide to relay to the French government about their missing scepter. That, however, is well over my head. I only ask that you keep the knowledge to yourselves. Something was stolen from this house, no need to go into what it was. For now, let us claim it was some silver."

Daisy nodded, only too glad to have a reason never to talk about the evening's circumstances again.

"Well," Sir Matthew said, with a longing glance toward the sliced ham on the sideboard, "I'd best be off."

"Might we not tempt you to have something before you go, Sir Matthew?" Daisy said kindly, certain the poor man had been run off his feet this night.

"Very kind, Miss Danworth," Sir Matthew said, his enthusiasm evident. "Very kind, indeed. I was just going into dinner when I was called away by Lady Montague. It has been an unexpectedly long evening."

Mrs. Jellops and Mrs. Phelps had risen as one. Mrs. Phelps said, "Mrs. Jellops, you have read my mind. We must accompany Sir Matthew to the sideboard and point out the dangers of that mustard. It could fell even the hardiest of men."

Mrs. Jellops nodded and said, "It appears that *you* have read *my* mind, Mrs. Phelps. After the long night the poor gentleman has had, it would not do to fall over on account of devilishly hot mustard."

And so, the two ladies escorted Sir Matthew to the board and supervised his filling of his plate.

As for Daisy, she had no thought to eat. She was content enough to listen to Mrs. Jellops and her new friend manage Sir Matthew's plate and watch Lord Burke's solicitousness of Miss Minkerton. Somehow, everything that had gone wrong was now put right. She supposed she would be asked to compose a statement for the inquest, but she had full confidence in Sir Matthew to guide them all through it.

Lord Dalton had left the room for some minutes, and now he returned and sat next to her.

"I have spoken to Mrs. Broadbent," he said. "As I suspected, the maids are all in a tizzy. The footmen are equally shaken though they claim they are not and would pound the lieutenant into the ground if he were not already dead. Mr. Flanagan is a bundle of nerves, though he claims he is only fretting about how his mustard is going over. Mrs. Broadbent is as unruffled as ever. I directed them all to have a small glass of brandy, and Mrs. Broadbent just as quickly overrode me and insisted it be a medium glass."

Daisy nodded and smiled to herself, remembering that when she'd first arrived to the house, she'd been so determined that the lord never direct her staff. Now, she was quite grateful for it.

"By the by," Lord Dalton said in a quieter voice, "Farthmore fell because he tripped over the cat."

Daisy looked up. "He tripped? Over the cat?"

Lord Dalton nodded.

Daisy felt laughter bubble up inside her. What could be more ridiculous? Lieutenant Farthmore, the devil who'd haunted her since she arrived to Ramsgate, had been killed by the cat.

She pressed her hand against her mouth to stop from laughing, as she knew very well this moment could not be one for levity.

"In her defense, she is a very clever cat and entirely unremorseful," Lord Dalton said.

"Yes," Daisy said, stifling a giggle, "it seems so."

"Now, you ought to eat. I'll fix you a plate. You really do not eat enough."

Lord Dalton rose and set off to the sideboard.

Daisy felt herself blushing, a circumstance so rare she did not know what to do about it. She willed the heat away from her cheeks. If it were noted, she supposed she might blame it on Mr. Flanagan's mustard.

⇶⋘

IN THE FOLLOWING days, this or that news came to the house regarding Lieutenant Farthmore's demise. Sir Matthew had informed the government of the stolen scepter and, as he had thought, it was not to be mentioned. Not by anybody, not at the inquest, and not in any official papers. He did not know what would be done about it and doubted very much he would ever be told.

That did not stop all the talk surrounding the incidents of that night. As it turned out, the government had not cared at all about keeping Lady Montague's stolen jewels a secret. What was known by people who heard anything about it was that the lieutenant had gone on a wild criminal jaunt. He'd stolen from Lady Montague and then, as he was making off with some silver from Miss Danworth's house, he fell upon the rocks. His conspirators, whoever they had been, had made off with the loot.

As all bits of gossip were prone to do, over time there was much added to the story. It was speculated that Miss Danworth's house had only been the second stop in what was likely to be a town-wide thievery. The lieutenant was supposed to have plans to rob absolutely everybody. The tale was told across card tables and at parties, creating a delicious shiver in all who discovered they had made a narrow escape.

Daisy heard most of this from Betsy, who heard it from all her acquaintances in town, most of whom were lady's maids and house-keepers. According to Betsy, the whole circumstance had provided a wonderful opportunity for butlers and footmen everywhere to speculate on what sort of derring-do they might have committed, had the lieutenant attempted a break-in of their own premises.

Aside from the interest of these stories, Daisy's days had returned to what they had been. There were afternoons in the garden with Lord Dalton, Lord Burke and Miss Minkerton, overseen by a sleeping Mrs. Jellops. Daisy no longer had to send Lord Burke and Miss Minkerton off to examine a flower, as they were now perfectly capable of sending themselves off. Despite everybody's turns round the garden, nobody went near the gate that led to the steps. It had been soldered shut, and it would stay that way until the crumbling steps could be properly destroyed, the gate removed, and the gap filled in with solid stone.

Of course, Daisy now viewed the cat in an entirely different light. She supposed she should not give the creature credit for what was certain to have been an accident on the feline's part. And yet, she could not wholly dismiss the cat's intent. She was entirely dedicated to Lord Dalton, always under his chair and winding round his legs, and so might she not have sensed the danger to him and done her part? Daisy could not say, but she'd since directed Mr. Flanagan to prepare her special meals of ground up raw fish or an elegant fanning of sardines which she seemed to particularly approve of.

It was now just such a usual day. It was overcast enough that the sun was not in one's eyes, but not gloomy either, and the clouds scudded overhead, pushed by a brisk breeze off the water. It was still warm, but there was something in the air that hinted of a change of season on the way.

Lord Burke and Miss Minkerton had returned from one of their strolls, Mrs. Jellops had awoken at the sound of tea being poured, and Lord Dalton scratched the cat's ears under the table. All was exceedingly comfortable, until Mr. Bellamy rushed to their little wood table in the garden, pale and looking as if he'd had a great shock.

Daisy put down the teapot. "Goodness, Bellamy, what is it?"

"It is Lady Montague," Bellamy said, glancing behind him. "She has arrived. I've said you were not at home, but she pointed at Miss Minkerton's carriage and told me I'd better not dare to go on with such nonsense. She awaits you in the drawing room."

Daisy felt as if her heart were freezing solid in her chest. She could not imagine what the lady wanted; she could only be sure it would be deeply unpleasant.

"She may wait there all day long," Daisy said resolutely. "I will not see her."

Bellamy nodded. "She has already informed me that she is prepared for that eventuality and nothing shall drive her out," he said.

Daisy looked to Lord Dalton. He said, "Show her out here, then. We will not be inconvenienced by the lady. Further, she is not to imagine she will corner Miss Danworth alone and attempt to run over her."

"I hardly think she will run over me," Daisy said, though it was not really true.

"You know what I mean," Lord Dalton said quietly.

And of course Daisy did know what he meant. She was grateful she was not to face the lady alone.

"She is unpleasant," Lord Burke said, "but not nearly as powerful as she once was. Further, *we* are not responsible for her cousin's actions. I shouldn't worry about anything she says or does."

Daisy would like to believe that, but she could not quite. She thought she understood Lady Montague's modus. There were plenty of people in the world whose power was not very powerful. The lady sought them out and gave them the vague feeling that if they did not see things her way, they would lose whatever little power they had. As Lord Hampton had once said, Lady Montague attacked down, never up.

The lady could, if she set her mind to it, turn a great deal of people against Daisy. Only a month ago, Daisy would not have cared. But she was becoming more and more convinced that isolating herself in Brighton, removing herself from all society, might not be as attractive as she'd originally thought. She had come to no conclusion about how she *did* wish to live, but she could not rule out a return to London. And it was London that was Lady Montague's favored hunting ground.

As well, Daisy found herself so very tired of conflict and danger. She really did not feel up to facing whatever the lady had to say.

Lady Montague, in the full regalia of seaside fashions, topped by a pink beribboned bonnet best worn by a girl of sixteen, strode into the garden.

There were no extra chairs, nor cups for that matter. Daisy noted Bellamy looking at her as if to be sent to make arrangements for the lady. She did not send him for anything and left the lady standing.

"Lady Montague," Daisy said.

The others repeated her name in the same fashion, nobody sounding as if it were a pleasure to encounter her. Even Miss Minkerton, so prone to pleasant cheerfulness, said her name as if it were a chore. None of them had bothered to rise at her approach and Daisy felt it was the boldest bit of discourtesy she had ever dared.

Lady Montague looked around for a chair, then said, "I see I am to be left standing."

"I am certain you will not be here long enough for it to become a burden," Lord Dalton said, stretching his legs out as if to communicate his own comfort in being seated.

Lady Montague sniffed and looked disapprovingly at the cat, who'd decided to make a sudden appearance by way of front paws on the table and peering at her.

Daisy thought of how exactly disapproving the lady would be if she knew that she just now looked upon the feline murderess of her cousin. As it was, the only three people who knew of the cat's involvement in the lieutenant's demise were herself, Lord Dalton, and Lord Burke.

"Miss Danworth, I am sure you are acquainted with the circumstances of my cousin's unfortunate actions on the night he...expired," Lady Montague said. "Though Sir Matthew has explained it all to me, I find I am more mystified than ever. Why should the lieutenant come here for a paltry amount of silver when he was already in possession of my very costly jewels?"

"I have no idea, Lady Montague," Daisy said. "How is one to understand what goes through a criminal's mind?"

"It does not make sense, though," Lady Montague plowed on. "Why bring a boat here, only for some silver? Hearing of Lord Childress the things that I have, I cannot even imagine it being *good* silver. No, I am sure he was after something else and am equally sure you know what it was. I feel, that in some way, the answer to that may absolve my cousin somehow."

Daisy suppressed a shiver, as Lady Montague was drifting far too close to the truth.

Lord Dalton stood and said, "I can clear up a few things for you, Lady Montague. I will inform you to cease your wondering. For, I can assure you if you continue to delve into this matter, it will not excuse your cousin at all. What it will result in, should the matter become fully and publicly understood, is you and your lord being stripped of your title by the regent for harboring a treasonous individual. That is, assuming you knew what he was all along, which I would be happy to claim that you did."

Lady Montague had paled. "I hardly think—"

"You think too much," Lord Dalton said. "My advice is you slink back to Yorkshire and explain to your husband that your no-good cousin has stolen your jewels. This is unlikely to come as a surprise to poor Lord Montague, as I am sure he is entirely inured to your near-constant missteps. If I hear that you have placed one foot out of line, I will go to the regent myself. And that, Lady Montague, will really be the end of you."

"I will back Lord Dalton, if it becomes necessary," Lord Burke said. "I do not think I would tell any tales either. I think you certainly did know what your cousin was capable of and kept him around for your own convenient purposes."

Lady Montague staggered a bit on the uneven grass. Regaining her footing, she said, "I certainly did not know he was capable of stealing!"

"So says *you*, I say otherwise," Lord Dalton said, beginning to look bored with the conversation. "Pack up and be gone and do not trouble us again or it will be at your peril."

Lady Montague huffed and seemed as if she would say more, but no words came out.

Bellamy, who had remained standing behind the lady, said, "May I show you the way out, Mrs. Montague?"

She turned on him and screeched, "It is *Lady* Montague!"

Bellamy had already started his walk back to the house and Daisy heard him say quietly, "So it is. For now."

Lady Montague clutched her ridiculous bonnet against the breeze and hurried after the butler, pink ribbons flapping behind her.

CHAPTER FIFTEEN

D AISY WATCHED LADY Montague storm out of the garden, refusing Bellamy's arm to be helped up the steps and staggering up them herself. The back doors slammed behind her.

"That went well, I thought," Lord Dalton said.

Daisy nodded, with a great sigh of relief. She did not know if that would be the end of trouble coming from Lady Montague, but she at least had hope for it. She could not imagine what would threaten the lady more than losing her rank. The prince had already warned her against stirring pots all over his realm and were she to delve more deeply into this circumstance, she would stir a very large pot indeed. Daisy had faced down the dragon and come out relatively unscathed.

Daisy blushed, as was becoming a common occurrence, as it dawned on her that she'd not faced down the dragon at all. Lord Dalton had done it.

She was becoming more and more reliant on him. On his protection. Really, on his company. What was she to do when he was gone? He would not stay forever, hanging about in the garden and chasing off her enemies.

Daisy was not at all certain of her feelings. It was very strange, as whatever she felt for him, it was not anything that had happened to her before. She looked forward to seeing him, was not at all put off by his frequently dour temperament, and often regretful that she'd declared in the beginning that he ought not to eat his dinner in the house.

She was not at all afraid of him. Perhaps that was the feeling that affected her so much. He was a man, and she was not afraid of him. He was a man who often frightened people, but she was not afraid of him. She felt she knew that underneath his grumpiness and hard-edged exterior, he would never hurt her. How odd, to think that of a man.

It had been a habit, for weeks, to blow out the last candle and gaze out the window at him. He sat on the bench with his brandy, his jacket off and sleeves rolled up, the cat lounging on his lap or next to him.

He was so handsome, but in a different way than she had known him in town. He was at once looking rather rakish in his state of déshabillé, but also endearing in his care for the cat.

Her ventures to the window had been unnoticed until the night of the lieutenant's death. That night, Lord Dalton had looked up and seen her by the light of the full moon. Mortified that she'd been spotted spying on him, she'd called out that she often preferred to have some night air before retiring. It had been the most ridiculous thing in the world and she'd promptly shut her window and jumped in her bed.

But then, she had not given up the habit of staying by the window. She thought he might know it, though he pretended he did not.

She could see from the markings the bench had made on the grass that he had moved it closer to the house. Only a foot or so, but closer. How close would he come?

She knew she ought not allow her thoughts to travel in any particular direction in regard to Lord Dalton. It was soon to be shooting season and Daisy would be packed off to the duke's estate while the lord made the rounds of house parties.

Lord Burke and Miss Minkerton had been chattering on about their wedding ever since Lady Montague had stormed off. Of course, they had been talking of their wedding ever since the engagement and it seemed the appearance of Lady Montague was not enough to put them off it. It was to take place in a month in Somerset and there was much to arrange. It was not to be a small affair; they would have friends and relatives coming far and wide and expected more than a hundred at the wedding breakfast—every large house in the county would be commandeered to accommodate the guests.

The Minkertons and their soon to be son-in-law would set off for home earlier than they had planned on account of it. Daisy was delighted for them, though she would miss Belle's company.

They rose and Miss Minkerton said, "We will be off to town now. I have explained to Lord Burke that there is a perfectly charming bonnet that ought to be included in my trousseau and he has insisted I have it."

Daisy smiled. "Of course he has insisted."

"And anything else she likes," Lord Burke said. "Now is a time for weddings and the frippery that must come along with it. We may safely leave all unpleasantness behind, I think."

"Agreed," Lord Dalton said.

"Agreed?" Lord Burke said. "I had not thought to hear that sentiment from you, my friend."

Lord Dalton fed the cat a choice piece of ham and said, "I have grown weary of plots, whether they be Farthmore's or Lady Montague's. Or even my own. You may have noticed I did not do a thing to stop you chaining yourself. Let us finally have done with it all."

"Well said," Lord Burke said.

"Though, *chaining*, Lord Dalton?" Miss Minkerton said. "Lord Burke is not *chaining* himself."

"I am, and happily," Lord Burke said.

"Well, as long as it's happily," Miss Minkerton said, with an adorable shrug.

As Lord Burke escorted Miss Minkerton out of the garden, Daisy was amused to hear him inquire, yet again, on the state of her by now long-healed ankle.

"I will be sorry to see them go," Mrs. Jellops said. "Though wherever we are to be in a month, I hope we can attend the wedding. Mrs. Phelps will be there, her house is very nearby. She'd said I ought to stay with her and she will show me her own recipe for mustard, which is a deal more civil than Mr. Flanagan's, and we might entertain ourselves with piquet of an evening."

Despite being tickled by the idea of Mrs. Jellops further corrupting Mrs. Phelps' ideas about piquet, Daisy did not laugh. The subject of what was to be done with her and her companion in the next months had been raised and she waited to hear what Lord Dalton would say.

He took so long to say anything that Daisy began to wonder if he'd given it any thought at all.

Finally, he said, "Yes, as to that…I had thought I'd write to the hostesses that have kindly invited me to stay for shooting and let them know you would come as well. But then I thought…"

Daisy felt as if her heart was dropping. He had thought to bring them along with him, but then he'd thought…

"Then I thought, well it is very pleasant here and the notion that nobody can stay at the seaside beyond a certain date is nonsense and does it not become tedious to always spend one's days shooting game for somebody else's table?"

"I would find it alarming to shoot anything at all," Mrs. Jellops said. "But do you say that we ought to stay here, Lord Dalton?"

"I suppose here is as good as anywhere," Lord Dalton said. "You've got to be somewhere until Miss Danworth reaches her majority. Unless, of course, you prefer the estate in Shropshire."

Both Daisy and Mrs. Jellops recoiled at the idea. Daisy wished never to walk through those doors again. It had been the scene of her unhappy childhood and would still smell of her father's tobacco.

"I see that is not a preference," Lord Dalton said.

"If you do not mind staying here," Daisy said, "I certainly do not mind it. Mrs. Jellops, do you mind it?"

"Goodness, no," the lady said. "Though I still hold out hope that we may travel to Somerset for the wedding."

"Burke is one of my oldest friends," Lord Dalton said. "I suppose since he's asked, I must go."

"I am relieved," Mrs. Jellops said. "I had thought, what with your ideas of marriage...there were rumors of one of your friends being locked up to prevent one? I thought you might not be keen on the idea."

"I will not attempt to prevent the marriage," Lord Dalton said, "my efforts in that direction have only resulted in failure. Though I would not go so far as *keen*."

"But," Daisy said, "you do like Miss Minkerton?"

"Yes, yes," Lord Dalton said, waving his hands, "it is just..."

"That you have said you will never..." Daisy trailed off.

"As have you," Lord Dalton said.

There seemed to be nothing to say after that, and so the party grew silent. Daisy twisted her hands under the table. They were to stay here. It was not a circumstance she would have imagined. It was not unwelcome.

But why? Why should they stay here? Why did not Lord Dalton go off to his rounds of country house parties? Was not shooting at things the highlight of a man's year? Is that not what they talked about at their clubs? Her father and his cronies had spent hours talking about what they'd bagged, as if they had hunted tigers and not pheasants or foxes.

As well, had it not always been the case, at the beginning of the London season, for ladies to be complaining that their husbands were still off shooting? Why should Lord Dalton suddenly pretend he found it tedious?

She did not know, but she found herself very glad of it. She had no idea what she would have done if she were dragged from house to house. Would she keep to her rooms, pretending at deep mourning? Would she throw off the dark clothes and face down any remarks about it? Here, she could go on as she had done, appearing as herself with no pretense. Here, she would have time to think through what she wanted to make of her life.

DALTON HAD LEFT the garden and gone back to his cottage to await his dinner, the cat following close behind. He supposed the one benefit of dining alone, or with only the company of a cat, was that he need not change clothes for it. He gazed around the shabby abode, realizing it was to be his home for some months more. What had he been thinking? He was near-certain the chimney would kill him with smoke once the weather made lighting a fire necessary.

He sighed. He knew what he'd been thinking. He'd thought Miss Danworth would despise being dragged from place to place, being asked to smile pleasantly and go along with whatever hare-brained schemes the hostess had cooked up for the ladies. As far as he understood it, when the women were not piled into a cart to watch the shooting from afar, they were led on long walks for picnics or driven through some local village to shop for ribbons they might have bought before they got there. The evenings consisted of dinner and then, hopefully, cards or pool or some other sensible activity. A few hostesses were not so sensible and, in a bid for originality he assumed, came up with some more painful plan, the worst of which was charades. Finally, there was the inevitable ball toward the end of it where everybody pretended to be more delighted than they actually were. This was followed by packing up and moving onto the next house, where the same would commence all over again.

It was not just Miss Danworth who would find the whole proce-dure tedious, he would as well. He used to think all the nonsense was worth it because of the shooting. But he had distinctly noticed that these days he preferred to be well away from the sound of a gun firing. It set him on edge.

He did not know what Miss Danworth thought of gunfire, but he sensed that she was on edge about something herself. It was not Farthmore, that rogue was dead. It was not Lady Montague, that lady had been dispatched to everybody's satisfaction and had since decamped to Yorkshire to deliver the bad news about her jewels to her long-suffering lord.

There was something else. The night they'd received Lady Grayson's letter and discovered what the Dagobert was, and that it was in the house posing as a bedpost, she had seemed to be overcome in some way. In the moment he'd spoken of her father having some agreement with Farthmore to wait until her majority, something had flashed in her eyes, some sudden knowing. It seemed as if she'd understood why her father would wish to wait until she was of age, though it remained unfathomable to him. She'd said nothing, but the mention of it had sparked something in her—some idea, or some recollection.

She'd gone white as a sheet and gripped the arm of her chair, as if she understood and was horrified.

Had she experienced some sort of memory, long forgotten? He suspected that whatever she had realized still haunted her, even if the two parties to it were long gone. There were times in the garden, when she did not know anybody was watching, that she looked as if she saw nothing, as if her mind's eye was very far away.

He found it irked him that he did not know what she thought about.

As for his extended stay in this hovel, what was done was done. He'd stay here, and in a month he'd take Miss Danworth and Mrs. Jellops to Somerset for Burke's wedding and then...then, he did not know what he would do. He presumed his father would write with some new set of directions, and threats about giving everything that was unentailed to his idiot cousin Herbert if he did not comply.

The cat suddenly dug her nails into his calf. He pulled her away by the scruff of her neck and set her down. It seemed whenever she decided that dinner was running late, she expressed her irritation with a scratch. "I am not your prey, you wretch."

The cat sat implacably staring at him.

"Oh, I know what you think," he said. "You think I make too many arrangements to suit Daisy…Miss Danworth. You think my father's outrageous plan is working. You think I grow fond of the lady and *that's* why I've put myself in this ridiculous situation."

The cat did not comment one way or the other, but only turned and strolled away, waving her tail high in the air.

"I haven't," he called after her. "No more than in the usual way."

Was that exactly true, though? Had he not allowed himself to grow a little too fond of Miss Danworth? Had he not found it adorable, or at least a deal less icy than was her usual habit, that she spied on him every night? On the night of Farthmore's death, under the full moon when she'd been caught out, she'd claimed she preferred to take in the night air. A ridiculous and charming ruse.

He'd since pretended he did not note her there at her window, but of course he had. He always watched while the candles burned in her room and then looked away when the last candle was tamped out.

He could, he'd realized, keep his head down and, in the darkness, she would not realize his eyes occasionally looked up. He also could move the bench closer to the house by subtle degrees. Or not so subtle degrees, as the case might be. It would be extraordinary if she had not noticed, though she had not commented on it.

Was it a game? Or was he developing feelings that were growing a little too strong to ignore? What if those feelings were leading somewhere? That *somewhere* being a place he'd claimed he would never go?

If it were so, there would be certain…hurdles to jump.

For one, she had insisted she would never marry.

For another, *he* had insisted he would never marry. Loudly. Vociferously. Repeatedly.

For another, he had taken certain steps to stop his friends from marrying.

His had been a firm decision, well thought out. Was he just to throw it over? How would it even be done? What was he to say to his friends?

See here, I realize I have been against the thing, but now I find I'm not. And if you will be so good as to not remind me of anything I have said, and definitely not remind me of anything I have done, *that would be convenient.*

His scar burned just thinking about it.

Charles paused. It occurred to him that what he'd just been thinking about had nothing to do with his original impediments. He was supposed to be opposed to marriage because of what he'd seen in the war. He was supposed to remain firm in not producing children who might go off to war themselves. That had been the beginning of everything.

Where had that idea gone? Why was the impediment now to be what his friends, or everybody who ever knew him, would make of it? Was that really an impediment at all? Might not a man develop different opinions over time? Was a man to be saddled with a particular opinion for a lifetime? Should one's friends hold a person to an opinion forever?

Charles stood up and paced the small sitting room. "I think not," he said. "And as to that, might not a woman change her opinion too? After all, must they not be given the same rights?"

"Must who be given the same rights, my lord?"

Charles spun around and found Bellamy standing in his doorframe, carrying a tray.

"Nobody, never mind," Charles said.

As Bellamy carried the tray to the rickety table he dined on, Charles said, "By the by, we will remain here for another month, then to Somerset to Lord Burke's wedding. I know not where we go after that."

Bellamy set the tray down with a clatter. "Here? We stay here? I was sure we were to be off. The boys and me would go to the London house while you fanned about the countryside for the shooting."

"I don't *fan about* anywhere," Charles said.

Bellamy uncovered the tray and looked sadly down at the beef and roasted vegetables that sat on the plate. "I was counting on leaving the plaguey tornado behind!"

"I presume by that colorful description that you are still being overcome by Mrs. Broadbent."

"As ever," Bellamy said. "It's like we've all joined a militia—one step out of line and a string of what-fors rains down upon our heads."

"It can't be all bad," Charles said, finding some amusement in his butler's defeat. "You did win the argument about the drinking chocolate."

Bellamy straightened himself and got a faraway look, as if he were a retired general recalling a successful campaign fought against all odds. "Indeed I did. *Decisively*, I might add. Furthermore, as the weather cools, I will demand an increase. If she dares cross me on the subject, *I* will be the one raining down the what-fors! Just see if I don't!"

The butler turned on his heel and marched out, steaming back to the house. The cat had got to the tray as soon as it was uncovered, sniffed at the vegetables, and slinked off with a large slab of beef. Charles assumed she was eating it under his bed, as that seemed to be her preferred dining room.

So this was what his life had come to—the uncomfortable knowledge that he might have gone slightly offtrack with his vow to stay a bachelor forever, a butler who thought he might air his grievances at any and all hours, and a cat who made off with a good part of his dinner.

Thank God Flanagan had sent over a bottle of wine.

※»※«※

FOR SOME DAYS, Daisy had watched Lord Dalton's bench inch closer to the house. Not even inching, as it had been, now it was progressing by feet at a time.

It was alarming, but she was not unhappy about it. She just did not quite understand it. Where was he going? What was he doing? How close would he come?

As had been her habit all summer, she blew out the last candle and sat by the open window, moving the curtain aside ever so slowly and quietly.

She ought not to be doing it, not because there was anything particularly wrong in it, but it really was getting too cool at night for it to be at all sensible. The change in the weather had come on suddenly, as it often did. The mild nights had been changed to crisper and cooler, with a distinct feeling that autumn was not far off. She was wrapped in a heavy dressing gown as if it were January and had requested the housemaids build a fire, all to sit by an open window. They likely thought she was mad.

Lord Dalton did not come in only his shirtsleeves rolled up anymore, but kept on his coat. It could not be comfortable sitting there of an evening, even when one had a glass of brandy at one's side.

His bench had now come so close that she might have thrown something down to him. Where once he had been so distant across the garden that she could hardly make out his features, now she saw him more clearly by the light that shined from the kitchen windows.

"Getting the air again?" he said.

He'd startled her, and she pulled back and let the curtain fall to hide her.

"No need for excessive modesty," he said.

Daisy did not know if she were being excessively modest or not, but she *did* know the idea of her taking in the night air in such weather was ridiculous.

"I do not suppose," he went on, "that there is anything disreputable about a window open or talking across a distance."

Daisy slowly pulled the curtain aside once more. "No," she said. "The night air is...bracing. Certainly, nobody could claim I am compromised by any conversation that accompanied it."

"Conversation does pass the time, after all."

"Indeed," Daisy said. "I suppose we might talk of anything, within bounds."

"Whatever I am, I am hardly known for going *out* of bounds," Lord Dalton said.

"No, of course not," Daisy said. She knew that was perfectly true. Lord Dalton was not a breezy, carefree individual, but he was a gentleman through and through. There had been some talk of the bizarre steps he'd taken to stop his friends from getting married, but never a whisper of anything over-forward to do with a lady. Though he did not say so, she thought he had spent far too much time dodging them to have caused any of those sorts of offenses.

She gripped the curtains a little less tightly at the idea.

"I was wondering," Lord Dalton said.

He'd trailed off and the only sounds were the quiet waves washing up on the rocks. What was he wondering? Why did he not speak?

"Though," he said, "perhaps that subject would be out of bounds after all."

"What would be out of bounds?" Daisy asked.

"Do not answer if you do not wish to. The night we discovered the nature of the Dagobert, and I told everyone of the agreement between your father and Farthmore, the agreement that something was to happen when you reached your majority...you seemed as if you understood it, though I still cannot work it out. Why would your father wish to wait until the very moment when he would have lost all power over you?"

Daisy had not had the first idea of what he'd been wondering, but it certainly had not been that. Of all people, though, she thought Lord Dalton might understand what her father really had been.

"I questioned myself, not certain if it would be obvious to others," she said, "then I concluded it would not be, unless a person understood my father's particular type of depravity."

Though Daisy had not ever said half of it aloud, she told Lord Dalton of what had really happened to her mother. The slow death by insult and neglect and occasional fist. Then how he had turned on Daisy, how he'd schemed to get hold of her inheritance and been furious when he could not.

"So you see," Daisy said, "he could only have had one plan in mind. When I reached my majority, if I were to die intestate, he would inherit my money as the closest living relative. My father planned to murder me for his convenience. Should you wish to confirm the truth of it, you must only know that while I was horrified at understanding the scheme, I was not exactly surprised."

"My God," Lord Dalton said quietly.

"I will retire now," Daisy said hurriedly. She shut the window and closed the curtain and threw herself on the bed.

Why had she told him all of that? Now he knew her. Really knew her. He knew those things about her that she'd kept so well hidden. He knew the important things. The things only Betsy and Mrs. Jellops knew.

She sighed. It was both disturbing and freeing. Perhaps she need not prevaricate anymore. Or hide anymore. She had been built by adversity. Her coolness, as people called it, had been instilled by fear. She was as she was, and perhaps she need not pretend otherwise.

Daisy did not know what she and Lord Dalton would talk about on the morrow, but she would be at the window to find out.

And so began the nightly conversations that would go on for some weeks.

CHAPTER SIXTEEN

THOUGH DAISY HAD retired, which had prompted Lord Dalton to go back to his ramshackle cottage, the lights still burned in the kitchens.

It had not, perhaps, been the household staff's intention to listen in on the lord and Miss Danworth talking in the darkness, but they had not been terribly successful at ignoring it. Or shutting the open window so they would not hear it. After all, it *was* the kitchens and very warm even on a cool night.

Tom had been reading from *The Mysteries of Udolpho* but had silently closed it and laid it down. The rest of the occupants round the table might have even slightly leaned themselves toward the errant open window.

Now, the lord and Miss Danworth had ended their conversation, the lady shutting her window with a decided thump and the lord marching back to his cottage. They sat in silence, a horror hanging over them.

"That poor dove," Mrs. Broadbent said.

"For once," Bellamy said, "we are in agreement."

"A most unnatural father," Mr. Flanagan said. "I feel myself going red in the face just thinking of it. I wouldn't mind digging the old scoundrel up and beating him about the head with my pots and pans."

"But," Gerald stuttered, "can a pa really be that devilish to his own flesh and blood?"

"He can," Betsy said, being the resident authority on the matter, "and he was. I could tell you stories that would curl your hair and set it on fire."

The Mysteries of Udolpho clattered to the floor and nobody bothered to pick it up. In a confidential tone, Betsy regaled them with tales of what she had witnessed, and perhaps things she had not witnessed and only thought the master capable of.

The tales were dark and threatening and had put a chill down their spines as no mere story in a book could. They retired to their respective rooms with candles held high in front of them in case the dead man was to rise again and catch them in the halls. For all their trepidation, every single one of them planned to be conveniently nearby an open window on the following night. There might be further horrors to come.

AND SO THEY did gather the next night, and remained so every night. Their drinking chocolate in hand and leaning toward the open window, they sat silent and listened to Lord Dalton and Miss Danworth.

It was not every evening that they heard some terrible tale. In truth, most nights were quite usual conversations that flitted from subject to subject. Lord Dalton and Miss Danworth exchanged views on everything from politics to the cat to sidesaddles to India muslin to preferred newspapers. They were in hearty agreement that Brighton was superior to Ramsgate, though Miss Danworth had yet to even visit that town. They even discussed the recent news of the streets of Birmingham having been lit by gas lamps, Miss Danworth thinking it might appear cheery and Lord Dalton thinking it might appear blown to bits one day soon. Mr. Flanagan said they'd begun to sound like an old married couple, which struck everybody harder than he would have thought.

They had almost decided to go back to *The Mysteries of Udolpho* when one evening, Miss Danworth was heard to say, "Lord Dalton, if I might ask, what made you decide you would not marry? Are your mother and father terribly unhappy?"

The servants round the table froze. They were intrigued to view Bellamy's reaction to that question.

He shook his head vigorously and whispered, "That's not the reason."

They were even more intrigued to hear where the conversation went from there.

DAISY HAD FOUND a strange comfort in her nightly talks with Lord Dalton. The only uncomfortable part was that she knew she was allowing her feelings to run on ahead of her.

Suddenly, the idea of marriage did not seem so frightening. At least, not frightening if a particular individual was considered.

She'd already admitted to herself that she'd always been a little in love with Lord Dalton. She had always felt more like herself with him than she ever had attempting to converse with an over-cheerful fop. A little in love had been perhaps as much as she'd ever allowed herself to be. But, she knew her feelings were more than *a little* these days.

She knew so much about him now. That was, she knew so much but for the big question. Why had he sworn he'd never marry?

What would she do when she found out? Would it cool her feelings, which were beginning to run far hotter than was quite safe? What was she to do when they both went their separate ways? Would she remove to Brighton alone, as she said she would? The whole idea had begun to seem most unsatisfactory!

If she were honest with herself, she would marry him if she could. But only him. There could not be another like him.

She was setting herself up for heartbreak and she knew it, but she could not stop. Her feelings had become a runaway carriage barreling down a steep hill. Only the inevitable crash would halt them.

Still, she pressed on.

The night was the coldest yet and aside from her heaviest dressing gown and a well-built fire, she had piled a thick blanket on her lap. It was so chill out of doors that she wondered if he would come. Certainly, he would have to give it up at some point.

He did come, though.

They talked of this or that, though Daisy could hardly keep her attention on it. Then, she said what had been on her mind for so long. "Lord Dalton, if I might ask, what made you decide you would not marry? Are your father and mother terribly unhappy?"

"The duke and duchess?" Lord Dalton said, almost sounding amused. "They go on well enough. He does what she says when it comes to social engagements and she leaves him alone about his clubs. They are fond of one another, I think. At least, it has always seemed so to me."

Daisy was silent for some moments. She supposed she had assumed his determination to remain a bachelor must be connected to an unhappy household, as that was what she herself had experienced. But if it were not that, what on earth was it?

She hoped it was not solely due to the Dukes' Pact. It was true that the whole idea of the old dukes pushing their heirs into penury to get them married was ludicrous. But it would be somehow boyish to vow he would cross his father and never produce an heir, only in an effort to thwart him. It would not be a worthy reason for Lord Dalton. There must be something else. Something she did not understand.

"Then why?" she asked softly.

She was not certain he heard her, as he did not answer for some moments. Finally he said, "I am not at all sure I should tell you the story. Sometimes it is not right to put a burden on someone else and create a memory that is unpleasant and was never their own to carry."

"I do not mind," Daisy said. "I have enough of my own, I will not be overcome by one more."

Daisy saw his dark head nod in the gloom. He said, "When I fought at Quatre Bras, there was a French fellow I came upon. He really looked too young to be there, but I suppose he was not. We came at one another with swords and he fought like the devil though he was not nearly skilled enough to have been sent into the fray.

"I wounded him, but I did not kill him. I thought to leave him there and he might make his way out to live another day. As I turned away, I heard something behind me. The fool had risen and had his sword raised. I was taken by surprise and did not react quick enough."

Lord Dalton paused and ran his hand down the scar on his face. "That is how I got this embellishment on my cheek—he sliced me before I knew what was happening. In my anger, I dealt him a deadly blow. He died at my feet."

"But what choice did you have?" Daisy asked, hardly daring to breathe.

"None, I suppose. But the last thing he said was *Ma pauvre femme, elle est enceinte.*"

"My poor wife, she is with child," Daisy said softly.

"Yes, and so you see I decided I would not bring any boys like him into the world only so they might go out like that. I saw plenty of men die, but none with the look of fear that he had."

Daisy felt as if her heart skipped beats in her chest. She'd known all along it would come to this. She'd find out why he would never marry and that would be the end of it. He might have gotten over a parents' unhappy union, but he would never get over what he had just described. Whether or not he was right in it would not matter. It had not just left a scar on his face, it had left a scar on his soul.

"I have given it up, though. Funnily enough," Lord Dalton said.

Daisy clutched the blanket to her chest. "Given it up?" she said.

"Given up what?"

"My vow to never marry," Lord Dalton said.

"Why?" Daisy asked, her own voice sounding as if she were choking.

"I think you know."

She did know. Only a moment ago, she had been certain he'd never give it up. Just as quickly, he'd said he *had* given it up.

He had given it up for her.

All her life Daisy had looked for a way to be happy. A chance to be happy. Here it was. She knew chances did not come raining down from the sky. If one were to spy a chance, one had better reach for it before it disappeared from view.

"Do not move!" she cried. She threw off the blanket and fled toward the door and down the stairs. She made her way down the dark corridor that led to the servants' entrance and ran outside.

Lord Dalton stood under the lights from the kitchens. She threw herself into his arms.

"Daisy," he said softly.

"Daisy?" she said, burying her face in his coat. "You have never called me that."

"I have," he whispered in her ear. "Often, in my thoughts." He used his index finger to lift her chin and kissed her softly.

It was not like anything she had ever experienced. She had, until recently, recoiled from the idea of a man touching her, of a man getting so close to her that she could feel his breath. But this man could not come close enough.

"Do not ever stop kissing me," she said.

He smiled, one of his rare smiles, and said, "I am happy to comply, Daisy Danworth." He kissed her again.

Daisy could not have said how much time passed, only that eventually she was wrapped inside his coat and against his shirt and could feel his heartbeat and it was very cold outside and she was very warm.

"You will have to ask permission from my guardian, you know," Daisy whispered.

"I will *ask* my father nothing," Lord Dalton said in a growly voice. "I will inform him that we are to wed and he will be suitably delighted."

"Oh dear," Daisy said, "but then you will also have to live it down with your friends, I'm afraid. You did vow you would never—"

"What care I for those idiots," Lord Dalton said. "I have been clever enough to win the real prize."

There was a sudden loud whisper floating through the night air that was not their own.

"See? They are standing right there!"

The voice was unmistakably her lady's maid's. Daisy pulled herself away from the inside of Lord Dalton's coat in time to see faces illuminated at the kitchen windows—Betsy, Mrs. Broadbent, Bellamy, and Mr. Flanagan peered out. Seeing they were spotted, Bellamy blew out the candle and the scene went dark.

"Scoundrels," Lord Dalton said, pulling her close again. "We ought to go indoors. We can go to the cottage."

Daisy was all too willing, but for propriety's sake she said, "Only if you promise you will not ravage me."

Lord Dalton laughed rather loud at this and said, "Not until you marry me and have taken to calling me Charles when we are alone. Then, I cannot say what I might do."

Daisy nodded as if she were quite approving of this. In truth, she was not certain she would mind being ravaged at this moment. However, one of the things that had made her fall in love with Lord Dalton, or *Charles*, was that she was certain he would never do the wrong thing by her. He might be a plague to his friends and frighten many a hostess with his oft-grim visage, but he would not do wrong by *her*.

He took her hand and led her back to the cottage and they talked until the sun rose over the rooftops and she fell asleep in his lap. As Lord Dalton had promised, no clothing was removed during the long hours of night, though the various pieces of armor both parties had been accustomed to wear began to melt away like blocks of ice in the summer sun.

CHARLES WROTE HIS father the following day and, just as he'd promised, he merely informed his father that he was to wed Miss Danworth. He couched it very matter of fact and would not give the old schemer his due in having had a hand in it.

He did, however, put off the banns being read until after Burke's wedding. There was no getting round the idea that his friends would not only be shocked—they might well be mocking of any past statements he had made on the subject of marriage. Or worse, any actions he might have taken to uphold that particular opinion. They would all attend the nuptials, and he was determined to face them down in person and deliver the news himself.

He did not, however, spend much of his time thinking of it as so much else took up his attention. After Mrs. Jellops had been apprised of the engagement, she needed more than a little convincing that it was actually wanted. All along, she had taken Daisy at her word and never envisioned that her charge would marry. Or, at least not so soon. Or, at least not to Lord Dalton. Her incredulousness felt like a hint of things to come.

Still, through numerous conversations with Daisy, she was finally convinced and she was not unhappy. Mrs. Jellops was particularly not unhappy when Charles described to her the rooms she would be given in his various houses, her generous allowance, and that she might come and go as she pleased with the use of his own carriages. Once the lady was assured of her charge's affection for the gentleman, Mrs.

Jellops rather relished the idea of jaunting across England in a carriage emblazoned with the lord's crest, visiting friends old and new, and spending that generous allowance on fripperies and gewgaws as she went.

The schedule of their days in Ramsgate was not so very different than they had been, with only a few changes made. Charles now dined in the house, to the initial irritation of the cat. Though, the cat being enterprising, she made it her business to overcome Mr. Flanagan and so was often lounging in the warmth of the kitchens and stealing whatever she fancied. Charles also suspected the cat had thrown him over for the sanctuary of one of the footmen's beds, as she wandered off when the night grew too cold and Mrs. Broadbent was forever scolding Gerald for the telltale cat hairs on his coat.

Daisy had twice suggested that Charles move into the house entirely. The cat had done so and just as everyone predicted, the chimney in the cottage was useless. This, he thought a step too far and stayed where he was. It was horrendously uncomfortable as day by day the weather cooled, but it was not forever, so he bore it with good humor.

During the day, if Charles was not in the house with Daisy, Daisy was in the cottage with him. The servants went about looking very pleased with themselves, seeming convinced they'd personally arranged the engagement. Even Bellamy put a good face on it and appeared resigned to having Mrs. Broadbent hiding round every corner forevermore.

Daisy had thrown off the darkest of her mourning clothes and did not particularly care who said what about it. As Charles had pointed out, she would be a duchess someday and might run through the streets naked and society would pretend they had not noticed or deem her delightfully eccentric.

The month had passed by far more quickly than either Charles or Daisy had expected and suddenly it was time to make their way to

Somerset for Lord Burke's wedding. The servants, aside from Betsy and Tate, would stay behind. Mrs. Broadbent would supervise, though Bellamy remained under the illusion that he was at least nominally in charge. Charles thought they might battle it out at their leisure, as their only vital job was making certain the cat was fed.

Four days of travel passed by while Mrs. Jellops endlessly speculated on everything she viewed out the carriage window, asked the coachman to slow down so she might get a better look, insisted that nobody should eat in a carriage that was moving, and needed endless stops to stretch her legs. Finally, they delivered the lady to her friend Mrs. Phelps' house.

Once arrived to her destination, Mrs. Jellops began to fret over the idea that Charles and Miss Danworth would be quite alone in their carriage, with only Betsy and Tate following in the second carriage. The as-yet unmarried couple would be unchaperoned for nearly twenty minutes! Perhaps twenty-five if they encountered a delay.

Mrs. Phelps did not help in that regard, as she was in the habit of heartily agreeing with her friend and took to murmuring, "You have gone straight to the point, my dear."

Mrs. Jellops was both soothed and shocked when Charles assured her that the thing she worried about could not be done proper in only twenty minutes, or even twenty-five. This had left every lady in the vicinity blushing, the footmen red-faced, and the coachmen snorting, but it got them on their way.

Now, they drove through the gates of Burke's estate.

Daisy squeezed his hand. "How shall you break the news?" she asked.

"I have no idea," he said.

"Well," Daisy said, laughing, "please do not give anybody a black eye if they find too much amusement in it."

"I will try, Daisy," Charles said. "I will try."

⇶⟫⟪⇷

DAISY REALLY DID not know how Charles was to break the news of his engagement to his friends. He was a genial gentleman, once one got more acquainted with him, but she did not think he would suffer being overly teased and laughed at. He preferred a certain dignity, as she did herself—neither of them relished appearing silly.

When she'd hinted that he ought not give anybody a black eye, it was because she could see how things might go in that direction if his friends expressed too much glee over his being so wrong in his past opinions. Especially Lord Grayson, who was always too much in the habit of cheerful mockery.

They'd been admitted to the house and led to their respective bedchambers and she had not seen him since. She had not seen anybody and only understood that everybody was to gather in the drawing room at seven before dinner. The *everybody* noted were all of Burke's particular friends—the lords Hampton, Lockwood, Ashworth, Cabot, and Grayson, and their respective wives. They would see the Minkertons and their friends and relatives on the following day, but this was to be a small party of old friends.

Daisy did not consider herself one of these old friends, though some of them she knew better than others. She particularly looked forward to seeing Kitty. Though just now, her thoughts were far more taken up with how poor Charles was to get through his gauntlet.

Still, he must do it. These were the only people that really mattered to Charles, and so it was the ideal time to relay his news.

On the other hand, the dinner had been advertised as Burke's idea of saying goodbye to the last of the willing bachelors, everybody apparently putting Lord Dalton into the *unwilling* category. Her poor, dear Charles.

Daisy had donned a satin dress that was some shade between red and dark orange, its vibrant color not having a thing to do with sadness. She thought it might communicate that her mourning, if she had ever mourned, was over. It might stop the inevitable condolences that she never really knew how to receive. In any case, it made her feel more like herself and she had no intention of hiding again.

She waited until the last possible moment to go down. She did not wish to have any awkward conversations—the entire party would view her as the cool Miss Danworth that Lord Dalton had been forced to drag from place to place.

Well, with the exception of Lord Burke, possibly, though even he did not know their secret.

The drawing room, though large, was already crowded. Charles stood with Lord Ashworth, Lord Hampton, and Lord Lockwood nearby a window. Lord Grayson and Lord Cabot were having an animated conversation with Lord Burke. Most of the ladies sat together on a long sofa, so engaged with one another that her entrance was not noted. But Kitty spotted Daisy at once and made her way over.

"Dear Daisy!" she said. "I did not know if Lord Dalton would bring you or not, but then Lord Burke told me you'd struck up a friendship with Miss Minkerton and he was sure you would come. I was so delighted to know it. Also, when we have a moment alone, I must know more about the mystery of the Dagobert! Was it indeed the scepter? How did you come across it? What has happened to it?"

Daisy nodded at Kitty's enthusiastic stream of questions, keeping one eye on her intended, who was looking decidedly uncomfortable. She said to Kitty, "It is more mysterious than you would imagine, and do not repeat the name Dagobert anywhere—it is to remain a very great secret. I will tell you why when I can."

Kitty appeared delighted with the idea that there was something further mysterious to know. She surely would have pressed on, had not Lord Burke sent champagne round and now tapped his crystal glass with a silver letter opener to quiet everyone.

All eyes turned to Lord Burke and conversations stopped. "My friends, I cannot tell you how happy I am that you have all traveled far and wide for my wedding. It was a long time coming, as some of you know and some of you don't, but I have been in love with Belle Minkerton for as long as I can remember. It was the reason, perhaps, that I was sometimes able to give out such level-headed counsel to my friends—I was always standing outside the fray, my heart safely left behind in Somerset."

"Here, here," Lord Lockwood said.

"Now," Lord Burke continued, "we will wed, and I will be surrounded by friends who wish for my happiness."

"And the miracle of it," Lord Grayson said, laughing, "is that for once, Dalton didn't do anything to stop it."

The entire party found great mirth in this idea, though Daisy did not so much. The teasing had begun and Charles hadn't even told them of his engagement to her. She was afraid the whole thing could turn remarkably dreadful.

"As to that," Lord Dalton said, "I told Burke I had decided not to interfere. And, I will just point out that a man may change his mind on occasion. In fact, an educated man often does. It is only the dull and stupid who do not occasionally reflect on their opinions and make adjustments where necessary."

Daisy gripped Kitty's hand. Kitty squeezed back but looked entirely perplexed as to why her hand was being squeezed so tightly.

"Furthermore, when a man changes his mind," Lord Dalton went on, "a man's friends ought to go along with it without unnecessary debate. Or risk a black eye."

Good Lord, he was threatening black eyes already and had not even said why.

"We'll all happily go along with your ceasing your meddling in our affairs," Lord Ashworth said, "however late you are to the idea. No reason to threaten black eyes over it."

"Indeed," Cassandra said, "even I have forgiven you and think no more about it."

"As have I," Sybil said.

"I think you rather helped me than not," Lily said, "though it was not your purpose."

"My lord and I are far too busy with our horses to give it much thought," Penny said.

"Well, I am still a *little* annoyed," Kitty said, still clasping Daisy's hand, "but I won't hold a grudge forever. It would not be very intellectual to do so, I do not think."

"There, you see?" Lord Cabot said, "no harm done in the end, Dalton. You may retire your threats of black eyes."

"We'll see," Lord Dalton said darkly, staring down the company as if they were enemy forces on the verge of an attack. "You are to know that I have engaged myself to Miss Danworth, and if anybody has anything to say about it, black eyes are back on the table."

Daisy sighed in relief. He'd said it, now they only need brace themselves for the jokes and hope those jokes didn't go so far beyond the mark that black eyes would actually result.

The room was silent for a moment, everyone seeming to have some difficulty in taking in Lord Dalton's words, so strange they were. En masse, the party turned to Daisy for confirmation of this extraordinary news.

She nodded. "It is true, we are to be married. I hope we can count on your congratulations regarding this development."

"I knew it!" Burke said, "did I not say you were suited? Congratulations indeed, old boy!" Burke grabbed Lord Dalton's hand and shook it heartily.

There were general exclamations, most along the lines of: *I am not surprised at all, of course they have always been well suited, did I not speculate on it last season and nobody believed me?*

As Dalton was congratulated by his friends, and treated far more kindly than he had a right to be, Kitty leaned close to Daisy and whispered, "Is it true? You will really wed Lord Dalton? And nobody is forcing you to?"

Daisy laughed at the idea. "Indeed, nobody forces me *or* him."

"I am just so surprised," Kitty said. "Others seem not so taken off guard, as I think they see you as similar temperaments."

"We *are* similar," Daisy said. "We have been two blocks of ice who have had a very slow thawing."

"Goodness," Kitty said, sounding nearly breathless, "one never does know how these things will turn out."

"No," Daisy said, laughing, "one never does."

AT DINNER, THE party were remarkably cheerful, including Lord Dalton. Once he'd got over the danger of being teased into blacking eyes, it seemed the last of his cares were shed from him. He still was not an open book to his friends, as evidenced when Grayson inquired of him how he had pressed his suit to win Miss Danworth. He would not say, and Grayson thought to tease him by inventing strange scenarios until Lord Dalton glared at him with such ferocity that it was understood that black eyes might yet be back on the table.

Daisy was grateful he would not divulge how it had been. Their odd wooing at the window might stay just between them. And also the rascally servants who'd listened in.

Most of the dinner was passed with exchanging news. Cassandra, Lady Hampton, told Daisy that she and the other ladies had a regular correspondence amongst one another and now she was to be brought into the fold. It seemed somewhat remarkable to Daisy, as she had known all of the ladies from past seasons, but most very distantly. If she recalled rightly, she might even have been rather cool to Cassandra. It had only been Kitty who'd managed to make some cracks in her walls.

She was to be married and have a circle of friends. She had not seen her life taking such a turn. Always, she had been intent on just surviving and then retiring to quiet and safety. This was to be an entirely different life than the one she had envisioned.

As the dinner went merrily on, Lord Dalton stole glances at her and she stole glances back and the last hurdle had been jumped. They would marry in a month. As for the idea she'd told Kitty, that they'd both been blocks of ice on the thaw, it seemed they were well on their way to melting.

Dignified still, but melting all the same.

EPILOGUE

C HARLES AND DAISY did indeed marry in a month, and quietly, unlike Lord Burke's large celebration. They married at the duke's estate, which of course had undergone no renovations whatsoever.

The duke might have boasted to his son about his hand in arranging the whole thing, but the dowager was a more discerning sort and warned him against it. Nobody made comments or expressed surprise, which suited Lord Dalton very well. In any case, the duke would have his opportunity to crow when he would next meet with the other dukes, their pact now fully realized.

Daisy was not certain if she would have been particularly put out if the duke *had* claimed his hand in pushing them together. After all, he had indeed done it, with rather wonderful results. She found her new father-in-law a rather doting old fellow and Charles' mother an energetic and helpful woman. The dowager, of course, was everything marvelous—sprightly and devilish and reminding Daisy of her own dear departed grandmother. While it took some time to become used to being surrounded in kindness, she was well-satisfied with the family she'd married into.

To her further delight, she was equally well-satisfied with the particular gentleman she'd married. Charles had told no tales when he'd informed Mrs. Jellops that a particular thing could not be done proper in twenty minutes. The duke's servants were scandalized at their luxurious mornings abed and how late they descended the stairs each day, the time being closer to noon than morning.

They spent a month under the duke's roof, walking the gardens and discussing the practicalities of a household. Daisy had thought there would be much to debate and decide between them, but it seemed that things were to go all her own way. When she had first noticed it, she'd playfully wondered aloud if pink silk curtains, or perhaps a print of palm trees and parrots, might not do well in his library. Charles had nodded and said it would be as she wished, though he had been mightily relieved to discover she had not actually meant it. It had been the first teasing between them, but was not the last.

Mrs. Jellops and Mrs. Phelps came to stay at the duke's estate for a fortnight. Charles informed his mother and father of the ladies' interesting mode of playing piquet, which became an amusing diversion. If six people played cards in the drawing room, two of them stumbled forward with ever-changing ideas on scoring while the rest stifled their laughter. Those two ladies had become such fast friends that they had plans already to visit one another often.

Charles, well-knowing the sort of insults and cruelty Daisy had endured at the hands of her father, took every step to ensure she would never suffer such again. The London house was re-made from top to bottom to her liking, and Charles was endlessly surprised to find a new carpet or draperies having arrived but took it in with good humor.

The house was re-made in temperament too—there were no drunken staff, no intemperate indulgences, no harsh words, no low acquaintances making themselves comfortable in her drawing room. The mistress' house was inviolate and nothing untoward was to occur. Though, Daisy kindly left her husband's library alone and it remained a clutter of open books on every surface.

Charles sometimes smiled to himself, knowing full well that with

Mrs. Broadbent at the helm and Mrs. Jellops in the wings, anything out of bounds would have been stopped in its tracks anyway. They hired another butler after Bellamy retired to a cottage on the duke's estate, where he was assured of having as much wine as he liked.

Mr. Roberts had come into the role severe and strong, but after enduring a series of relentless what-fors, questions, notations, and comments, that fellow was entirely outmanned by Mrs. Broadbent.

In truth, the only being in the house who was not very attentive to Mrs. Broadbent's directives was the cat. That feline had various names at various times, though was mostly just called *the wretch*. She made herself free with laps and beds, pulled down curtains for her amusement, and shredded chair covers with reckless abandon. She and Mr. Flanagan had a tense relationship, as whatever she could make off with from the kitchens was gone in a trice and she eventually grew very fat. Her only exercise was being chased off for some infraction, though she usually left the scene of the crime in a rather unapologetic leisurely stroll, waving her tail high in the air.

Not a year after Charles and Daisy were married, a bit of gossip traveled to their doors by way of Lady Grayson, who was a regular visitor along with the rest of the ladies of the pact. The season had begun with no sign of Lady Montague and it was discovered that Lord Montague had finally put his foot down. He'd sold his London house and forbade her to return to town. It was reported that Lady Montague was in a frenzy over it and writing letters everywhere, hinting she ought to be invited as a houseguest. Kitty was confident that she would receive no replies and she was right. Lady Montague was never seen in London again.

While both Daisy and her lord went forward perhaps still a bit too dignified for their own good, that could not hold when children arrived. When that blessed event came to pass, they had both thought to carry on as was the custom—hiring an army of nannies and governesses to manage the nursery. Yet, they found themselves constantly drifting into that youthful sanctuary. Eventually, they found themselves eating an exceedingly early and unimaginative dinner there, on very short chairs, on nights they did not go out. Then, whenever there was laughter or tears heard somewhere in the house, they both felt an urgent need to investigate. There was no entertainment to be had that surpassed what their children were able to provide.

It was very hard to maintain a serious and dignified manner when one was surrounded by ridiculous naughtiness, outrageous hi-jinks, and the heartfelt speeches of regret and sorrow that inevitably followed.

Daisy could not help but laugh when Marigold made off with her brother's toy soldiers and they were discovered in the un-soldiery location of her collection of cotton bunnies. Her brother was suitably outraged to find his generals lounging on the lap of an overstuffed and irritatingly fluffy rabbit.

Charles could not help but laugh when the younger Charles swore he'd not touched the sponge cake that had been left to cool on Mr. Flanagan's kitchen counter, despite the fact that the only remains of it were the crumbs on his face.

Neither Daisy nor her lord could successfully remain stone-faced when they found both children in tears, only to discover they had dared one another to take a spoonful of Mr. Flanagan's mustard.

Whatever nonsense they got up to, Daisy was determined in making sure that her children's world was soft and cushioned. They might *do* wrong, and delight in it until they were caught, but they could never *be* wrong in who they were. Their house was both their bedrock and their feathered mattress to fall on.

The family summers in Brighton were made brighter by two children who made laughing runs at waves, or jealously collected their own piles of shells and sea glass, or marveled at a sailing ship in the distance and then argued over who would make the better captain.

And, after all, was there anything more charming than two children fighting to keep their eyes open after a day of salt and sun?

Aside from the well-apportioned Brighton house, a cottage was built, not much bigger than the one the lord had uncomfortably occupied at Ramsgate. At least twice a week in the summers they would travel to this humble abode to have a picnic dinner, never caring that there was often more sand in the sitting room than there was on the beach.

Their friends often joined them in Brighton. At times, all of them arrived together, overrunning the house and straining even Mrs. Broadbent's determined arrangements. These young parents were always under great pressure to come, as a visit to the house was considered a highlight amongst their various offspring. Traipsing down to the cottage, nannies were dismissed and the evening's entertainment was a lively game of cards the children invented called *Catch the Pirate*. The rules of the game were so ever-changing that nobody over the age of eight, except for Mrs. Jellops who was often responsible for a changed rule, had ever a chance to keep up. Great amounts of farthings changed hands and the game was not over until the last pirate had fallen asleep.

The children sometimes marveled at the scar that ran down the side of Lord Dalton's face, traced it with their pudgy fingers, and demanded to be told what had caused it. As Charles had finally been able to leave that time of his life in the past where it belonged, he told them various stories having to do with dragons and ogres. He did not think he was particularly lying, as Quatre Bras had been full of them. He had even been one of them.

The London season was all well and good, but it was the summer and the seaside that called them always.

Lord Dalton's softened edges were attributed to age and the mellowing of time. Daisy's warmer nature was thought to be an ease at finding herself settled. Between themselves, though, they knew the truth.

It was the children—their joy of being alive, their high spirits, their innocent transgressions—that brought back an enduring faith in mankind and its potential for good. Of course, it all would have been for naught if they hadn't first developed an enduring faith in one another.

And so, the six gentlemen of the pact who vowed never to marry all did marry in the end. That Lord Dalton was the very last of them surprised nobody. That he may have ended the happiest of them all, certainly *did* surprise. But then, when one has the furthest distance to travel, arriving is all the sweeter.

The End

P.S. The Scepter of Dagobert was indeed stolen from the Basilica of Sant-Denis. It has never been found—check your bedposts!

About the Author

By the time I was eleven, my Irish Nana and I had formed a book club of sorts. On a timetable only known to herself, Nana would grab her blackthorn walking stick and steam down to the local Woolworth's. There, she would buy the latest Barbara Cartland romance, hurry home to read it accompanied by viciously strong wine, (Wild Irish Rose, if you're wondering) and then pass the book on to me. Though I was not particularly interested in real boys yet, I was *very* interested in the gentlemen in those stories—daring, bold, and often enraging and unaccountable. After my Barbara Cartland phase, I went on to Georgette Heyer, Jane Austen and so many other gifted authors blessed with the ability to bring the Georgian and Regency eras to life.

I would like nothing more than to time travel back to the Regency (and time travel back to my twenties as long as we're going somewhere) to take my chances at a ball. Who would take the first? Who would escort me into supper? What sort of meaningful looks would be exchanged? I would hope, having made the trip, to encounter a gentleman who would give me a very hard time. He ought to be vexatious in the extreme, and *worth* every vexation, to make the journey worthwhile.

I most likely won't be able to work out the time travel gambit, so I will content myself with writing stories of adventure and romance in my beloved time period. There are lives to be created, marvelous gowns to wear, jewels to don, instant attractions that inevitably come with a difficulty, and hearts to break before putting them back together again. In traditional Regency fashion, my stories are clean—the action happens in a drawing room, rather than a bedroom.

As I muse over what will happen next to my H and h, and wish I were there with them, I will occasionally remind myself that it's also nice to have a microwave, Netflix, cheese popcorn, and steaming hot showers.

Come see me on Facebook! @KateArcherAuthor

Made in the USA
Middletown, DE
23 September 2021